THE GHOST
AND THE TWINS

HAUNTING DANIELLE

THE GHOST
AND THE TWINS

USA TODAY BESTSELLING AUTHOR
BOBBI HOLMES

The Ghost and the Twins
(Haunting Danielle, Book 33)
A Novel
By Bobbi Holmes
Cover Design: Elizabeth Mackey

ISBN: 978-1-949977-76-9
A

Dedicated to my readers.
Without your encouragement,
I wouldn't be releasing Book 33 of the
Haunting Danielle series. Thank you!

ONE

Homer stood in the far corner of the ER patient room and watched the nurse hook the unconscious man up to monitors. When the nurse had inserted the IV minutes earlier, Homer looked away. He could never stomach the sight of needles puncturing flesh.

"How is he?" Flora asked from the open doorway. Flora, a plain-looking middle-aged woman was, in Homer's opinion, responsible for this mess. If she had just completed the DNR, instead of the nurse wasting her time on the patient, he might be at the funeral home. After all, without medical intervention, how long could he last?

"The same. We hope to move him to his own hospital room within the hour. Did you contact the family?" the nurse asked.

"It's just two nieces and a nephew. But no. I haven't been able to reach them yet, but I left messages."

"I don't see any of them rushing to their dear uncle's side," Homer grumbled.

If Flora heard Homer's comment, she didn't respond.

The nurse turned from the monitors to the hospital bed and

studied the unconscious patient, his breathing labored. "How long have you been his caretaker?"

"About six years. It was a few months after they diagnosed him with Alzheimer's."

"And he doesn't have family in Frederickport? No one?"

Flora shook her head. "No. His one niece, Camilla, used to live here. She's the one who arranged for me to take care of him."

The nurse looked from her patient to Flora. "Does she visit often?"

Homer laughed at the question while Flora said, "To be honest, I only met her that one time when she hired me. Of course, we talk on the phone periodically. I've never met her brother or sister, but I have their numbers as contacts, and I have spoken to them on the phone."

The nurse shrugged. "That's sad. I've seen that happen many times before. Family members stop visiting when the Alzheimer's patient no longer remembers them."

"To be honest, they never visited, even back when he might have still remembered them. But the niece who hired me, her ex-husband used to come see him every week."

"That's nice."

"I thought so. The niece, the one who hired me, she left town a couple of years before I met her. But her ex was fond of her uncle, and he'd visit him for a few hours each week, and they'd play cribbage. But after a year, well, the Alzheimer's worsened, and he no longer understood how to play the game, and eventually he no longer recognized his cribbage partner. Unfortunately, visits after that upset Mr. Carter, so I suggested it be best if he stopped coming."

"Does he still live in Frederickport?"

"Yes. In fact, he's a police officer in town. Perhaps I should call him. He might know another way to contact the family."

THE ONLY WAY Danielle could fit comfortably in the booth at Pier Café was to shove the table toward Brian and Heather's side, giving her growing belly more room. She found it difficult to get comfortable no matter where she sat these days.

Instead of weaving her long brown hair into a fishtail braid that morning, Danielle had pulled her hair into a quick ponytail. She did not have the energy to fuss with her hair. These days, her normal wardrobe included stretch pants and oversized blouses or T-shirts. Next to her in the booth sat her husband, Walt, whose attire was far more put together than hers. Today he wore gray slacks and a gray and white striped dress shirt, its top button unfastened.

"Are you sure you're only seven months pregnant?" Heather asked as she popped a french fry in her mouth. A few years younger than Danielle, and considerably younger than her boyfriend, Brian Henderson, Heather wore her long jet-black hair free, falling past her bare shoulders. Heather referred to the long dress she wore as a sundress, which Brian found amusing, considering its color matched her hair.

Danielle glanced down at her belly and then looked back at Heather with a sigh. "Almost eight months."

"Twins usually come early," Heather chirped. She grabbed another french fry.

Brian let out a snort and shook his head. "Are you picking on Danielle?"

Danielle chuckled. "Actually, I'm okay with them coming early, as long as they're both healthy."

"Well, if they come early, and you can't get to the hospital in time, Brian can always help if he's here," Heather said.

Danielle arched her brows. "Brian?"

"Sure, he's delivered babies before. Sometimes cops have to."

Brian chuckled. "I doubt Danielle wants me to deliver her babies. I'm sure she'll get to the hospital in time."

Danielle cringed. "Yeah, um, that would be rather awkward."

"Have you really had to deliver a baby when on the job?" Walt asked.

Brian nodded. "Twice."

They chatted a few minutes more about Brian's experiences delivering babies before shifting the conversation to their friend Lily and Lily's pregnancy.

"I'm surprised Laura's not sticking around until Lily has her baby. It's only four more months," Heather said. Laura, Lily's sister, had been staying at Marlow House with Walt and Danielle across the street from Lily and Ian's house.

Noticing Danielle's cringe in response to Heather's comment, Brian laughed before saying, "Is that houseguest beginning to smell like fish?"

Danielle shrugged. "It's not that. But, well, it will be nice to have our house back, especially now. After all, Heather is right. These babies could come early. I'd rather we have everything set up—and no houseguest."

Heather gave a nod. "True. And it's not like she can stay with her sister. They have the house torn up with the addition."

"Didn't I hear something about Lily and Ian moving into Marlow House while they add onto their house?" Brian asked.

"We made the offer," Walt said, "but they decided they really didn't need to."

"And I think Lily felt a little funny with Laura staying with us for so long. She mentioned how Walt and I need time alone before the babies arrive," Danielle said.

"When does she leave for Europe?" Brian asked.

Danielle looked at Brian. "She flies to New York on Wednesday."

"I still can't believe Charlie Cramer was in town all that time, getting chummy with Laura." Heather cringed at the thought.

"It about got her killed," Danielle said.

Heather leaned forward, placed her elbows on the tabletop, and rested her chin on her right palm. "What really annoys me, right after they arrested Cramer, he confessed to the murders, but then his attorney got the confession tossed out. So instead of going straight to prison, he's in a jail waiting for trial. If he hadn't been in that jail, he probably wouldn't have escaped, and he wouldn't have come here and terrorized Danielle and Laura."

"And he would still be alive," Brian reminded her.

Heather smiled at him. "You always know how to make me feel better." She leaned over and gave him a quick kiss. Before Brian could respond, his cellphone rang. He picked up the cellphone and looked to see who was calling. He frowned and answered the phone. "Flora?"

Walt, Danielle, and Heather quietly ate their lunch while Brian talked on his cellphone. After Brian ended the call a few minutes later, he set the cellphone on the table.

"Is everything okay?" Heather asked.

"Remember when I told you about my friend Carter who has Alzheimer's." Brian asked. He then looked across the table to Walt and Danielle. "He's also my ex-wife's uncle. Carter and I go back a long way. In fact, I knew him before I met my second wife. He lives in Frederickport and has Alzheimer's." Brian looked back at Heather and said, "That was his caretaker. Carter had a heart attack, and he's in the hospital. Flora's been trying to get ahold of Camilla and her brother and sister." Brian looked back at Walt and Danielle and added, "That's the only family Carter has. When Flora couldn't get ahold of them, she called me."

"What does she want you to do? Does she think you can get ahold of Camilla?" Heather asked.

Brian shrugged. "She thought I might have another number for them. I don't."

"How's he doing?" Walt asked.

"Not well. Flora says he may not make it through the night. I hate the idea of Carter dying alone."

"Why don't you go see him?" Heather said.

Brian considered Heather's suggestion a moment before saying, "I think I should." He looked back at Walt and Danielle. "Like I said, Carter and I go back a long way. He was always a character; I really liked him. After Camilla and I split, and she left town, I visited him once a week; we'd play cribbage."

"But that pissed off his ex," Heather told Walt and Danielle.

Brian flashed Heather a smile, looked back to Walt and Danielle and continued, "It did. Carter mentioned something to Camilla

5

about our weekly cribbage games. Camilla called and reminded me Carter was her uncle, and I needed to find someone else to play cribbage with."

"Why did she care?" Danielle asked.

"Carter doesn't have family aside from my ex-wife and her brother and sister. He has some money and a house that's paid for. I know he set up a trust back when Camilla and I were married, dividing the estate between Camilla and her two siblings, with her as the trustee. From what Flora has told me, Camilla hasn't been back since she arranged for Carter's care. Flora's never met Camilla's brother or sister. Carter wasn't happy when she divorced me. He was the one who introduced us."

"Camilla was worried Brian would end up inheriting her uncle's estate," Heather interjected.

Brian gave Heather's comment a nod and looked back at Walt and Danielle. "That's pretty much what Carter and I thought."

"You discussed it with him?" Walt asked.

"Yes, when I told him about her phone call."

"So you continued seeing him?" Danielle asked.

"Yes. On Camilla's next phone call to her uncle, he brought up the subject. He reminded her we were friends before she ever met me. He told her he didn't appreciate her interfering with his life. Camilla never called me again about it. I think she was afraid to. I imagine after that call she probably realized it wasn't the smartest thing to say. Carter didn't like to be told what to do."

"I'm assuming the Alzheimer's stopped the cribbage games?" Danielle asked.

Brian nodded. "A little over six years ago, I noticed there was a problem. I called Camilla. I thought she should know. Like I said, after our divorce, she had left town and never returned. Not even to visit her uncle. But she called him every week. I'll give her that." Brian picked up his iced tea and took a sip. "After I called her, she came back to town and arranged care for her uncle."

"How long had she been gone at this point?" Danielle asked.

"About four years." Brian set his glass of iced tea back on the table. "Anyway, before Camilla arrived, I convinced Carter to go to his doctor. A year later, Carter had no clue who I was."

AFTER LUNCH, Brian decided to visit Carter. Heather sat quietly in the passenger seat as Brian drove them to the hospital. She had offered to go with him. Brian had accepted the offer, rather liking the idea of a chance to talk to Carter again—through Heather—if he passed when they were at the hospital.

Fifteen minutes later, they were on the second floor of the Frederickport Hospital. Before leaving Pier Café, Flora had called Brian a second time, telling him Camilla's uncle had moved to room 210.

As Brian and Heather walked down the hallway toward room 210, Heather stopped abruptly when an elderly man exited the room. The fact he had moved through the door without opening it gave her pause.

Brian, preoccupied with his own thoughts, failed to notice Heather trailing behind him. Just as Heather caught up to him, the old man looked at Brian and shouted, "Brian, you came!"

The next moment, Brian walked through the old man and opened the door to room 210. The old man vanished.

TWO

U*ncle Carter is dead,* Heather told herself as she quietly followed Brian into the hospital room. She wanted to grab him before he stepped inside room 210, but he had been too quick and had already opened the door and stepped inside before she could do anything. Plus, voices came from inside the room. Heather soon discovered the voices belonged to a doctor and a woman later introduced as Carter's caretaker.

"You came." Flora sounded relieved as she greeted Brian, giving him an awkward hug. Both she and the doctor stood with their backs to the hospital bed, with the doctor scribbling notes on a piece of paper affixed to a clipboard. Heather ignored the inquiring frown Flora gave her before the caregiver turned her attention back to Brian. Heather glanced over to the hospital bed, where Carter's body remained, his face turned from view.

"Of course I came. And I'd like you to meet my friend Heather Donovan." Brian reached out and grabbed hold of Heather's right hand, pulling her closer to him. "Heather, this is Flora Bennett, Carter's caregiver."

Flora smiled weakly in Heather's direction, gave an unconvincing, "Nice to meet you," and turned back to Brian and said, "This is Dr. Morgan."

Heather said nothing, feeling awkward, since Brian proceeded as if Carter still lived. She waited for them to tell Brian.

Dr. Morgan glanced up from his clipboard and gave Brian a smile. "I've met Officer Henderson before."

"How's he doing?" Brian asked the doctor.

He's dead. That's how he's doing, Heather silently answered. Normally, Heather would find those words harsh when talking about someone Brian so clearly cared about. But Heather understood Carter was not only old, but Alzheimer's had trapped him inside his body for over six years. Moving over to the other side and starting the next leg of his journey would be a relief, in her opinion.

"His vitals are good," the doctor said.

Heather jerked her head around and looked at the doctor, whose attention was focused on Brian. She looked back over at the bed with Carter and then at the monitors. Action on the monitors confirmed the doctor's claims. While Brian talked to Flora and the doctor, Heather slowly walked toward the hospital bed. The three did not seem to notice her departure from Brian's side and her sudden interest in the patient.

If he's alive, who is the ghost who greeted us at the door? Heather asked herself. *He obviously knew Brian. But that's no biggie. Everyone in town seems to know Brian, even the doctor. I wonder, is our ghost newly departed? Is his body still in the hospital? Or has he been haunting these halls for years?*

Heather inched her way to the hospital bed as the questions ran through her head. When she reached Carter's bedside, she moved over to the other side of the bed to get a better look at his face. To her surprise, the man sleeping in the bed looked just like the ghost who had greeted Brian in the hallway.

"Holy crap," Heather muttered. She looked up from the bed and glanced around the room. *Carter is obviously having an out-of-body experience. Is he in a coma like Lily and Chris were? Where did he go?*

A few minutes later, the doctor left the room, leaving just Flora and Brian chatting amongst themselves. Silently, Heather returned to Brian's side.

A sound from the bed interrupted the discussion. The three turned to the hospital bed in time to see Uncle Carter open his eyes and look around the room in confusion. Both Flora and Brian moved to his bedside.

"Mr. Carter?" Flora asked as she took his hand.

He looked at her and blinked several times before asking, "Where am I?"

I guess his spirit jumped back into his body, Heather told herself. *No reason to search the hospital for him after we leave.*

"You're in the hospital. You got a little sick, and they're taking good care of you here," Flora explained.

Brian moved next to Flora and smiled down at the elderly man. "Hello, Carter. How are you feeling?"

Carter frowned. "Who are you?"

Brian smiled sadly. "My name's Brian. Brian Henderson."

"Do I know you?"

"You did once. We used to play cribbage together. Once a week."

"I used to play cribbage with my dad. You're not my dad." Carter looked at Flora. "Where is my dad?"

"He's with your mom. You'll see him later," Flora told him.

Carter considered Flora's words a moment and then looked at Heather, who stood to one side of Brian. "Who are you? Have we met?"

"This is Heather. You've never met her before," Brian explained.

Carter looked from Heather to Brian and asked, "Is she your daughter?"

Heather grinned while Flora let out a snort.

Ignoring Flora's reaction, Heather stepped closer to Carter and said, "It's nice to meet you, Mr. Carter. No, I'm not Brian's daughter, just a friend. And he was worried about you, so I offered to come with him to check on you. I hope you're feeling better."

"I don't remember him," Carter said as he glanced from Heather to Brian, back to Heather. "You're pretty. I'd remember you."

Just as Heather flashed Carter a grin, a raspy voice called out,

"Criminy, old man, she's young enough to be your granddaughter." Heather, being the only one in the room who heard, looked up from Carter to find the ghost she had seen earlier standing by the hospital window, looking their way. Confused, she glanced from the ghost to Carter. *They look like twins. Did Carter have a twin? One who passed before his brother*, Heather wondered.

While thoughts ricocheted around in Heather's brain, Brian and Flora chatted with a confused Carter.

"I don't remember you," Carter once again told Brian.

"It's Brian, you idiot," the ghost shouted. "I swear, watching you like this drives me crazy!" The ghost turned to Flora and said, "It's all your fault! If you had simply gotten the DNR, I don't believe we'd all be here right now. I can't move on as long as he's sitting in that damn hospital bed sounding like an idiot!"

Distracted by the ranting ghost, Heather found it impossible to follow Brian and Flora's conversation. A moment later, Carter closed his eyes and fell back to sleep. Flora and Brian moved away from the hospital bed to discuss the patient. While Brian and Flora quietly chatted, Heather silently moved toward the window and the still ranting ghost.

Heather stood in front of the window. If Brian or Flora looked her way, they would assume she was looking outside. She stared at the ghost, who could not ignore the woman now standing inches from him, looking into his eyes. He frowned. "You can see me?"

Heather nodded.

"Who are you?" he asked. "What are you to Brian?"

"I'm his girlfriend," Heather whispered. "Who are you?"

The ghost's eyes widened. "His girlfriend?" The ghost looked from Heather to Brian, who stood on the other side of the room, still talking to Flora. He looked back at Heather. "How old are you?"

Heather flashed the ghost a scowl. "Old enough."

"Does Camilla know about you?" the ghost asked.

"He's no longer married to Camilla. They haven't been married for years."

"I know that," the ghost snapped. "But does Camilla know about you?"

"I doubt it. He hasn't seen her for years," Heather whispered.

"I'd like to be there when she sees you." The ghost chuckled. "She didn't treat Brian right. Broke his heart. Don't break his heart."

"Who are you?" Heather asked.

The ghost glanced at the hospital bed and then back to Heather. "Seriously? You don't know?"

"I assume you're Carter's twin brother, who passed before him. I'm just surprised Brian never mentioned he was a twin."

The ghost laughed and then said, "I'm Homer. Homer Carter." The next minute he disappeared.

Heather glanced around and turned from the window.

"Thanks again for coming," Heather heard Flora say when she returned to Brian's side. "While you're technically not family, Mr. Carter always called you family. And frankly, in his current condition, I think he deserves to have family with him."

"I'm sure Camilla will call you back. Maybe she went away for the weekend and her phone doesn't have service," Brian suggested.

"I also called her brother and sister. They haven't called me back."

"In fairness to them, they probably expect Camilla to handle it and assume she'll be calling you. When you left a message, did you tell them you've been trying to contact Camilla?"

Flora nodded. "Yes."

"If you don't hear from Camilla by tomorrow, call me. I'll try to get ahold of her brother. We always got along well."

They chatted a few more minutes while Heather silently listened, eager for Brian to say goodbye to Flora so she could ask him about Homer Carter. Ten minutes later, Brian and Heather were finally alone as they walked down the hallway toward the elevator.

"Who is Homer Carter?"

Brian glanced at Heather and frowned. "Umm… you just met him."

They stopped in front of the elevator, and Brian pushed the button. The elevator door opened. It was empty. As they stepped inside, Heather asked, "Was that a question or a statement?"

Now standing in the elevator, Brian glanced at Heather as the elevator door closed. "What are you talking about?"

"Who. Is. Homer. Carter?"

Brian frowned at Heather. "He's my ex-wife's uncle. You just met him."

The elevator stopped. The door opened, and Brian stepped out onto the first floor. Heather remained standing in the elevator, a confused look on her face.

When Brian realized Heather hadn't moved out of the elevator, he turned to face her. "What's wrong?" Brian asked.

The elevator door started to close. Brian moved his hand between the doors. The doors opened. Zombie-like, Heather stepped from the elevator.

"Heather? What's going on?"

"I'm so confused." Heather took Brian's right hand. "We need to go somewhere private to talk."

Thirty minutes later, Brian and Heather sat in Brian's car, still parked in the hospital parking lot. Heather had finished telling Brian about her encounter with the ghost. After answering a series of questions Brian asked, they now sat quietly, rethinking their conversation.

Finally, Brian said, "I don't understand."

Heather shrugged. "I don't either. If the dude in the bed had been sleeping while the ghost ranted, I would assume he was simply having an out-of-body experience."

"I have to say, being with you is never boring." Brian let out a sigh. "Now what?"

"Now we talk to Eva. If anyone knows what just happened, she will."

THREE

It was the first Saturday of April. After saying goodbye to Heather and Brian at Pier Café, Walt had driven Danielle to the grocery store in the Ford Flex. Danielle wanted to buy baking supplies. Her plan was to stock up on all their favorite homemade treats before the babies arrived next month. She didn't imagine she would have much time to bake with newborn twins in the house. Last week, they'd had a new freezer delivered, which Walt had easily moved to the basement using his telekinetic gift.

Initially, Walt had discouraged Danielle's plan, not wanting her on her feet for that long. She soon explained Marie had offered to help her, which would allow Danielle to remain seated during the process. Walt found Marie's offer generous, as Marie had not been fond of cooking during her lifetime, aside from her legendary Christmas divinity and peanut brittle. He doubted she had developed a love of baking during her death.

Just as Walt pulled into the grocery store parking lot, Danielle's cellphone rang. She answered the call. Walt pulled into a parking spot, turned off the ignition, and waited silently for Danielle to finish her call.

"That was Lily," Danielle explained as she returned the phone to her purse.

"That's what I assumed."

"She's planning a bon voyage party for Laura on Tuesday night."

Walt arched his brows. "Bon voyage party?"

"It's a going-away party. Basically, it's just dinner at a restaurant. Lily and Ian are treating. She wanted to make sure we can go. It's a surprise. Laura thinks she's going out Tuesday night with Kelly. Kelly will bring her to the restaurant."

"Rather late notice." Walt opened his car door.

"Lily said with all that's been going on the last few months, she didn't think about doing something special for Laura until this morning."

FIFTEEN MINUTES LATER, Danielle pushed a shopping cart down the cereal aisle en route to the baking section. Walt trailed alongside her. Halfway down the aisle, they spied Evan MacDonald, the police chief's youngest son and fellow medium. He was also one of the few people in Frederickport who knew the truth about Walt and his fellow mediums.

Ten-year-old Evan failed to notice Walt and Danielle's approach. So focused on a box of cereal on the top shelf, he stood on tiptoes and reached upwards. Despite his efforts, the box of cereal remained out of reach. Just as he was about to give up, the box floated off the shelf, hovering a moment above Evan's head before moving downward, within Evan's grasp.

Instead of freaking out about a flying box of cereal, Evan snatched the box in midair and swung around and faced Walt and Danielle. He grinned broadly. "I knew it was you!"

Danielle chuckled while Walt smiled at the boy, who ran to them with his box of cereal.

"Most people would scream if they saw food literally flying off the shelf," Danielle teased.

Evan shrugged. "I just figured it was Walt. I suppose it could have been Marie, but ghosts don't usually go grocery shopping."

"You here with your dad?" Walt asked.

Before Evan answered the question, a familiar voice called out, "Hey, what did I tell you about talking to strangers?"

The three looked over to the voice and saw a smiling Police Chief MacDonald walking in their direction, pushing a half-filled shopping cart.

"Hey, Chief," Danielle greeted.

"Edward," Walt said with a nod.

The adults chatted for a few minutes while Evan dropped his box of cereal in his father's shopping cart. The chief explained his older son, Eddy, hadn't wanted to go grocery shopping, so he stayed home. They discussed the reason for Walt and Danielle's shopping trip, and the chief teased he would need to stop over and help taste test Danielle's baked goods.

When they ended their brief visit, Evan and the chief headed in one direction, with Evan pushing the shopping cart, and Walt and Danielle went in the opposite direction, with Walt pushing their cart.

Just as Walt and Danielle were about to leave the aisle, they heard a frantic Evan call out, "Dad!"

Walt and Danielle quickly turned and saw the chief sprawled on the floor, his son crouching by his side.

Walt sprinted toward the chief and Evan, while Danielle followed at a slower pace, now pushing their cart.

"What happened?" Walt asked when he reached them.

The chief sat on the floor, rubbing his right knee, and grimaced before saying, "This damn knee gave out."

Walt stood over the chief. "You think you can stand up?"

Danielle pulled up beside them, parking her cart next to the chief's. "What happened?"

"Dad's knee went out again."

"Again?" Walt offered the chief a hand.

Danielle looked down at the chief as he took hold of Walt's hand. "I didn't realize you were having problems with your knee."

Instead of answering Danielle, Edward struggled to stand up, but found the task impossible.

Walt saw the chief couldn't stand with a hand up alone, so he focused his energy on the fallen man and telepathically lifted him to his feet.

"Whoa!" the chief blurted when he first felt his body lifting from the floor.

"It's just Walt, Dad," Evan told his father.

No longer struggling, the chief passively allowed Walt's energy to lift him to his feet. Applying most of his weight on his good leg, Edward held onto his nearby shopping cart. He let out a sigh of relief. "Thanks, Walt."

"What's going on with your knee?" Danielle asked.

"It's been bothering me lately." The chief reached down and rubbed his right knee.

"Have you seen a doctor?" Danielle asked.

"No, but I have an appointment on Monday."

"He fell at home last week," Evan told them.

NOT LONG AFTER Walt and Danielle arrived at Marlow House with their groceries and started putting them away, rose petals fell from the kitchen ceiling, disappearing as they reached the floor.

Danielle paused for a moment and glanced upwards. "Hi, Eva. What happened to snowflakes?"

"She's eager for spring," Marie explained when she materialized a moment later. Marie, the image of an elderly woman wearing a floral sundress and straw hat, stood by the sink, waiting for Eva to show herself. "Eva enjoys the color."

A moment later, the spirit of Eva Thorndike, onetime silent screen star and childhood friend of Walt Marlow from his first life, with an uncanny resemblance to Charles Dana Gibson's drawing known as the Gibson girl, materialized just as the last rose petal vanished.

Eva looked at the groceries Walt had already removed from the paper sacks and arranged on the kitchen counter. She arched her brows. "That's a lot of sugar and chocolate chips."

"Danielle's doing some baking before the babies arrive, and I'm helping," Marie said.

Eva turned to Marie. "You loathe baking."

Marie smiled. "But I enjoy helping Danielle."

Danielle grinned at the spirits. "And I appreciate it. And hello to both of you."

As Danielle and Walt finished putting away the groceries, Marie and Eva each took a seat at the kitchen table and listened as Danielle told them about Edward's fall at the grocery store.

"I did notice Edward was looking a little bowlegged lately," Marie said.

Danielle frowned. "Bowlegged?"

Marie nodded. "Yes. I was almost going to ask him if he took up horseback riding. But he wouldn't have heard me, anyway." Marie gave a shrug.

"I hadn't noticed," Danielle said.

Danielle's cellphone rang. She picked up the phone, looked at it, and before answering, said, "It's Heather."

Walt continued putting away the groceries while Danielle answered the call. "Hey, Heather... What?... Eva?" Danielle looked at Eva. "She's here. Why?... Laura?... No, she's not here. I don't expect her back until this evening... Okay, I'll tell her." Danielle ended the call and set her phone back on the kitchen counter.

"What was that all about?" Eva asked.

"Heather asked if I knew where she could find you. I told her you were here. She wants you to wait for her. She and Brian are coming over. They need to ask you something. She said it's important."

"What was that about Laura?" Marie asked.

"She doesn't want to talk to Eva with Laura here. That would be awkward," Danielle said.

ABOUT THIRTY-FIVE MINUTES LATER, Walt, Danielle, Heather, Brian, Marie, and Eva sat in the living room at Marlow House. Heather had just recounted their experience at the hospital. Brian was the only one in the group who could not see and hear Marie or Eva, yet he was aware of their presence.

"That is strange," Danielle said. She sat on the sofa next to Walt, with her cat, Max, curled up between them, sleeping. Heather and Brian sat on the chairs facing them, while the two spirits sat in imaginary chairs next to the sofa and chairs.

"Are you certain he was conscious when the spirit was talking?" Walt asked.

"They were both talking at the same time," Heather said. "Obviously, they both can't be Homer Carter."

"But didn't you say he has Alzheimer's?" Eva asked.

"Yes," Heather said. "But I'm not sure why that matters."

"Of course it matters," Eva insisted. "It makes all the difference in the world."

"How so?" Danielle asked.

Eva looked at Danielle. "I'm surprised you've never encountered this before."

"Encountered what?" Heather frowned.

With a sigh, Eva leaned back in the imaginary chair. "As you all understand, your body is nothing more than a vessel to hold your spirit."

Heather shrugged. "Uh… so?"

"When a spirit suffers from memory issues like Alzheimer's or dementia, it's not an ailment of the spirit—it's a defect of the body. The body can no longer process the needs of the spirit in the same way as it did before. For example, defects of the aging body, not of the spirit, suppress memories. The spirit remains whole. When a person who suffers from Alzheimer's or dementia dies, they are once again able to process—or remember all those memories their failing body suppressed," Eva explained.

"What does that have to do with the ghost I met?" Heather asked.

"For one thing, he is not a ghost—at least not yet. I suspect who you met was the spirit of Homer Carter, who stepped out of his body, not so different from any out-of-body experience," Eva said.

"But it is different," Heather insisted. "Homer's spirit was still in his body. He was talking to Brian at the same time the ghost rambled on."

"Ahh, but you see, it's not unusual for the spirit of a person who struggles with memory issues caused by a deteriorating body to break free from that body and communicate with a medium. Even while the person—in your case, the man in the hospital bed—was talking," Eva explained.

"What is she saying?" Brian asked.

"It makes little sense to me," Heather grumbled before repeating all Eva had said to Brian.

"That's an interesting theory," Danielle muttered after Heather did her best to retell Eva's explanation.

Eva looked to Danielle and smiled. "It's not a theory, and it's not uncommon. Think of it this way, the vessel holding a spirit has a crack in it. A crack caused from Alzheimer's. While it continues to hold the spirit, some of it slips out. Just as water might leak out from a cracked vase."

Brian's cellphone rang. He pulled it out of his jacket pocket and looked at it. "It's Flora," he said before answering the call. The others remained quiet. After a moment he said, "He's dead?"

"Carter's dead?" Heather whispered.

Brian gave her a nod while still talking on the phone. After he finished the call, he tossed his cellphone on the end table.

"What happened?" Heather asked.

"He had another heart attack, and that was it," Brian explained.

"Now he's a ghost," Eva said. "Unless he's already moved on."

FOUR

On Sunday afternoon, Heather gave Marlow House's kitchen door a cursory knock before reaching for the doorknob. Through the window, she saw Danielle sitting at the table, flipping through a cookbook. Heather smiled when she found the door unlocked.

Danielle looked up from the notebook. "Hey, Heather."

"I assumed I'd find you and Marie baking up a storm." After stepping into the kitchen, Heather closed the door behind her and walked toward Danielle.

Danielle closed the cookbook and set it on the table. "Actually, I'm waiting for Marie. She should be here any minute. We're going over some recipes I want to make. But we won't start until after Laura leaves on Wednesday."

"Ahh, to avoid her walking in on floating baking supplies?" Heather sat down at the table with Danielle.

"Something like that." Danielle grinned. "Laura's across the street right now. She's having dinner there tonight. She's trying to spend as much time as she can with her sister before she leaves."

"I noticed her crossing the street when I was walking here. By the way, Lily invited Brian and me to the surprise going-away party on Tuesday."

"So you'll be there?"

"Yep. And on Thursday, I'm going with Brian to his friend's funeral."

"The guy with Alzheimer's?"

Heather nodded. "Which means I'll be meeting Brian's ex-wife."

"That should be interesting."

"I'm surprised they already arranged the funeral. He died yesterday, and it's a weekend."

"I take it the caretaker finally got ahold of his ex-wife?"

"About an hour after Brian got the call about him passing away, his ex finally returned Flora's call. Flora's the caregiver. I guess his ex's brother and sister are coming too. They're both married and have kids, but according to Brian, he thinks they'll come alone."

"I'm here!" Marie appeared in the middle of the kitchen.

After greeting Marie, Danielle quickly recapped what they had been discussing.

"Ahh, so you'll meet Camilla?" Marie took a seat at the table.

"You knew her?" Heather asked.

"Of course. Brian was married to her for twenty-five years. They split up not long after their twenty-fifth wedding anniversary. We weren't friends or anything. But we knew each other."

"I heard about them breaking up after twenty-five years of marriage. That's a long time to be with someone," Heather said.

"Obviously, Camilla felt it was long enough." Marie chuckled.

Danielle looked at Marie. "What was she like?"

Marie considered the question a moment before answering, "To begin with, much closer to Brian's age."

"Yeah, I've heard that too," Heather grumbled.

Marie leaned back in her chair and sighed before saying, "In all seriousness, Camilla Henderson was a striking woman. In some ways, she reminded me a little of Beverly Klein. I always suspected that's why Brian was initially attracted to Beverly."

"You mean Camilla tried to kill Brian like Beverly killed her ex?" Heather snarked.

Marie chuckled. "No. I was referring to her appearance. Bev was always impeccably groomed, classy clothes, someone you expect to be wearing a single strand of pearls and tastefully applied makeup."

"Not black lipstick or polish?" Heather glanced at her own nails, painted dark burgundy, almost black.

Once again, Marie chuckled. "While people considered Camilla an attractive woman, if I want to be brutally honest…"

"Be brutally honest," Heather urged.

"Camilla isn't what I would call a natural beauty. But she knew how to use what God gave her and definitely had a knack for applying makeup."

"What was her personality like?" Danielle asked.

"Frankly, I didn't care for her. I always felt she came across as disingenuous. Something of a phony. But the men seemed to like her. She was a bit of a flirt."

"How did Brian deal with that?" Danielle asked.

Instead of answering the question, Marie studied Heather for a moment. "You know, Brian's attraction to Heather makes much more sense now that I think about it."

Heather frowned at Marie. "What is that supposed to mean?"

"For one thing, you are the polar opposite of Camilla."

"Gee, thanks. What, I'm unattractive, with no sense of style, and don't know how to wear makeup?"

Marie laughed. "No, dear. You are genuine. You never put on a pretense for anyone. And as I mentioned, Camilla is not a natural beauty, while you look lovely, even when you go jogging in the morning without bothering to put on any makeup."

"I guess that's a compliment," Heather muttered under her breath.

"You said she was a flirt. Is that why they broke up? Did she leave him for someone else?" Danielle asked.

"Not sure if there was another man. It wouldn't surprise me, considering how she openly flirted. But if there were rumors about her and someone else, they never got back to me. Despite everything, before she left him, they seemed to have a solid marriage. But one never knows what goes on behind closed doors."

"Brian rarely talks about her, and I don't ask," Heather said.

"He's obviously gotten over it, but back then, I understood it blindsided him. Quite broken up. Of course, that was about ten years ago," Marie explained. "I wonder if she ever remarried."

"She hasn't," Heather said. "Brian told me that according to Flora, she never remarried and still goes by Henderson. Which I find weird. Even if she's still single, why not go by her maiden name? I sure wouldn't use my ex's surname. Of course, I don't plan to ever get married."

"Remember, they were married for twenty-five years. That's a long time. Not unusual for a woman of that generation to keep her ex's name," Marie reminded her.

"Danielle didn't keep her husband's name after he died. And they didn't even divorce," Heather said.

"I'm not in that generation. Plus, Lucas and I hadn't been married that long," Danielle said. "And if he hadn't died, I wouldn't have stayed with him—or kept his name—not after learning of his mistress."

Heather let out a sigh. "True."

Marie looked at Heather. "Are you serious when you say you'll never get married?"

Heather shrugged. "What's the point? I've never wanted kids. Even if I didn't have messed-up genes, I don't really see myself as a mom. If not for having kids, I'm not sure; what's the point of marriage?"

ANNE ROBERTS SAT on the vanity bench and watched as her roommate Camilla Henderson filled the open suitcases on the bed with the clothes from Camilla's wardrobe. Camilla meticulously folded each item before adding it to the suitcase.

"What did your broker say when you gave notice?" Anne asked.

"I softened the blow by giving him my client list and told him I just expected a referral fee from my current listings."

"Was it wise to hand over your client list? After all, what happens if you want to come back?"

Camilla leaned over the bed, closed the suitcase, and looked over to Anne. "I'm not moving back. And I'm not sure I want to keep selling real estate. With the inheritance from my uncle, I might just retire." Camilla sat on the side of the bed and faced Anne.

"I understand that. But aren't you sort of repeating the past?"

Camilla frowned. "What do you mean?"

"How you left Frederickport... and your marriage of twenty-five years?"

"And never looked back?" Camilla hesitantly added.

"Oh, you looked back." Anne gave a snort. "I can't count how many times over the years you've cried on Sarah's and my shoulders over your ex-husband. And how leaving him was the biggest mistake of your life."

"I do get dramatic when I drink."

"Admit it, unresolved feelings for Brian are the real reason you're moving back to Frederickport."

Camilla shrugged. "If I wanted to see Brian, I could have always gone back under the pretense of seeing my uncle."

"Yeah, but when going back for a visit, there's no guarantee you'll run into him. And going there for a couple of days is nothing like moving back full time."

"What are you saying?" Camilla asked.

"I see what you're doing. I know you, girl. This is your opportunity to move back to Frederickport. It's a small town, so you're bound to run into your ex. You already have a house there—well, your uncle's house. If you don't have to worry about working, you'll have plenty of time to figure out ways to run into him. But before you make this big move, are you sure he hasn't remarried? It's been ten years."

"Yes, it has been ten years. So it's silly to assume I'm going back there now, after all this time, for Brian."

Anne resisted the temptation to point out Camilla's obsession with Brian had increased in recent years, which Anne believed had to do with Camilla's series of failed relationships. Anne also believed Camilla viewed her memories of Brian through a skewed lens. "Does this mean you aren't sure if he's in a relationship?"

"I haven't heard if he's in a relationship. But I'm certain he never remarried. After all, if he'd gotten married, there would have been some mention in the local paper."

Anne knew Camilla subscribed to the *Frederickport Press*. But she also knew Camilla kept in contact with a few people back in Frederickport, and had Brian remarried, Anne doubted Camilla would have to wait to read about it in the newspaper.

WHEN ANNE finally left Camilla alone in the room, Camilla removed the suitcases from her bed and set them in the corner. Her plan was to leave first thing in the morning for Frederickport. Aside from her clothes, she had already boxed up what she intended to take with her and what would fit in her car. She packed and stored the rest of her personal items in the garage, ready to be shipped. She wasn't planning on taking any of her furniture with her. That, she had already given to her roommates. She wanted to start fresh in Frederickport, and she had the money to do that.

Camilla walked from her bedroom into the adjacent bathroom and looked into the mirror, studying her reflection. With a smile, she ran her fingertips along the edge of her cheekbones. She wondered what Brian would think when he saw her. They would undoubtably see each other at her Uncle Homer's funeral service on Thursday. He would expect her to look a decade older. But she didn't, thanks to one of the most talented plastic surgeons in the country. While it had been costly, she believed the money was well spent.

FIVE

On Monday morning, Police Chief MacDonald sat on his doctor's examining table, wearing his shirt and boxers under the hospital gown the nurse had given him.

The doctor stood before him, examining his right knee. "How long has it been hurting?"

"The last few years, if it bothered me, I would wear a brace, and that seemed to take care of it."

The doctor glanced up from the knee to Edward's face. "There is nothing in your medical records about your knee bothering you."

Edward shrugged. "It didn't seem to be that big a deal, and the brace always helped. Not like it bothered me constantly. It was a random thing. If the brace hadn't helped and it kept hurting, I would have come in earlier. But the last few months, it's gotten worse, and when I fell last week, I thought I'd better have you look at it."

"And you fell again this past weekend?" the doctor asked.

Edward nodded. "On Saturday, at the grocery store."

"We need to get an X-ray."

Less than an hour later, after the chief returned from the X-ray room, he sat on a chair while the doctor viewed his X-rays on a monitor overhead.

"What do you see?"

The doctor looked at him. "I'm referring you to an orthopedic surgeon."

The chief groaned. "Are you saying I need surgery?"

"It depends on what the surgeon says. But looking at these X-rays, your knee is bone on bone. I'm surprised you're getting along as well as you are."

BEFORE LEAVING the doctor's office on Monday morning, the chief was told the orthopedic surgeon's office would contact him to set up an appointment within the week. He was told it could take over a month to get an appointment. The chief returned to his office, and much to his surprise, the surgeon's scheduler called to set up the appointment.

"I called you as soon as I received your referral," the woman's voice on the other end of the call explained. "This morning we had a cancelation for this afternoon. I already called the other people on our waiting list, and they can't take the appointment. I can give you this one, but if it's too last minute for you, the next opening is in June."

"June?" The chief frowned. He glanced at his calendar. It was April 8. He then looked at his wall clock. "What time today?"

"In thirty minutes."

"I NEED A NEW KNEE?" The chief repeated the diagnosis given to him by the orthopedic surgeon. The chief sat on the examining table while the surgeon sat nearby on a rolling stool.

To explain the current condition of Edward's right knee, along with the proposed surgery, the surgeon quickly scribbled illustrations on a pad of paper, showing it to Edward as he continued adding to the drawing while elaborating on his explanation.

Finally, the doctor asked if the chief had any questions.

"How soon do I need to do this? What would you do if it were your knee?"

"You'll need to talk to our person in scheduling. But if it were me, I'd want to take care of it as soon as possible."

LATE MONDAY AFTERNOON, Police Chief MacDonald sat alone at his desk, looking at the calendar pulled up on the computer. While he wasn't surprised to hear he needed a knee replacement, he hadn't fully appreciated the impact the surgery would have on his life and those around him—until now.

A knock on the open door broke his concentration. He looked up to see Brian Henderson standing in his doorway.

"Hey, Chief, anything going on we should know about?" Brian asked.

Edward waved Brian into his office.

"Funny you should ask that." Edward let out a sigh, pointed to the empty seat, leaned back in his office chair, and watched as Brian sat down.

"You've been in and out of the office most of the day, and on the phone most of the afternoon. What's going on?"

"I had to go to the doctor today and then a specialist," the chief began.

Brian sat up straight. "Oh crap, are you okay?"

The chief waved his right hand dismissively. "I'm okay, nothing life threatening, just a major pain in the butt. I have to have knee replacement surgery."

Brian winced. "I've had a few friends who've gone through that, and they say the physical therapy can definitely be a major pain in the butt. But from what I understand, it's a lot easier than it used to be."

"Oh, I'm not concerned about the physical therapy or even the surgery, but I'm going to be off work for at least four months."

"Joe and I can hold down the fort," Brian told him.

"Yeah, that's what I thought at first. From what the doctor told me, I'll be going home the same day as the surgery. While I obviously won't be running marathons until I'm completely healed—which, according to the doctor, can take between six months and a year—I figured I could still come into the office after a couple of weeks, oversee things with your help and Joe's."

"And you can't?" Brian asked.

The chief shook his head. "I had several long phone conversations with Fred Lyons today. Unfortunately, he had knee replacement surgery five years ago." Fred Lyons was the city manager.

"What does that have to do with anything?"

"He insists there's no way I'm returning to the office for at least twelve weeks, and he suggested our insurance might have a problem with me returning to work prematurely. If I injured myself by coming back too soon, and the city allowed it, he worries they would be liable. The fact he had the surgery himself, well, I guess he was laid up for a long time."

"I suppose I can understand his concerns." Brian leaned back in the chair.

"One problem, as you're aware, we're currently understaffed. Fred doesn't want me to pull you or Joe from your duties to cover for me. He wants to bring someone in from the outside to serve as an interim police chief. Someone who can stay and act as my second-in-command. Which is obviously what he feels will fix our understaffing issue."

"Really? And where would he find this replacement?"

"He's already found one. That's one reason I've been on the phone all day. He wants to hire Clay Bowman."

Abruptly, Brian sat up straighter. "Clay Bowman? The same Clay Bowman who used to work here years ago?"

The chief nodded.

"How is he qualified to be a police chief? Or even assistant police chief? I know he's Lyons's brother-in-law. But isn't that pushing nepotism a little too far?"

"According to Fred, Bowman is currently working as assistant police chief at the station he's at. But he's not happy there. Both Bowman and his wife miss living on the coast, and she wants to live close to her sister again. I guess Bowman called Fred a few months ago and told him that if there was ever an opening here, he'd like a shot at the job."

"There's been openings here for a few months. Why hasn't he applied already?"

The chief smiled weakly. "I didn't ask Fred, and he didn't say, but I suspect Bowman was talking about if I ever left. He wanted my job."

"Even if he comes, he'll only have your job for a short time."

"But he'll be assistant chief when I come back, second-in-command, ready to take my job if I decide to retire. Standing in the wings," the chief said dully.

"That kind of screws Joe," Brian grumbled. "I always figured Joe would advance to chief when you retired. And isn't this hiring your call?"

"Yes and no."

WHEN BRIAN GOT off work on Monday, he went straight to Heather's house for dinner. While waiting for the dinner to finish cooking, they sat together at the kitchen table, each drinking a beer while rehashing their day. Brian had just finished telling Heather about his conversation with the chief before leaving the station thirty minutes earlier.

"So who is this Bowman dude?" Heather asked. "How do you know him?"

"He used to work with us. He's a couple of years older than Joe. Honestly, I never cared for the guy. He always rubbed me the wrong way. He thought a lot of himself." Brian took a drink of his beer.

"You seem to be especially annoyed how him getting his temporary job could screw Joe's chances of moving up when the chief eventually retires. But you never seem to care about yourself."

Brian laughed and set his beer on the table. "Unless you haven't noticed, I'm older than the chief. I suspect I'll retire before him."

Heather studied Brian for a moment, cocking her head from side to side. "You never had dreams of moving up in the ranks and making chief someday?"

Brian smiled at Heather. "Will you think less of me if I say no?"

Heather returned his smile. "No. But I am curious."

"Years ago, I turned down a promotion at the station. In retrospect, that probably had something to do with the demise of my second marriage."

Heather arched her brows. "Why did you turn it down?"

"My ex asked the same thing." Brian picked up his beer and took another drink and then continued, "I enjoy my job, but I have —had—no desire to be a police chief. I'm comfortable and will be content doing what I do until I eventually retire."

"Is that what you told your wife?"

"You mean ex-wife?" Brian grinned.

Heather nodded.

"Pretty much. It took a while for it to sink in, but I eventually realized Camilla wanted someone who was more ambitious. At least, as ambitious as she was. When she told me she wanted a divorce, one reason she gave, she didn't want to make more than her husband someday."

"Seriously?"

Brian nodded. "I thought we were living a pretty good life. We had two decent incomes and good benefits."

"What did Camilla do for a job?"

"She was an escrow officer. But she talked about getting her real estate license someday. After she moved, Homer told me he paid for her real estate classes so she could get her license. From what I understand, that's what she does now. She sells real estate."

"Can I ask you a personal question?"

"Sure."

"You told me once that you and your second wife decided not to have kids. Did you ever want kids?"

"I grew up thinking people got married and had kids. That it was expected. But having kids wasn't really something I thought about. Before I married Camilla, she told me she didn't know if she ever wanted children. I was sorta surprised. I figured all women wanted children. But it got me to thinking. I realized I would be okay child-free. So we agreed to give our marriage a few years, revisit the topic of children, and if she still didn't want them, I'd have a vasectomy."

"So that's when you had your vasectomy?"

"Actually, about a year after we got married, she was diagnosed with endometriosis and had a hysterectomy."

"Umm… if Camilla had a hysterectomy, why did you get a vasectomy?" Early in Brian and Heather's relationship, Brian had told Heather he could never father children, as he had gotten a vasectomy during his second marriage.

"It wasn't because I wanted to cheat on my wife," Brian assured her.

"I remember you telling me you had your vasectomy years ago, when you were with your second wife. I assumed it was because you both decided not to have kids."

"Remember, when I got my vasectomy it was during a time in our marriage Camilla wanted to be with me. I think the only thing that bothered Camilla about her hysterectomy was that someday I might decide I wanted kids, and I might leave her for another woman who could give me babies. I tried to assure her I was fine with never having kids. But it bothered her. Finally, she asked me to have a vasectomy. I agreed."

SIX

Late Tuesday afternoon, Danielle stood in the downstairs bathroom of Marlow House, looking into the mirror, her blouse pulled up while she ran her hands over her extended belly. She had finished using the bathroom a moment earlier, and after pulling up her stretch pants, she found herself in front of the mirror, inspecting the progress of her pregnancy. She looked nine months pregnant, while she wasn't quite eight months along. But that was to be expected, she thought. After all, she carried twins.

She wondered if she'd make it to her May 15 due date. Her belly button was now an outie, and she couldn't remember the last time she'd had a solid night's rest. Fortunately, she had gotten past the morning sickness stage.

A loud knock came at the door. "Danielle, are you alright?"

Danielle turned from the mirror, let her blouse drop back into place, and opened the door. She looked into the anxious face of her husband.

"I'm fine." Danielle grinned up at Walt.

"You were in there forever. I was worried."

Flashing Walt a grin, Danielle stood on her tiptoes and gave him a quick kiss on the lips before saying, "I was checking out my belly. I look like I'm ready to pop."

"But you're okay?"

"I'm fine." Danielle stepped out of the powder room into the entry hall with Walt.

"Laura took the last load of her laundry out of the dryer. She's in her room, packing." Walt nodded toward the downstairs bedroom.

Danielle glanced at her watch. "Kelly should be picking Laura up pretty soon."

"Does Laura have any idea?"

Danielle shook her head. "If she does, she's a good actress."

After Lily had decided to throw her sister a bon voyage party, she'd called the beauty shop and asked if she could get an appointment for her sister late Tuesday afternoon, explaining she was leaving for New York the next day, en route to Europe. Once the beauty shop had scheduled the appointment, Lily had set the plan in motion. She would pay for Laura to have her hair done as a going-away gift. Kelly would offer to take her, and after the appointment, they would stop at the Italian restaurant under the pretense they were picking up pizza Lily had supposedly ordered and return to Lily's house for dinner.

Of course, Lily had not ordered pizza. She had reserved a private room at the restaurant for the party. When Laura walked into the restaurant with Kelly to pick up the pizza, she would be surprised by all the friends she had met in Frederickport gathered for her bon voyage going-away party.

The doorbell rang ten minutes later, and Danielle answered the door. Kelly stood on the front doorstep.

"I'm here to pick up Laura."

Danielle opened the door wider. "Come on in. She's in her room, packing. She's been doing laundry all day."

"Yeah, she told me." Kelly dropped her voice to a whisper and asked, "Does she know anything's up?"

"Like I told Walt, if she does, she's a good actress."

A few moments later, Kelly and Danielle stood in front of the closed door of the downstairs bedroom. Danielle knocked on the door.

"Come in!" Laura called from inside the room.

Danielle opened the door.

Laura stood by the side of her bed, filling her suitcase with clean, folded clothes. She looked at Danielle and Kelly. "As soon as I finish this, we can go."

Kelly walked into the room and looked Laura up and down. "You're going to wear that?"

Danielle stood silently, just inside the bedroom, listening to the exchange. She had to agree with what she assumed Kelly was thinking—Laura would die if she walked into her surprise party wearing that outfit.

Laura glanced down at her worn jogging pants and faded T-shirt. "I'm only getting my hair done. And I did all my laundry already. I don't want to dirty anything."

"But we're stopping at the restaurant to pick up pizza? You really going to walk in wearing that? You told me you were getting rid of those pants."

Laura glanced down at her pants again and then looked back at Kelly. "Yeah, I was going to throw them away before I left. I didn't want to use up all my outfits. I have no idea when I'll be able to do laundry again. And I can stay in the car while you pick up the pizza."

Kelly let out a sigh. "Come on, wear that new outfit we bought last week. I was hoping we could take some pictures tonight at your sister's. It's your last night here."

Laura glanced down at her outfit again and looked back at Kelly and shrugged. "I guess this looks kinda tacky. Okay, I'll change. I really don't want to take pictures in this." Laura looked at Danielle and asked, "You sure you and Walt don't want to join us all for pizza at my sister's?"

"I'm not feeling that great," Danielle lied. "I'm afraid the smell of pizza will get me."

"I guess I'll see you in the morning before I leave."

"We'll have breakfast ready for you," Danielle promised.

"I don't want you to go to any trouble, especially if you aren't feeling well," Laura insisted.

"If I don't feel good, I'll make Walt cook."

Laura laughed.

"I'll go out in the hall, and you get dressed," Kelly told Laura. "But hurry, you don't want to be late for your appointment."

When Kelly and Danielle stepped back into the hallway and closed the door behind them, Danielle looked at Kelly and said, "That was quick thinking. Good job."

"I was prepared," Kelly confessed. "I was a little worried that Laura might decide to slum it her last night in Frederickport."

"YOU LOOK SO cute with that haircut," Kelly told Laura after they left the beauty shop.

"Thanks. I'm really glad Lily thought of this. I should have thought of it myself."

"I'm going to miss you," Kelly told Laura as she unlocked the driver's side of her car.

"I'll be back to Frederickport," Laura promised.

When Kelly and Laura walked into the Italian restaurant some fifteen minutes later, Laura was a little confused when Kelly headed toward the dining room instead of stopping at the counter to pick up the pizzas Lily claimed to have ordered.

Laura followed Kelly. "Kelly, I'm sure we're supposed to pick up the pizzas in the front."

"Your sister said they'd be back here," Kelly told her as she walked through an open double doorway leading to one of the private party rooms.

Laura followed Kelly and stopped abruptly when welcomed by a loud chorus of, "Surprise!"

Laura looked around at the sea of familiar faces, along with bon voyage party decor scattered around the room. One of the smiling faces was Danielle—who earlier that day had claimed she didn't feel good. Standing next to Danielle was Lily grinning in her direction.

Speechless, Laura looked to Kelly.

"It was your sister's idea. I was just an enlisted co-conspirator."

Laura hugged Kelly and whispered, "Thanks for making me change my clothes." A moment later, Laura gave her sister a hug.

LILY HAD INVITED Police Chief MacDonald and his sons to the party. He sat at a table with Walt, Danielle, Chris, Brian, and Heather, while his sons sat at a table nearby with Connor, eating pizza.

"I can't believe you're having knee replacement surgery next Friday. That's so fast," Danielle said. "Is your knee that bad?"

"It is fast. But that has nothing to do with the severity of my knee. More about some poor guy who had a heart attack."

"Heart attack?" Heather asked.

"One of my doctor's patients was scheduled for surgery next Friday. This last Monday was his pre-op appointment. But on Sunday, he had a heart attack. He's okay. Or he will be. But they can't operate right now. They fit me in on Monday—I took his pre-op appointment. And they offered me his surgery date. If I didn't take it, I'd have to wait a few months. I really don't want to wait."

"I'm surprised they told you that the other patient had a heart attack," Chris said. "They aren't supposed to discuss other patients."

"They didn't tell me why the patient cancelled. I overheard two of the nurses talking about it," the chief explained.

"You mentioned they're bringing in someone to replace you while you're out?" Walt asked.

"Yeah. A guy who used to be on the department here," the chief said. "It was about ten years ago. He quit around the time Evan was born. I was a little annoyed because I had planned to take some extra time off to help Cindy, but he left abruptly. Supposedly, he had a great job offer he couldn't pass up. Currently, he's assistant chief."

"And he's going to leave his job there?" Danielle asked. "He can leave that fast? No two weeks' notice?"

"To be honest, one reason I accepted next Friday's surgery date,

I figured that would kill the idea. I couldn't imagine he could get here that quick. And you didn't hear me say that."

"The replacement is the city manager's brother-in-law," Brian added.

"Nepotism?" Danielle asked.

"The city manager insists it's our good fortune to have someone who is not only experienced but is familiar with Frederickport and can get here on Monday," the chief explained.

"Wow. That's quick," Heather said. "Doesn't sound like he gave his current employer much notice."

"He didn't give his last employer much notice either," Brian snarked.

"Does he have a family?" Danielle asked. "That would be a quick move for a family."

"The last time it was him and his wife. From what I was told, he and his wife have two sons now. Twins." The chief looked at Danielle.

"Twins?" Danielle repeated.

"They're a little younger than Evan. From what I understand, his wife was pregnant when they left Frederickport. Anyway, I can't imagine pulling Evan and Eddy out of their school and taking them away from their friends at a moment's notice."

———

CAMILLA OFFERED TO DRIVE TONIGHT. After all, unlike her brother and sister, she had once lived in Frederickport, and she knew the streets better than they did. There wasn't much food in their uncle's house, and Flora hadn't moved out yet. Plus, none of them wanted to cook. With her sister in the passenger seat and her brother in the back seat, Camilla pulled her car into the restaurant parking lot. Last night, she had picked up takeout at Beach Taco after arriving in town. Her brother and sister had arrived this afternoon, and they all had agreed on Italian food.

SEVEN

"Looks like someone's having a party," Camilla's brother, Ted, said after picking up a menu from the center of the table. They had just sat down in the back of the restaurant, next to the event room, its double doors wide open, so they could see inside. Camilla and her sister glanced to the open doorway and back to their menus.

"Speaking of parties, are we going to have some sort of wake?" Camilla's sister, Lucy, asked.

Ted looked at his younger sister. "What do you mean?"

Lucy set her menu on the table. "After the service, it's customary to go back to the family's home."

"You saw Uncle Homer's house. It needs a good cleaning. Not sure what Flora's been doing every day," Camilla said.

"Obviously not cleaning," Ted snarked.

"We need to do something," Lucy insisted.

Camilla glanced over her menu to her sister. "Pastor Chad said the meeting room would be open, and the church's Ladies' Auxiliary will make coffee and bring cookies, so his friends who want to share a moment after the service can do it at the church. That's basically the wake."

"Did Uncle Homer still go to church?" Ted asked.

Camilla shrugged. "For a while, after Flora came to live with him, she took him to church. But that didn't even last a year. After the Alzheimer's progressed, according to Flora, it was too difficult to take him anywhere. Of course, you would have known that had you bothered checking in with Flora to see how he was doing."

"I called a few times. But you were the one who hired the woman. I didn't think you'd want me to interfere," Ted said. "After all, Uncle Homer left you in charge. You were always the favorite."

"Let's not argue. This is the first time in a couple of years we've all been together, the three of us. But I am curious about the funeral." Lucy turned to Camilla. "You said Uncle Homer had already arranged everything?"

"Yes. Remember when Uncle Homer updated his will and sent us all a copy? I think it was the year before his Alzheimer's diagnosis."

Camilla's siblings nodded in response.

"I called him after I received my copy. He told me he had also made the arrangements for his funeral. He said when the time came, all we had to do was call the local funeral home and Pastor Chad from his church. I explained all this to Flora when I hired her, and she made the calls after Uncle Homer passed away."

"You gotta give it to Uncle Homer. He made everything easy for us. I appreciate the fact he set up the trust. Easier and faster to settle the estate." Ted looked at Camilla and said, "I hope you didn't go crazy spending money to take care of him. Aside from paying Flora, which wasn't cheap, it's not like he needed new clothes each year or money to go out to dinner. I imagine he spent most of his time sitting around in his bathrobe."

AFTER FINISHING HER DINNER, Lily moved to Danielle's table. The two women sat together and visited with the guests who made it their way. These days Danielle avoided spending too much time on her feet. While Lily's pregnancy wasn't as far along as Danielle's, she didn't feel like standing on her feet either.

Walt had left Danielle's side to get her another beverage, while Heather had moved to the children's table, where she held Connor on her lap while she talked to Evan and Eddy. Brian and Joe huddled together, each drinking a beer, discussing the new temporary police chief, while Ian chatted with his father and the chief. Ian's father, John, shared with MacDonald his own personal experience with knee replacement surgery, while Kelly talked with her mother, who kept looking over at Heather, making sure Heather didn't drop her grandson. Meanwhile, the guest of honor shamelessly flirted with Chris.

Eventually, Joe drifted over to Kelly, and Brian to Heather.

Now standing behind Heather, who still held Connor on her lap while the boy colored on a disposable menu sitting on the table, Brian leaned over and whispered, "I'm going to the restroom. Are you about ready to leave?"

"Let me finish this picture with Connor, and when you come back, we can say goodbye to everyone," Heather said.

"IS THAT BRIAN?" Ted blurted when he spied a familiar face coming out of the event room.

Both Camilla and Lucy looked toward the double doors leading to the party room.

Not waiting for a response, Ted stood up and yelled, "Hey, Brian!"

Brian stopped walking and turned to the voice. There, sitting at a nearby table, was Brian's ex-brother-in-law, ex-sister-in-law, and ex-wife. He stood motionless for a moment, making no response. Finally, he took a breath, exhaled, smiled, and walked toward the table.

Ted met Brian halfway, shook his hand, and led him back to the table where he had left his sisters. Both women remained sitting. Brian made no attempt to give either woman a hug or handshake;

he simply gave them both a nod, said hello, and expressed his condolences for the loss of their uncle.

Ted sat back down in his seat and insisted Brian sit down in the empty chair. Reluctantly, Brian complied.

"You look good, Brian," Lucy said.

"So do you," Brian returned. "How is your family?"

"Wonderful. Our youngest started college this fall. Ted's oldest starts next year."

"Wow. They were little kids the last time I saw them."

Lucy glanced at her sister and then back at Brian. "Doesn't Cam look amazing? I swear, she doesn't age. I'd love to know her secret."

Brian smiled and said, "So how long are you all staying?"

"Ted and I flew in. We rented a car together in Portland. We're heading back the day before Easter." She looked to Camilla and said, "Umm, I'm not sure about Cam." Lucy looked back to Brian. "Ted and I got into Frederickport late this afternoon. Cam was already here. She drove in. Ted and I stopped at Uncle Homer's first, dropped off our suitcases, and came here to eat dinner. We haven't had a chance to learn Cam's plans."

Brian arched his brows at Camilla. "You didn't fly? Wow, that's a long trip to make for a few days."

Camilla smiled at Brian. "I'm not staying for just a few days. I'm moving back to Frederickport."

"Moving back?" Ted and Lucy chorused.

Camilla looked at her siblings. "Yes. That's why I drove."

"Where are you going to live?" Ted asked.

"Uncle Homer's house, of course," Camilla explained.

"But we're selling the house," Ted reminded her. "You mean you're staying in the house while it's for sale? When it sells, are you going to buy something here or rent?"

"I planned to discuss this with you later. But I'm not selling Uncle Homer's house," Camilla said.

"It's not exactly Uncle Homer's house anymore," Lucy reminded her.

"No. It's our house now," Camilla said. "And I hope you both visit as often as you can. Thankfully, it's a spacious house, room for all of us."

Ted shook his head. "I don't want a vacation home. But if you want to buy out my share, that's fine with me."

Camilla was about to suggest they discuss the topic later when she noticed a young woman with straight black hair, pale skin, and an outfit that could only be described as Goth walking toward their table. Without pause, the peculiar woman walked up behind Brian. Had the woman not exited the same room as Brian, Camilla might have assumed she was someone Brian had once arrested, and she was stopping by to harass him.

Instead, the woman placed her hands on Brian's shoulders and said, "So this is where you went."

Brian glanced over his shoulder at the woman, smiled, and patted one of her hands before looking back at the people now sitting in silence at the table with him, staring at the stranger.

Brian stood and pulled Heather to his side. "Heather, this is my ex-wife Camilla, and her brother, Ted, and sister, Lucy."

Heather smiled at the people sitting at the table, staring in her direction. "Nice to meet you. I'm sorry about your uncle Homer."

"You know about Uncle Homer?" Lucy blurted.

"After Homer had his heart attack and Flora couldn't get ahold of you, she called me. I dropped by the hospital to see him. Heather came with me. I talked to Homer. He didn't recognize me, of course."

"Is Heather one of your friends' daughters?" Camilla asked.

Heather chuckled. "No. I'm his girlfriend." She turned to Brian. "If you want to stick around and visit, I can hitch a ride home. It's okay."

Camilla frowned and thought, *If this girl really is Brian's girlfriend, she doesn't sound annoyed at the prospect of him leaving her to visit with the ex-wife. No way is she his girlfriend. What is he up to?*

Brian looked at Heather and grinned. "No, I'm ready to go." Brian glanced back at the table. "It was nice to see you all."

"See you at the funeral," Heather called as they walked away, hand in hand.

"THEY CAN'T BE SERIOUS," Lucy said after Brian and Heather were out of earshot.

"I never imagined Brian was so kinky," Ted said with a laugh.

Camilla scowled at her brother. "What is that supposed to mean?"

"She's hot—and weird. Weird in sort of a hot way," Ted explained.

"She's a child," Camilla spat.

"I wouldn't call her a child. I imagine she's in her thirties," Lucy said.

"Still young enough to be his daughter," Camilla said.

"What do you care?" Ted asked. "You walked away from Brian years ago. Good for him; he's found a cute little honey."

"She's not his girlfriend," Camilla insisted. "He's doing this to bug me."

"You haven't seen him in years," Ted reminded her. "Why would you imagine he's showing up with her for your benefit?"

"Think about it. Does she look like Brian's type? No. Did she even sound remotely upset about her boyfriend staying here with his ex while she finds her own way home? No."

"For as long as I knew Brian, you were the only woman he was with, and she's definitely nothing like you," Lucy said.

Camilla nodded. "Exactly."

"It's been a long time since Brian was with our sister," Ted reminded her.

"Brian expected us to be here for Uncle Homer's funeral. I bet anything that girl is someone Brian's arrested in the past, and he got her to pretend to be his girlfriend. Girls like that find it in their best interest to do favors for cops."

"This is Frederickport, not New York City," Ted snarked.

"And he knew we would be here?" Lucy asked.

"I left a note for Flora telling her where we were going for dinner. It's entirely possible he called her, under the guise of asking something about the funeral, and if we arrived yet. And she told him where we'd be."

"But they were at that party," Lucy reminded him.

"Brian's a cop. He can crash a party like that and pretend he's just making sure everyone is behaving—or some lame excuse like that. No way is that girl really his girlfriend. He's trying to make me jealous." Camilla laughed.

EIGHT

Laura rolled her suitcases from the downstairs bedroom at Marlow House into the entrance hall, lining them neatly by the wall next to the front door. She returned to the bedroom for her purse. In the bedroom, she looked around, making sure she had forgotten nothing. After picking up her purse from the dresser, she made her way to the attached bathroom to give it a final once-over. Satisfied she had forgotten nothing, she returned to the hallway and set her purse on one of her suitcases. She glanced at her watch. Lily and Ian should be here any minute to pick her up to take her to the Portland airport.

From the entrance hall, she walked to the kitchen, where she found Walt and Danielle sitting at the kitchen table, eating breakfast. They looked in her direction and smiled.

"Are you sure we can't get you anything to eat?" Danielle asked from the table.

"Thanks, but no. I'm just not hungry. I think I'm too anxious to eat." Laura poured herself a cup of coffee and joined them at the table.

"I can understand that. If you get hungry, you can always get something to eat at the airport after you check in," Danielle said. "They have a lot of restaurants at the airport."

"I want to thank you both for everything. I really wish you would let me pay for my room." Laura took a sip of her coffee.

"We appreciate the offer, but that's not necessary," Walt said. "It was nice having you."

"But I expect you to post daily pictures on your Facebook page so we can travel vicariously with you through Europe," Danielle said.

"You sound like my sister." Laura set her cup of coffee on the table. "You guys are going to have your hands full pretty soon. I should feel guilty about traipsing all over Europe while you'll be dealing with two babies—and so will Lily and Ian!"

"What do they say, the consequences of our actions?" Walt laughed.

A loud "hello" called out from the direction of the hallway.

"Sounds like Lily and Ian are here," Walt said.

Lily walked into the kitchen a few moments later and looked at her sister. "Ian's loading your suitcases into the car. Ready?"

"Let me go to the bathroom one more time." Laura stood up and ran from the kitchen.

"I meant to say something before. You guys want to leave Connor with us?" Danielle asked.

"Thanks, but June's over at our house watching him. She offered last night at the going-away party."

"You want to bring Sadie over here?" Walt suggested, knowing June felt uncomfortable with the golden retriever around her grandson.

"No, that's okay." Lily smiled. "Ever since you had a talk with Sadie about not licking Connor when June's at our house and staying out of his bedroom, there hasn't been a problem."

When Laura returned to the kitchen from the bathroom, Walt and Danielle got up from the table and walked with Lily and Laura back into the entry hall, where they found Ian, who had just finished loading Laura's suitcases into the car. They exchanged goodbye hugs, thank yous from Laura, and well-wishes from Walt and Danielle.

AFTER IAN and Lily drove away with Laura, Walt and Danielle returned to the kitchen. Danielle sat down while Walt cleared the table and hand-washed the breakfast dishes. Walt was just finishing up the dishes when a knock came at the back door before it opened. Heather walked into the house, closing the door behind her.

"I saw Ian's car leaving with Laura and Lily. I imagine they're off to the airport." Heather helped herself to a cup of coffee.

"There's tea in the pantry," Danielle offered.

"Thanks, but I sorta feel like coffee. It's one reason I came over. I didn't want to make an entire pot for one cup." Heather took a seat at the table.

"Did Brian drink an entire pot this morning?" Walt joined them at the table.

"He didn't stay last night. He had to work this morning, and he needed to get back to his place and wash some clothes for work."

"You should have washed them. That's woman's work," Walt teased.

"Hey, I saw you doing the morning dishes," Heather countered. "If I were his wife, he'd be washing his own clothes."

"You've washed Chris's clothes before," Walt reminded her.

"Yeah, but he pays really well." Heather grinned. "And speaking of wives, I met Brian's ex last night." Heather told them about her meeting with Camilla Henderson at the Italian restaurant.

"I wish I'd known she was there. I'm curious to see what she looks like. What did you think?" Danielle asked.

"She looks super young. Supposedly she's only a couple of years younger than Brian, but she looks way younger. Attractive woman." Heather took a sip of her coffee. "But I have to admit, the bitchy way she looked at me is probably why I blurted out that I was his girlfriend."

"How did she react to that?" Walt asked.

"I guess the best way to describe it, shock, disbelief, speechless. Not just her; her brother and sister looked stunned, too. I thought it might annoy Brian how I handled it. You know, just blurting it out like that."

"Was he annoyed?" Danielle asked.

"Umm, considering he broke into laughter after we left the restaurant, I don't think he was upset. But when we got in the car and started back to my house, he told me how he ran into her. He also said she's moving back to Frederickport, which he didn't seem happy about."

"What does she do for a living?" Danielle asked.

"She's a real estate agent." Heather looked at Walt and added, "Like you used to be."

"Cute." Walt chuckled.

"I try." Heather grinned and then added, "You guys happy to have your privacy back?"

"Who said we got our privacy back?" Walt teased. "There's always someone from the neighborhood walking in and helping themselves to our coffee."

"MRS. HENDERSON, you can't expect me to move out by the end of the week," Flora told Camilla.

Camilla stood at the kitchen counter of what had been her uncle's home. She had just turned on the coffeepot while Flora stood nearby, wringing her hands. Camilla turned from the counter and looked at Flora. "There's no reason for you to stay here any longer. Your services are no longer needed. I think I've been generous, letting you stay until after our uncle's funeral. I expect you to be out by Sunday. And if you're worried about your last check, it should be ready Friday."

"Where am I supposed to go?" Flora asked.

"It's not my concern. I hired you to take care of my uncle. I don't know why you expect us to let you stay when we no longer need your services."

"I don't expect you to let me live here indefinitely. But I thought you'd let me stay until I can secure another job, or at least find a place to live."

Ted and Lucy heard loudly raised voices coming from the kitchen yet couldn't make out the conversation. They walked into the room. Flora and Camilla stopped talking and looked at them.

"What's going on?" Ted asked.

"I was just explaining to Flora, we expect her to move out by Sunday," Camilla explained.

"Mrs. Henderson, I need more time. But if you insist I move out by this weekend, you should probably get an eviction notice. Which means you can expect me to be here for at least another month." Flora turned abruptly and left the room.

Lucy looked from the doorway where Flora had just exited to her sister. "What was that about?"

"It means Flora won't be moving out for another month." Ted walked over to the counter and pulled a coffee cup from the overhead cabinet.

Lucy frowned. "I don't understand."

"That woman is making it difficult." Camilla grabbed a coffee cup from the overhead counter and waited with her brother for the coffee to finish brewing.

Five minutes later, the three siblings sat at the kitchen table, each with a hot mug of coffee.

"Maybe if you would have handled her differently, not insisted she leave this weekend, she'd be leaving of her own accord in a couple of weeks. But I have a feeling, even if she finds something, she'll stay for the entire thirty days of the eviction notice," Ted said.

"I don't want a roommate," Camilla grumbled.

"And I want to sell this house," Ted countered.

"I agree with Ted. You can't be serious about moving in here. It's not fair. It doesn't belong to you," Lucy said.

"It belongs to me. A third of it," Camilla insisted.

"Yes, and two-thirds belong to Ted and me. And we want to sell," Lucy said.

"We already covered this last night," Camilla reminded her.

"According to the terms of Uncle Homer's will, we can only sell the house if all three agree. No one is stopping you from moving in here with me."

"I thought you said you didn't want a roommate," Ted reminded her.

"She knows we aren't moving in. Unlike Cam, we have our own lives—our own families. And not in Oregon."

"Come on, Lucy, this will give you a vacation home. You can come visit with your family. There are plenty of bedrooms." Camilla flashed her sister an insincere smile.

Ted let out a sigh and set his coffee cup on the table. "Come on, Cam, don't be this way. This house is huge. Too big for one person. I never understood why Uncle Homer stayed here. We can sell it, split the money. Your share should be enough to buy something else in Frederickport. Something smaller and more appropriate for one person."

"If Flora intends to stay here, it's going to be difficult to sell, even if Cam changes her mind," Lucy pointed out.

Ted looked at Lucy. "I can talk to Flora, soothe her ruffled feathers. I don't see why she can't stay while we have the house on the market. Once it sells, it'll probably take at least thirty days to go through escrow. We can get Flora to sign something to agree to leave before the house closes escrow. It will be a win for her, because it'll give her over thirty days before she has to move—which she'd have to do if we serve her an eviction notice."

"Not selling. I like this house and want to live here." Camilla stood up from the table. "And I don't want Flora to stay for a month." Camilla turned from her siblings and left the kitchen, leaving her half-full coffee mug sitting on the table.

Ted and Lucy sat in silence for a few moments. Finally, Lucy said, "We can't keep this house. This is even overreaching for Cam. Who's going to pay for the upkeep and the taxes? Knowing our sister, she's intending to live here while we pay two-thirds of the property tax and maintenance on the property. When the house needs a new roof, she'll expect us to pay what she considers our share. And unfortunately, because of how Uncle Homer wrote his will, I'm not sure there is anything we can do about it. We don't even know what's left in Uncle Homer's bank account. As far as we know, Cam depleted that. Then what happens? We end up dipping into our own money so Cam can live rent-free in our house?"

"If I have my way, she will not live here." Ted picked up his mug and downed his coffee.

NINE

Danielle no longer walked—she waddled. These days she found it necessary to rest her right hand on her hip while waddling, which accentuated what had turned from baby bump to basketball belly. Walt had asked her not to use the stairs unless he was with her, which she found an unreasonable request, as she had no desire to be stranded on any level of Marlow House. She promised she would be extra careful when using the stairs and avoid making unnecessary trips up or down the staircase. Walt accepted her compromise, yet he or Marie seemed to magically appear on the staircase if she used it without first asking him or Marie to accompany her.

After breakfast on Thursday morning, Danielle retreated to the living room with a book. Walt was on his way to his attic office to get some work done when their housekeeper, Joanne Johnson, arrived. Joanne and Walt exchanged greetings before he headed upstairs, and she went to the living room to say hello to Danielle.

"Good morning," Joanne greeted from the doorway.

Danielle looked up from her book and smiled at the middle-aged woman. "Morning, Joanne."

"How are you feeling today?"

"Sorta like a beached whale."

Joanne laughed.

"Other than that, pretty good. Walt keeps spoiling me."

"As he should. I'm going to start in the downstairs bedroom. Did Laura get off okay?"

Danielle nodded. "Yep. She arrived in New York safely. Ian has a friend there she's staying with. He arranged theater tickets for the friend and Laura. Then she flies to London on Sunday."

"Sounds exciting. Well, I'm going to get started. Do you have your cellphone with you?"

Danielle frowned and glanced at the nearby table and then to Joanne. "Yeah. Why?"

"If you need anything, call me." Joanne turned and moved out of sight.

They all spoil me. Danielle grinned and glanced back to the iPhone sitting on the coffee table. She closed her book, tossed it on the table, and picked up the cellphone. They still had not decided on names for the babies. Like she had done a dozen times before, Danielle began surfing for name ideas on her phone. After ten minutes of surfing, a girl's name popped out at her. She paused a moment, considering the name.

"Addison?" She closed her eyes and said, "Addison Marie." Danielle smiled. If Walt agreed, Danielle had found the name for their baby girl. Now, all they needed was a boy's name.

A familiar voice called out, "Good morning," a moment before the spirit attached to said voice appeared in the living room, standing next to the coffee table.

Danielle looked up and smiled at Marie. Instead of wearing one of her favorite floral sundresses and straw hats, Marie looked as if she were heading to church.

"Morning, Marie. What are you dressed up for?" Danielle set her cellphone back on the coffee table.

"I'm going to a funeral this morning."

"So is Heather. Are you going to the same one?" Danielle asked.

"Yes. Homer Carter's. I haven't seen him around town since he passed, but I'd like to say hello if he hasn't moved on yet."

"Were you friends with him before he came down with Alzheimer's?" Danielle asked.

"Not really. I was more friends with his late wife. Of course, she died years ago. He never remarried. Before he started having memory issues, I'd see him around town. We were friendly, not close. But I want him to give my best to his wife when he passes over."

"THANKS FOR COMING WITH ME," Brian told Heather as he parked the car in front of the church.

"I suspect you want me more as an interpreter today than for moral support." Heather didn't sound offended at the possibility.

Brian shrugged. "Well, I have to admit, I am curious to find out what Homer is thinking about all this."

"He's thinking he's dead." Heather unbuckled her seatbelt.

Brian chuckled. "I'm also grateful Chris let you take a couple of hours off."

"And I'm forever grateful I ran into Chris's car. It landed me the best job." Heather grinned as she opened her car door.

"It did."

As they approached the church, Heather stopped walking. "He's here."

Brian stopped walking with Heather and glanced around. People were arriving at the church, with some just getting out of their cars in the parking lot, others making their way up the walkways, and some going into the church.

Brian glanced around. "Where?"

"And he's not alone."

"What do you mean?"

Heather nodded toward the entrance of the church. "Marie's with him. And by the way they're chatting it up, I have a feeling she's giving him the inside scoop on death, ghosts, and moving over to the other side."

Heather and Brian started walking again. After a few steps,

Heather said, "They're looking this way now. Homer is staring at us, and Marie is talking away. I have a feeling she's telling him about me."

"I used to hate funerals."

Heather glanced at Brian. "You don't anymore?"

Brian shrugged. "Attending a funeral with you is a little entertaining and sometimes more of a going-away party."

Heather chuckled.

Before they arrived at the front steps of the church, they encountered Homer's caretaker, Flora.

"Officer Henderson," Flora greeted.

Brian reached out and took Flora's hand for a moment and said, "Do you remember my friend Heather Donovan? Heather, this is Homer's caretaker, Flora Bennett. You met her at the hospital."

The two women exchanged brief nods and half smiles. Flora looked back to Brian and said, "I was his caretaker, past tense, as Mrs. Henderson reminds me."

"What do you mean?" Brian asked.

"I've been taking care of Mr. Carter for years. Which, of course, meant I needed to live in his house. Be on call twenty-four seven. A week ago, I had no idea Mr. Carter would pass away so suddenly. As far as I knew, he could have lived another ten years or more."

"What are you saying?" Brian asked.

"Mrs. Henderson expects me to move out on Sunday. Sunday. I've had less than a week to process the fact that I not only need to find a new job, but a place to live."

"That doesn't seem fair," Heather chimed in. "Why can't you stay a little longer while you find a new job and someplace to live?"

Flora flashed Heather a smile, her expression softening toward the younger woman. "She said they no longer need me. So I have to leave."

BY THE TIME Brian and Heather reached the church entrance, Marie and Homer were no longer there. Heather assumed they had gone inside. She conveyed this information to Brian as they walked up the steps.

Once they entered the church, Heather spied the pair again, this time standing by the open casket, watching mourners enter the church. Heather was about to tell Brian where Marie and Homer now stood, but froze when Camilla appeared out of nowhere, taking hold of Brian's arm and practically shoving Heather off to the side.

Stunned at the boldness of Brian's ex, Heather stared speechless at the pair.

"Brian, you need to sit up front with the family," Camilla insisted. Still holding onto Brian, she looked over her shoulder at Heather and smiled sweetly. "You can go home. You didn't even know Uncle Homer. I'm sure you have more fun things to do than attend the funeral of someone you don't know."

Brian, who himself was a bit taken aback by Camilla's assault, regained his composure and pulled his arm from her grasp. "Thank you, Camilla, for the offer, but I'm not family, and Heather and I will sit in the regular pews."

Camilla moved closer to Brian, her back to Heather. "Brian, Uncle Homer considered you family. He loved you. Your place is up front with the rest of us."

"Heather and I—" he began, only to be cut off by Camilla.

Moving even closer to Brian, Camilla lowered her voice and said, "Brian, stop this ridiculous charade. You're just making yourself look foolish. I know I hurt you. You have no idea how sorry I am for that. Why don't we go someplace after the service and talk about it? Just you and me."

While Camilla had lowered her voice and positioned herself between Heather and Brian, Heather could still hear what Brian's ex said, even if others around them could not. Instead of being incensed at the woman's behavior, it amused Heather, and she felt a little sorry for Brian.

Marie suddenly appeared by Heather's side. "What is going on with those two?"

Heather, who now stood with her arms crossed, directly behind

Camilla while looking over her shoulder at Brian, glanced at Marie and whispered, "I think she's hitting on Brian."

"I don't know what you think is going on here," Brian told Camilla.

"I think you paid some little tramp to…"

"Did she just call you a tramp?" Marie blurted, making it impossible for Heather to hear the rest of Camilla's sentence.

Heather nodded, and Marie turned toward the woman and smacked the side of her head. Marie instantly regretted her outburst, because in the next moment Camilla, who assumed Heather had assaulted her, twirled around and slapped Heather across the face.

Heather was not the only one who let out a gasp. Brian pushed Camilla to the side and pulled Heather, who now held her injured cheek with one palm, to his side.

"What the hell do you think you're doing?" Brian shouted at Camilla. "I should arrest you for assault."

Camilla pointed to Heather and screamed, "She hit me!"

"She did not!" Brian screamed back.

Camilla solicited affirmations of those now gathered around her that Heather had indeed struck her first. While no one could say they saw Heather strike Camilla, none could say she hadn't hit Camilla. Ted and Lucy appeared on the scene and pulled Camilla away from Brian.

"ARE YOU OKAY?" Brian asked Heather after the two sat down in a church pew. "I don't know what the hell Camilla was thinking. I don't remember her ever being violent before."

Rubbing her cheek, Heather glanced from Brian, who sat to her right, to Marie, who sat to the left.

Marie smiled sheepishly at Heather. "I really am sorry."

Heather rolled her eyes at Marie and looked back at Brian. "I hate to say this, because I'm not a fan of your ex, but that wasn't entirely her fault."

"What do you mean?" Brian asked.

"Marie joined us when Camilla started getting all in your face. When Camilla called me a tramp, well, that didn't sit well with Marie."

Brian cringed. "Marie did something to Camilla?"

Heather nodded. "Gave her a good smack upside her head."

AFTER PULLING Camilla away from Brian, Ted deposited her with Pastor Chad, telling the minister his sister was having an emotional time. Pastor Chad led Camilla into his office and closed the door, intending to help her deal with her grief before starting the service.

"I'm going to find out who she is and sue her," Camilla told the minister. "She hit me. Although, considering she's just some addict Brian hired, I wouldn't get much."

"Are you talking about Heather Donovan?" Pastor Chad asked.

"Yes, the woman who hit me. I think her name's Heather."

Pastor Chad frowned. "I'm not sure why you think Brian hired Heather, or that she's an addict."

"Do you know her?" Camilla asked.

"Yes. She's the personal assistant of Chris Johnson, who heads the Glandon Foundation. She's also Brian's girlfriend. They've been together for at least six months, if not more."

TEN

It wasn't a large funeral. Had Brian's ex-wife not slapped her face, Heather might suggest she and Brian move up a few pews, since there was no one else sitting on the pew with them, or behind them, and the rows in front of them were sparsely populated. But she had no desire to move up closer to the psycho ex.

Heather attributed the low attendance to the fact Homer Carter's family only included two nieces and a nephew, two of whom had never lived in Frederickport, and she imagined many of his friends had already passed away. Plus, he had been living in isolation for years because of his illness.

She watched as Pastor Chad walked down the aisle with Camilla. When passing their row, Camilla glared her way. For a moment Heather wondered if the woman might stop and start hitting her again, but Pastor Chad put his arm around Camilla's shoulder and gently nudged her along. When they finally reached the front pew, Camilla sat down with her brother and sister, while Flora sat in the pew behind them.

Pastor Chad walked to the podium to begin the service. Homer continued to stand by his casket. Marie, who had been sitting near Heather a moment earlier, repeatedly apologizing for getting

Heather slapped, was currently pew hopping, moving from place to place, eavesdropping on conversations. Heather assumed that now that Pastor Chad was beginning the service, Marie would stop moving around and return to her pew. She glanced over to the casket, and Homer disappeared.

"I'm sorry my niece slapped you," a voice told Heather. Glancing to her left, Heather looked into the face of Homer Carter. The ghost sat next to her in the pew where Marie had been sitting minutes earlier.

Heather smiled at the ghost and whispered, "She doesn't like me."

Brian looked at Heather and whispered, "Are you talking to Marie?"

"No. The guest of honor," Heather explained.

Brian arched his brows and leaned forward, looking at what appeared to be an empty spot on the pew next to Heather, and whispered, "Hello, Carter."

"He can see me too?"

Heather grinned. "No. But he understands you're there."

"I wanted to tell you how sorry I am that you had to spend your final years the way you did," Brian whispered to Carter. "I always liked and respected you."

"Tell Brian the feelings are mutual. As for the final years, yeah, they kinda sucked. But nobody's fault. It is what it is."

After Heather repeated Homer's words, Brian leaned back in the pew and turned his attention back to Pastor Chad, listening to the memorial.

Since no one was in the pew in front of her or behind her, Heather wasn't overly concerned someone might overhear her conversation with Homer. She just needed to whisper. And since all heads were turned to the front of the church, she doubted anyone would notice her seemingly talking to herself.

"I introduced them, you know," Carter told Heather. "Never knew they had problems."

"You never know what goes on behind closed doors," Marie said when she suddenly appeared next to Carter.

"Hello, Marie," Heather greeted.

"How is your cheek, dear? I'm so sorry for getting you slapped."

"Oh, I forgive you. It was sweet of you to try to protect my honor. Anyway, I totally understand wanting to give someone a good smack when they bug you. After all, I've been working on not doing that anymore."

Carter eyed Heather up and down. "In that hospital room, when I first saw you, you said you were Brian's girlfriend. I was sure I had misunderstood."

"I still don't understand how you were still alive and talking to Brian. But then, well, you were there, another you. Also talking away."

"There is a great deal I also don't understand. For example, I couldn't quite see you as Brian's girlfriend. But then Marie explained everything." Homer smiled.

"She did?"

Homer nodded.

"I told him about your little misadventure in the mountains," Marie explained.

"Brian is a good man," Homer said. "All that I care about is that he's happy. My niece hurt him. I regret ever playing matchmaker those many years ago."

"Your niece is moving back to Frederickport," Heather told Homer.

"Yes. I know. That's another regret, how I wrote my will."

"Why?"

"Because Camilla moving back to town is already causing problems with her brother and sister. I've been over to the house, checking in on things. Ted and Lucy want to sell. I don't blame them. They each have their own lives. And I'm afraid the slap my niece gave you isn't the only problem she's going to give you."

Heather frowned. "Why's that?"

Before answering, Homer leaned forward and took another look at Brian, whose attention was fully on Pastor Chad. Homer leaned back and looked at Heather. "Because my niece regrets her divorce. She wants Brian back."

"Really?" Heather and Marie chorused.

"They've been divorced for ten years," Heather reminded him.

Homer shrugged. "I suspect things didn't work out the way Camilla thought they would."

"You mean her life after she left Brian?" Heather asked.

"Yes. I never understood why she left him in the first place. I always felt they were happy. Maybe she was going through some mid-life crisis. I suppose women can have them too." Homer gave another shrug.

"And she thinks she can just show up after ten years and Brian will welcome her back?" Marie asked.

"Apparently she does." Homer looked at Heather. "But she wasn't expecting someone like you. She's convinced herself you must be someone Brian hired to make her jealous."

"Seriously?" Heather frowned.

Homer nodded. "When I stopped in to see how they were doing, she was on the phone talking to someone, probably her old roommate, because they were discussing shipping the rest of her things here. She mentioned you. Told her friend Brian hired someone to pretend to be his girlfriend. She said he did it so she wouldn't know he was still alone and to make her a little jealous."

Marie gave a snort. "She actually thought Brian would hire someone who looked like Heather to play his girlfriend?"

Heather narrowed her eyes at Marie. "What is that supposed to mean?"

"Think about it, dear."

Heather let out a sigh. "Yeah, I suppose you're right."

NINE-YEAR-OLD ZACK BOWMAN clutched the box of toys, refusing to budge from where he stood until his mother agreed to include the box with the items the family planned to take to Frederickport with them.

"I already explained," Debbie patiently told her son. "We are not taking everything now. But if we end up moving to Frederickport, we'll bring the rest of our things. Think of this as a vacation."

"If it's a vacation, does this mean we don't have to do schoolwork?" Zack's twin, Eric, asked his mother.

Debbie looked at Eric and shook her head. "It's not that kind of vacation."

"If we end up moving to Frederickport, can we go to the school there?" Eric asked.

"Why would moving mean no homeschool?" Debbie asked.

"How are we going to meet other kids?" Zack asked. "Franky said if we move to a new town, the only way to meet other kids is at a public school." Franky was a neighbor boy whose mother's low opinion on homeschooling spilled over to her son's conversations with the twins. Debbie tried to dissuade the boys' friendship, but they had known each other since they had been in diapers, back when she and Franky's mother were still friends, and before the boys started school. The neighbor had sent Franky off to public school while Zach and Eric stayed home with her to be homeschooled.

"Your aunt told me the current police chief has a ten-year-old son. I'm sure you can be friends with him. And then he can introduce you to more boys," Debbie suggested.

"Isn't Dad taking his job?" Eric asked.

"Yes, just for a few months while he recovers from surgery. But if your father decides he likes it there, then the current police chief will probably retire. But we don't need to talk to anyone about that. That's family business. And what do I tell you about family business?"

"Family business stays in the family," Zack and Eric chorused.

Debbie smiled and gave her sons a nod. "Exactly."

"Why wouldn't Dad like it?" Zack asked.

Debbie shrugged. "We probably will stay."

Zack stomped his right foot. "Then why can't I take all my stuff?"

Her cellphone ringing in another room of the house saved Debbie from having to answer the question. She told her sons to finish their math assignment, and then she dashed from the boys' bedroom to answer her phone.

"HOW'S THE PACKING GOING?" the caller asked.

Debbie held the phone by her ear and plopped down on her living room sofa. "It would be much easier if I could ship the boys off somewhere while I'm doing it. It's one time I wish I had put them in a public school. Of course, then it would make this move more complicated."

"I wish I could be there to help you."

"Thanks, I appreciate that." Debbie glanced to the hallway leading to her boys' room. She heard screaming, but she blocked it out, focusing on the phone call.

"I wanted to tell you, I went to Homer Carter's funeral this morning," the caller told Debbie.

"I imagine she was there."

"All three of them were."

Debbie kicked off her slippers and pulled her feet up on the sofa. "Weird he would die now."

"Why is that weird? He was old and sick for ages."

"I just mean him dying right before we're coming to town. A reason for her to show up. All those times we visited, I never worried about seeing her. But I suppose there shouldn't be a problem. I can't imagine she'll still be there when we arrive next week. There's no reason for her to stick around. And with her uncle dead, no reason for her to come back to Frederickport."

"That's what I wanted to tell you. I heard at the funeral that she intends to stay. She's moving into her uncle's house."

Debbie sat upright, moving her feet back onto the floor. She clutched the phone to her ear. "You're not serious?"

"I'm afraid so. I wanted to warn you."

Debbie frowned. "She doesn't know we're coming back to Frederickport, does she?"

"I doubt it. She's only been in town a couple of days. And it's

66

not common knowledge about MacDonald having surgery and taking off for a few months. In fact, no one asked us about it when we were at the funeral. I even ran into Millie Samson there, and she never said a word about MacDonald."

"From what I remember, Millie always seemed to know what was going on in town." Debbie snorted.

"But Millie told me something interesting. Apparently, there was some sort of physical altercation at the funeral between Camilla and her ex-husband's new girlfriend. I didn't see it, and neither did Millie. But one of her friends told her about it."

"Brian was at the funeral?" Debbie asked.

"Yes. And he brought his girlfriend with him."

"What happened with Camilla and the girlfriend?"

"First, the girlfriend is much younger than Brian. Much younger."

Debbie laughed.

"From what Camilla told Millie, the girlfriend physically attacked her."

"What did Camilla do?" Debbie asked.

"She slapped her. And then Brian started screaming at her."

"Who did he scream at? The girlfriend or ex-wife?"

"The ex-wife. He didn't believe his girlfriend hit Camilla."

"What did Millie say about all this?"

"I guess Millie knows the girlfriend. She used to volunteer at the museum, and while she could be a little outspoken, Millie didn't believe she would hit Camilla unprovoked."

ELEVEN

On Monday morning, Carla wore her bright fuchsia-colored hair pulled back in a low ponytail while she waited on her customers at Pier Café. She filled Chief MacDonald's cup with coffee. He sat alone in a booth. "You ready to order, Chief?"

"I'm waiting for Brian and Joe. I'll order after they get here."

Fifteen minutes later, Brian and Joe had arrived, Carla had taken their order, and after she left their booth, they briefly discussed her newest hair color, with Joe wondering when her hair was going to start falling out, noting that all that dying could not be good for her hair. After the men finished gossiping about the server, the topic turned to the chief's upcoming surgery.

"Bowman is supposed to arrive today," the chief explained.

"I still can't believe that jerk will be our boss." Brian picked up his mug of coffee and took a sip.

"When's your last day?" Joe asked.

"I intend to work through Thursday. The surgery's on Friday. No reason to take off sooner. Although, I'll be out of the office for a couple of hours this afternoon. I have a pre-op appointment at one."

"When does Bowman start?" Brian asked.

"Like I said, he's supposed to arrive in town today. I don't imagine he'll even bother coming into the station until tomorrow. He needs to get his family settled."

"Where's he staying? Doesn't he have a couple of kids now?" Joe asked.

MacDonald gave a nod. "Yes, twins. Nine-year-old boys. Lyons has a one-bedroom apartment over his garage that they'll be staying in until they find a rental."

Brian cringed. "Sounds crowded with two young boys."

Carla interrupted the chief when she showed up with their orders. As she placed the plates around the table, she looked at Brian and said, "What's this about Heather getting into a brawl at Homer Carter's funeral?"

"It wasn't a brawl," Brian scoffed.

Carla set the last plate on the table. "Word around town, Heather and your ex were throwing hands."

"What?" the chief and Joe chorused.

"Heather didn't hit anyone. But my psycho ex slapped her," Brian explained.

The chief looked at Brian. "Seriously? Camilla slapped Heather?"

"Unprovoked?" Joe asked.

"Yes. Unprovoked." Brian wanted to tell the chief the complete story, that Marie had smacked Camilla first, but since neither Carla nor Joe knew anything about the paranormal activities of Frederickport, he kept that part of the story to himself.

"That's not exactly what I heard." Carla stood over the booth with one hand resting on a hip. "From what your ex told a friend of mine, Heather hit her first. Whacked her across the side of her head while you were talking to her. Like Heather was jealous or some-thing. Your ex told my friend she didn't mean to slap her. It was a reflex."

"That's not what happened. I was there. And if anyone hit Camilla, she'd intentionally hit back, and it wouldn't be a reflex. But in this case, Heather didn't touch her."

"Really?" Carla frowned. "I like Heather, but I could so see her decking someone who pissed her off."

"Yeah, me too." Brian chuckled. "But in this case, Heather did nothing to deserve that slap."

"Heather didn't even slap her back?" Carla asked.

"No. I think she was too stunned." *Plus, she knew Camilla was simply reacting to Marie hitting her,* Brian thought.

"Why would Camilla hit Heather?" Joe asked Brian after Carla left the table.

"All I know, Camilla has it in her head that Heather isn't really my girlfriend. That I hired Heather to pretend to be my girlfriend to bug her."

WHEN CHIEF MACDONALD arrived at the police station on Monday morning, he found Fred Lyons waiting for him. He was not alone. Clay Bowman stood by his side, wearing a uniform identical to the chief's.

MacDonald greeted both men and showed them to his office. Silently, he noted the changes in Bowman since the last time he'd seen him. He remembered Clay had always worked out, and those years of workouts had obviously paid off, considering Clay was stockier than MacDonald remembered. The man's body hadn't softened over the years. It had gotten harder. With his buzz cut, Clay could easily pass for a marine, albeit a mature marine.

They exchanged pleasantries, and Lyons stuck around while MacDonald gave Clay a brief tour, while explaining two of his top officers, Brian Henderson and Joe Morelli, were currently out on duty, but would be back later that afternoon. When they returned to his office, the chief announced he needed to leave for a pre-op appointment within the next few hours. He was just telling them when he should be returning when Lyons announced, "You don't need to come back."

The chief frowned. "Excuse me?"

"I've already gone over this with the rest of the city council, and they agree. Clay's first day on the job as interim police chief begins today, as does your medical leave. So go to your doctor's appointment and then go home. Get some rest. I'm sure there's a lot you need to do this week to prepare for your surgery," Fred explained. "You have those two boys of yours to think about. You're going to be laid up for a while."

"That's not necessary," the chief argued.

"Yes, it is. And this is not up for discussion. We are thinking of you, Edward. And if Clay here has questions, you are just a phone call away. You go home, take care of yourself. Take care of your family. The police department will be in excellent hands." Fred reached over and gave Clay's back a pat as he said the last sentence.

Police Chief MacDonald didn't leave immediately. He ended up staying until it was time to go for his doctor's appointment. Lyons had left an hour earlier, giving Clay alone time with MacDonald to further discuss the department. Before leaving for his appointment, the chief set Clay up as a user on his computer and assigned him an email account.

CLAY BOWMAN SAT in the chief's chair and looked around the office and smiled. MacDonald had finally left. Finally. Alone in what was now his office, Clay leaned over the desktop and picked up MacDonald's nameplate. He looked at the nameplate, with MacDonald's name and title, and gave a shrug before tossing it into the nearby trash can. "You won't need that anymore."

Clay stood up. "Time to get this place in order." He walked to the open doorway, stepped into the hallway, and closed the door behind him. The first order of business, dealing with the front staff.

A few minutes later, he stood at the front desk, looking down at Colleen Harper, whom MacDonald had introduced him to during the tour of the station. She looked up at him and smiled. "Is there anything I can help you with, Officer Bowman?"

"You can start with addressing me as Police Chief Bowman."

His abrupt response startled Colleen, and her eyes widened. "Umm... yes, Police Chief Bowman."

"Where are the visitor logs?" he demanded.

She pointed to a clipboard on her desk. Brusquely, he picked up the clipboard and began flipping through the pages. After a moment, he looked down at Colleen. "We don't get many visitors, do we?"

She shrugged. "We don't sign everyone in."

Clay frowned down at her. "Why not?"

"If we know who they are, what's the point?"

"Everyone will sign in. Even your mother. Do you understand?" he snapped.

She nodded. "Yes, sir."

"Where are the visitors' name badges?"

"Umm... we don't really use those."

"Do we have them?" he demanded.

"Yes."

"Where are they? Get them!"

She bolted from her office chair and rushed over to the file cabinets, where she retrieved a plastic bag filled with unused name tags. She held out the bag to him.

"I don't want them. But I want you to start using them. Everyone, and I mean everyone, who does not work at the Frederickport Police Department is to sign the visitors' log and put on a name tag the moment they enter this section of the building. Do you understand?"

WALT AND DANIELLE had just finished running their errands when Danielle looked at her watch and said, "Hey, let's stop at the police station."

"Why?"

"The chief had his pre-op appointment today. He should be back in the office by now. I want to see how everything went."

THE MOMENT JOE and Brian walked into the police station on Monday afternoon, Colleen rushed over to them. "Thank god you're here!"

"What's wrong?" Brian asked.

"My son's coach called. Sean fell, and they think he broke his arm. I can't get ahold of my husband, but I called Betty, and she's coming in early. But she can't get here for another thirty minutes. I really need to leave."

"Go. We will deal with the phones until Betty gets here," Brian promised.

"Thank you!" Without another word, Colleen snatched up her purse and ran toward the exit door.

After she rushed off, Brian told Joe he would cover for Colleen until Betty arrived. Ten minutes later, Walt and Danielle walked into the station and found Brian alone at Colleen's desk.

"Are you the new front office person?" Danielle teased.

"I'm covering for Colleen. She had a family emergency."

"I'm going to run to the bathroom," Walt said. He gave Danielle a quick kiss, flashed Brian a smile, and told Danielle, "I'll meet you at the chief's office." He left for the bathroom.

"So you're here to see the chief?" Brian asked.

"I know his doctor's appointment was this afternoon. Is he back?"

"I'm not sure. I haven't been here that long." Brian glanced at the wall clock. "But he should be. His appointment was over two hours ago. He's probably in his office."

"Is the new guy here yet?" Danielle asked.

"I haven't seen him. The chief doesn't expect him to come in until tomorrow."

"I admit, I am a little curious to check him out."

Brian chuckled.

"I'll go see if the chief is in his office."

"Behave yourself," Brian called out as Danielle waddled down the hallway.

WHEN DANIELLE ARRIVED at the chief's office, its door was closed. She gave the door a quick knock, opened it, and peeked inside. The office was empty.

Just as she was about to step back and close the door, someone grabbed her left wrist and jerked her into the hallway. She found herself staring into the piercing eyes of an angry stranger, who continued to grip her wrist with his right hand, refusing to let go.

"Who are you?" he demanded.

She winced in pain. "Please let go; you're hurting me."

He squeezed harder and twisted it slightly. "Answer my question. Who are you?"

"Let me go!" Danielle screamed. "You're hurting me."

Moments earlier, Joe had stepped out of his office as Walt walked out of the men's room. The two men had exchanged greetings before heading down the hallway together. Just as they turned down the hallway leading to the chief's office, they witnessed Danielle struggling with a man in uniform in front of the chief's door.

When Walt heard Danielle's cry, "You're hurting me," he froze, his attention on the man gripping his wife's wrist. A second later, the man let out his own cry as his right hand released Danielle. The man flew into the wall next to the door leading into the chief's office. With a loud thud, the man slid down onto the floor after hitting the wall.

Brian, who had also heard Danielle's cry, raced down the hallway just in time to see a man hitting the wall. Danielle stood in the middle of the hallway while Joe and Walt ran in her direction.

TWELVE

C lay managed to get to his feet by the time Brian and Joe reached his side. He immediately recognized both officers. Once standing, Clay's left hand clutched his right wrist. It throbbed in pain. The pregnant woman he had caught breaking into his office now stood with a man whose arm protectively wrapped around her shoulders while she absently rubbed her left wrist. Neither the man nor woman wore visitor name tags. They, like his two officers, stared at him as if he had two heads.

"Clay?" Joe asked.

Now standing straight, Clay glared at Joe. "It's Chief Bowman, Morelli."

"What's going on?" Brian asked. He looked at Walt and Danielle and back to Bowman. "Where's the chief?"

"I'm sure you're aware that Chief MacDonald is out on medical leave, and I'm stepping in as his replacement. But we can discuss this later." He turned his attention to Danielle and pointed at her. "But first, arrest that woman and take her to lockup."

"What are you talking about?" Brian asked.

Clay turned to Brian. "Does she work here?"

"Danielle? No. She doesn't work here, but…"

"Then arrest her. I caught her breaking into my office. She's not wearing a visitor name tag, so she obviously broke into this section of the building." He turned his attention to Walt and said, "And if he doesn't work here, detain him. He doesn't have a name tag either."

"Name tag? What are you talking about?" Brian asked.

"We don't do visitor name tags," Joe said.

"We do now." Clay paused a moment and then groaned. "Did that incompetent Mrs. Harper forget to sign them in?"

"Colleen wasn't even here when Walt and Danielle arrived," Brian said.

Clay glared at Brian. "What are you talking about?"

"When Joe and I got back, Colleen needed to leave because of a family emergency, so I told her to go and we'd cover for her," Brian explained.

"You had no authority to make that decision. But we'll discuss that later." Clay turned to Danielle and said, "But I still want that woman arrested."

"On what grounds?" Joe asked.

"She attacked me."

"My wife did not attack you. When Joe and I walked down that hallway, you were holding onto my wife's wrist, and she asked you to let go because you were hurting her. She didn't touch you. I'm sure both your officers saw the same thing I did."

"Who are you?" Clay demanded.

"He's Walt Marlow, and this is his wife, Danielle," Brian introduced.

Clay looked unimpressed at Walt. "Mr. Marlow, you saw how she pushed me into that wall. Your wife attacked me. I simply detained her and asked her to identify herself, which she refused to do."

Walt arched his brows and smiled. "She attacked you? My very pregnant wife threw you against the wall?"

"I obviously wasn't expecting a pregnant woman to attack me. She caught me off guard."

"You probably slipped." Walt looked Clay up and down as if assessing the man. "You look a little clumsy."

Clay took a step toward Walt, and the next moment, his feet jerked out from under him, and once again, his body slammed against the wall. While Clay lay on the floor a moment later, Walt looked at Brian and said, "Danielle and I are going home."

Brian gave Walt a nod while Clay again stumbled to his feet.

"They're leaving! Stop them!" Clay shouted.

"You just proved Walt's point," Brian said.

Clay narrowed his eyes at Brian. "What are you talking about?"

"We just watched you fall again, and no one was near you. Perhaps the floor is slippery," Brian suggested.

Clay stood in silence for a moment before saying, "Get someone to watch the front desk. Sign in all visitors after checking for IDs and issue name tags. And then I want you both in my office in thirty minutes." Clay turned abruptly and marched into the chief's office, slamming the door behind him.

Now alone in the hallway with Joe, Brian turned to his friend, who looked dazed.

"Are you okay, Joe?" Brian asked.

"What just happened? He didn't slip. He literally flew into the wall, like someone picked him up and body-slammed him."

Brian smiled knowingly and put a hand on Joe's shoulder. "Let's go up front. We can hold down the fort until Betty gets here and discuss what just happened."

JOE SAT at Colleen's desk, leaning back in the chair while resting his chin on steepled fingers and staring blankly across the room. Brian sat on the edge of the desk next to him, his arms crossed.

"What happened out there?" Joe asked again. "That wasn't just a slip."

"Sure it was. What else could it be? He obviously slipped, tried to catch his balance, and ended up sending himself into the wall."

Joe's gaze looked up at Brian while his body remained perfectly still. "You honestly believe that?"

"What else could it be?" Brian smiled.

Shifting his eyes again to look across the room, Joe let out a sigh. "This isn't the first time something like this has happened. And you know what the common denominator has always been?"

"No. What?"

"Walt. Walt is always there when something like this happens."

Brian grinned and looked down at Joe, who continued to stare across the room away from him. "Hmmm. Interesting. What do you think that means?"

"I have no idea."

"Well, I'm not as concerned about Bowman's clumsy moves as I am about how he's technically our boss for the next few months. He wasn't even here half a day, and he wanted to arrest Danielle. Heck, I didn't even want to arrest her the first day we met."

"Yes, you did."

BRIAN AND JOE stood outside the chief's office. Brian knocked. Yet instead of going in after knocking, both officers remained in the hallway, waiting for Bowman to invite them inside. When Bowman did not respond, Brian knocked again.

"Come in!" Bowman yelled from inside the office.

Joe opened the door, and both officers walked inside. They found Bowman sitting at the desk.

"Close the door behind you. Then sit down." Bowman pointed to the two chairs facing him.

Brian closed the door and glanced around the office. He walked to one chair. The first thing he noticed, the photos of the chief's wife and children were no longer on the nearby shelf. He sat down.

Bowman started the conversation with, "So that is Walt and Danielle Marlow?"

"Yes. And they are both close friends of the chief," Brian explained.

"You mean Edward MacDonald? I'm currently the only chief around here."

Brian forced a smile. "He also walked Danielle down the aisle when she and Walt got married."

"I don't care how close someone is to a member of the Frederickport Police force. There are rules and procedures in place to ensure the safety of everyone. She should not have been in this section of the building without first signing in, nor should she be walking into my office."

"I'm sure Danielle assumed the chief was here. She often visits him. It's not uncommon for her to just knock and walk in," Joe explained.

"It may not be uncommon, but it is unacceptable." Clay stood and began pacing the office while he continued to talk. "Before accepting this assignment, I had a long talk with Fred Lyons. He has been very concerned with Frederickport's rise of crime—especially capital crimes—over the last five years. Coincidentally, that rise in crime seems to correspond to when Mrs. Marlow first moved to town. She was Danielle Boatman back then." Clay stopped walking and looked at Brian and Joe, as if waiting for confirmation.

"You knew her last name used to be Boatman?" Brian asked.

Clay nodded and started pacing again. "Yes. While I've been waiting for you two, I did a little internet search on my attacker. It was enlightening. Trouble seems to follow the woman. And her husband? The man claims to have amnesia." Clay stopped again and looked back at Joe and Brian. "What is he hiding?"

DANIELLE AND WALT sat with Chief MacDonald in his living room. Danielle had just finished telling the chief about their encounter with Bowman.

"I'm so sorry, Danielle," MacDonald said.

"I'm okay now. But for a minute there, I was afraid he might break my wrist."

"He seemed to be upset that we hadn't signed some visitors' log and weren't wearing name tags," Walt explained.

MacDonald let out a sigh. "I admit, we've become lax regarding visitor logs, and we rarely give out name tags or check IDs before they come back to my office. But considering Clay's experience, I understand why it's a hot button for him."

"What do you mean?" Danielle asked.

"I remember Lyons telling me, a couple of years ago, that the station Clay was at had an incident where someone on their staff was being stalked, and the stalker got into the offices without showing an ID and getting a visitor's badge. Clay noticed the guy poking around the offices and saw he didn't have a visitor's badge. When he approached him, the guy pulled a gun on Clay. Fortunately, Clay disarmed him with no one getting hurt."

"I can understand how he could disarm someone. I thought he was going to rip my hand off," Danielle grumbled as she again rubbed her bruised wrist.

MacDonald leaned back on the sofa. "This all happened too quick. To be honest, Lyons blindsided me when he told me he and the rest of the city council wanted to hire Clay. When I told him my surgery date, I figured that would kill his plans to hire his brother-in-law. I thought, no way could Clay put in his notice and then move in that short of time. The guy's married with two kids."

"Who did you think would cover for you?" Danielle asked.

"Joe and Brian. Even though I won't be able to do much physically, I don't know why I can't still come in and supervise. Hell, it's not like I'm in the field arresting people. I know we're shorthanded, but I figured we could be more aggressive with hiring."

"I doubt we'll be stopping by the station anytime soon," Walt said.

"So... umm... how did Clay handle being thrown to the wall—twice—by an invisible force?" MacDonald asked.

"I'm more concerned about what Joe thought," Danielle said.

MacDonald cringed. "I am sorry for all this."

Danielle flashed the chief a smile. "It's not your fault. But I didn't know you were already on medical leave."

"I didn't know I was starting my leave today, either. So, any special reason for stopping by my office?"

"I knew you had your pre-op appointment today. We just wanted to see how you were doing, and wondered if there was anything we could do for you," Danielle explained.

"Honestly, I haven't had time to think about everything. Maybe Lyons was right about one thing; I need this week to get things in order. Before I scheduled my surgery, we were going over to my sister's for Easter dinner on Sunday. But Sissy suggested making dinner over here instead. Which is probably a good idea. I was going to take Evan to the Easter egg hunt that morning. I figured it would probably be the last time he'd want to go. But that's not happening now."

"We could take him," Danielle offered. "Lily and Ian are taking Connor. We were thinking of going with them."

"That would be wonderful. I know Evan would love going with you."

"One reason I went ahead with the surgery this week, I thought it might be easier not having to worry about getting the boys off to school and dealing with homework since they have spring break. Of course, it may end up being more difficult." The chief laughed.

"Do you have to spend the night in the hospital?" Walt asked.

MacDonald shook his head. "No. I'm having it done at the surgery center, and I'll come home that afternoon. Sissy offered to take the day off work to get me to the surgery center and pick me up, but I'm going to try working out something else."

"Let me do it," Walt offered. "I can take you and pick you up."

MacDonald grinned at Walt. "I accept your offer. You'd be a good one to have around if I fall after I leave the surgery center."

THIRTEEN

The petite calico cat perched comfortably on Heather's shoulder while looking down at the pit bull, Hunny, trailing alongside them. When Heather reached Chris's car, she stopped and opened one of the back doors.

"Go on," Heather urged the dog, who eyed the cat suspiciously. After gentle urging, Hunny jumped into the back seat and walked all the way to the other passenger door, putting extra distance between her and the cat. Heather shut the back car door and then opened the passenger door. Just as she was about to get in, her cellphone rang. She tossed the cat onto the front passenger seat, dug her hand into the purse that hung from her shoulder, and retrieved her cellphone.

"Hello?" came Brian's familiar voice when she answered the call. "Have you started home yet?"

"I'm just getting in the car. Chris is still in the office. He forgot something. Why?"

"I'm stopping at Beach Taco and picking up something for dinner. Can I bring you something? I can pick up something for Chris, too."

"Sounds great. Only thing, we're stopping at the pharmacy real quick. My allergies are kicking my butt."

"Okay. I'll meet you at your house. What do you want me to get for you and Chris?" By the time Heather ended her call and tossed her phone back in her purse, Chris was getting into the driver's seat.

They carpooled to work more frequently these days. Heather tossed her purse on the floor by the passenger seat. She leaned into the vehicle, picked up Bella, sat on the seat, and then put the cat on her lap. After closing the door, she buckled her seatbelt. Once comfortably situated, she said, "Brian called. He's picking up some food at Beach Taco and going to my house. You're welcome to join us."

A few minutes later, they pulled up in front of the pharmacy and parked. Heather was about to get out of the vehicle when two women walked out of the pharmacy.

"Holy crap." Heather slouched down in her seat.

Chris looked over at Heather from the driver's seat and frowned. "What is it?"

"It's her. Brian's ex. She just walked out of the pharmacy."

Chris looked toward the front entrance and spied two women. "Which one?"

At that moment, the two women looked their way, and by the expression on one of the women's faces, he suspected that was Brian's ex, and she had definitely spied Heather.

"The one staring daggers at me." Heather sat up straighter in the seat. She figured the woman had already noticed her, so no use sulking down like she was afraid.

"I expected her to look older," Chris noted.

"WHAT'S WRONG?" Lucy asked her sister when she realized Camilla had stopped walking.

"It's the little savage," Camilla said, still staring at Heather. She looked over at the car's driver. "The savage gets around. I wonder who the hot guy is."

Lucy turned to look at what had captured her sister's attention. They stood just a few feet from a vehicle, where the driver and its passenger stared back at them. "Well, this is awkward."

Lucy started walking again, but when Camilla did not move, she stopped and looked back at her sister. "Come on. You can't just have a stare-down with her."

"Yes, I can." Camilla smiled.

The next moment, the passenger door opened, and Heather stepped out of the car. She tossed something on the seat, picked up her purse, and closed the door. When she turned around, Camilla was still standing in front of Chris's car, staring at her.

"Do you want something?" Heather asked.

"I'm curious. Does Brian know about him?" Camilla asked with a smirk. "Or are you really dating Brian?"

"My relationship with Brian is none of your business. What is your problem?"

"You hit me," Camilla accused.

"I did not hit you. But, whatever." Heather walked toward the pharmacy entrance, keeping a wide berth from Camilla, while the driver rolled down his driver's door window and watched from inside the car.

After Heather entered the pharmacy, Camilla turned her attention to the driver. She smiled at him and walked to his side of the vehicle. She stopped by the driver's door while her sister stood some distance away, watching curiously.

Camilla leaned toward the car and said, "You can really do better than her. And she's not exactly exclusive. Or do you and she have some other business arrangement?"

Before the driver could respond, a pit bull jumped up from the back seat, leaned over the driver's shoulder, stuck its head out the window, and barked. Camilla lurched back from the pit bull's sudden appearance. She turned and hurried away with her sister.

CLAY PULLED the police car in front of the pharmacy and parked two spaces down from another vehicle. When he got out of the car and started for the pharmacy, he spied a pit bull sticking his head out of the back window of the other car. In the front seat sat a man who appeared to be talking to his lap. The dog barked, and the man looked his way. The dog barked again.

"Is that dog on a leash?" Clay yelled at the man.

"On a leash? The dog's in the car." The man flashed him a smile and didn't sound the least intimidated, which irritated Clay.

"And the window is open. That dog could jump out of the car and rip some kid apart," Clay snapped back. He approached the vehicle, his right hand resting on the gun in his holster. Clay smiled when the back window rolled up. *That's better*, Clay thought. "If I see that dog around town, he'd better be on a leash or properly restrained. I'm not opposed to shooting it." He turned and made his way up to the front door of the pharmacy.

CLAY STROLLED INTO THE PHARMACY. He had spent the last hour visiting businesses in town and introducing himself as the new police chief. There had been changes since he had left town a decade earlier. The Hayman jewelry store, which had practically been a landmark, was now a shoe store. Presley house had burned down, which wasn't a bad thing from his perspective. He remembered how that place had been a magnet for every local teenage troublemaker during Halloween. Marlow House was no longer vacant, and he had met its new occupants. He wasn't impressed. He read about the tunnel found under Beach Drive, but what had him the most concerned was Frederickport's soaring capital crime rate. Clay attributed the rise in crime to Edward MacDonald's ineptness.

Clay figured he had three months to identify the defects in MacDonald's leadership, which shouldn't be too difficult since he had been on the job less than a day and had already witnessed how they played fast and loose at the police station. Anyone could walk into the back offices and take the staff hostage. If things worked out as Clay planned, MacDonald would take an early retirement instead of returning to the job.

Walking toward one aisle, he noticed a suspicious-looking young woman heading in the opposite direction. She dressed like a Satan worshiper, with pale skin and long jet-black hair. She wore black nail polish and a black long-sleeved lacy dress with a flowing skirt over black high-heeled boots. The only thing she wore that wasn't black was her red lipstick.

Clay followed the woman, careful not to get too close. She stopped by one section of the over-the-counter medicine aisle, picked up a bottle of medicine, looked at it, returned it, and then grabbed another. He noticed the open purse hanging over her shoulder. He watched as she pulled another bottle off the shelf, looked at the label, and then started to drop the bottle into the open purse. Without hesitation, he rushed to her side and grabbed her purse off her shoulder while saying, "Let me see that!"

HEATHER LET out a scream and tried jerking back her purse but stopped when she saw the person holding it was an angry-looking cop. At least he dressed like a cop. Maybe not like Brian's uniform, but it looked like the uniform Chief MacDonald wore.

Still holding onto her purse's strap, she asked, "What the hell do you think you're doing?"

Clay jerked the purse from her grasp, opened it, and said, "What do we have here?" From her purse, he pulled out an unopened bottle of medicine. "Shoplifting, huh?"

"I'm not shoplifting, you idiot. You just knocked that bottle in my purse. And you ripped my purse's strap! And my shoulder doesn't feel terrific either!"

"You're coming with me, young lady." He reached for her wrist, but she responded with an unholy scream, sounding more like an off-key opera singer trying to hold a note indefinitely while piercing all nearby ears.

The scream had its desired effect, and the next moment Cherry, the pharmacy manager, rushed over and asked, "What's going on?"

Before responding, Clay took a silent note of the pharmacy employee's name tag and the fact she was the manager. "I'm afraid I caught this woman shoplifting." He held up the unopened bottle of medicine.

"I was not shoplifting!"

Cherry looked at the officer and asked, "Who are you?"

He smiled. "I'm Police Chief Bowman."

Cherry looked confused.

"I'm replacing Police Chief MacDonald," he explained.

"I didn't know Police Chief MacDonald left," Cherry said.

"He didn't leave. He's getting his knee replaced, and he's going to be out for a couple of months." Heather flashed a glare at Bowman. "And I guess this is the Bozo who's standing in for him."

Bowman looked a little taken aback at Heather's words. Instead of asking how she knew about MacDonald's upcoming surgery, he said, "None of that matters at the moment. I caught this woman shoplifting, and I assume you want to press charges."

Cherry turned a confused look to Heather and asked, "What happened, Heather?"

"I came in to get some allergy medicine. I wanted to see if that bottle had the same ingredients as the last one you sold me, because it's a different brand. So I was comparing them. My old bottle was in my purse. And then this Rambo grabs my purse and knocks the bottle out of my hand, into the purse, and accuses me of shoplifting."

"That's a good story, but I don't think anyone is buying it." Clay snickered.

The manager smiled weakly, took the bottle from Clay and handed it back to Heather. "As I am sure you know, even if Heather here was shoplifting, we couldn't do anything to her until after she left the store with the stolen item. And she's still in the store."

Clay glared at Heather and reluctantly released hold of the purse before telling her, "I know what you were trying to do. I'll be keeping an eye on you."

FOURTEEN

"Are you okay?" Cherry asked Heather after Bowman moved out of earshot.

Heather absently rubbed her injured shoulder and shrugged. "Yeah, I'm okay."

"That guy is a major jerk. I don't think for a minute you were trying to steal anything. He obviously doesn't know how much you and Chris have done for this community."

Heather smiled. "It's the Glandon Foundation, not me."

"No, it's you too. Where did they find that guy, anyway? I like Chief MacDonald, but I'm not sure about his choice for interim police chief."

"He's the city manager's brother-in-law. I doubt the chief had much choice."

Cherry rolled her eyes. "That explains it. I hope Chief MacDonald isn't out for long. We don't need some overzealous cop coming into stores and harassing customers. Especially with the tourist season around the corner. And he should know you don't go accusing a customer of stealing when they're still in the store."

"I don't think he liked the way I look." Heather grinned.

"Well, in my opinion, you look terrific. Can I get you something for that shoulder?"

Heather smiled at Cherry and handed her the bottle of medicine that Bowman had knocked in her purse. "No, just this."

When Heather exited the store ten minutes later, she spied the police car parked a few spots down from Chris's car. Bowman sat in the driver's seat, watching her. She hurried to the passenger side of Chris's car and opened the door.

"Get me out of here," Heather said as she slid into the passenger seat and slammed the door shut. She was already putting on her seatbelt when she started telling Chris what had happened inside the store. Chris listened, and when she finished putting on her seatbelt, he placed Bella, who had been curled up on his lap, on her lap. He put the key in the ignition. He was pulling out of the parking lot when she finished her telling. Chris proceeded to share with her his interaction with the interim police chief.

When Chris finished, Heather said, "That guy is mental. I wonder what Brian's going to say when I tell him his boss wanted to shoot Hunny and tried to arrest me today."

Chris glanced in his rearview mirror. "He's following us." Heather turned around in the seat and saw the police car trailing some distance behind them.

"Is he actually following us?" Heather turned back around in the seat and looked forward.

"Let me see." Chris made a left turn.

"Where are you going?"

"I want to see if he's still behind us."

Heather turned around in the seat again. "He turned."

Chris made another left turn. He glanced in the rearview mirror. "He's still back there."

Heather turned back to face the windshield and slumped down in the seat. "What is his deal?"

"I have no idea. I'm going to make a few more turns and head home. But if he's still following us when I get to your place, I might just keep going and drive over to Chief MacDonald's house. This new guy is a loose cannon."

When they turned down the alley, Chris glanced in the rearview mirror. "He's still back there. I guess we go to the chief's."

"No!" Heather pointed toward her driveway. "Brian's at my house. He's standing by his car. He probably just got there. Go ahead and stop." It wasn't Brian's personal vehicle parked in Heather's driveway, but the police car he drove home on certain nights.

A few moments later, Chris pulled into Heather's driveway and parked a few feet away from Brian. Dressed in his uniform, Brian stood by his police car.

Chris parked his car, and Brian looked confused when Bowman pulled his police car into the driveway next, blocking Chris's vehicle. Bowman parked and got out of the vehicle, his right hand resting on the gun in his belt holster as he sauntered toward the others. Heather had just gotten out of her car with Bella in her arms, but Chris remained seated in his car with Hunny in the back seat and the windows rolled up.

"Do you need some help with these two?" Clay asked Brian as he walked toward them, reminding Heather of some dime-store cowboy getting ready for a gunfight. "What's going on over here?"

Confused, Brian stared at Clay.

"We met the guy covering for the chief," Heather said loudly. "He's a real ass." She walked to Brian and stood by his side, clutching Bella while glaring at Clay.

Now Clay was the one to look confused. He glanced over to Chris, who remained seated in his car with the windows rolled up and back to Brian and Heather, who stood together in the middle of the driveway by Brian's police car.

"What is going on, Henderson?" Clay demanded.

"I am so confused right now," Brian said.

"A simple question. Why are you here? Are you arresting them?" Clay asked.

"Why would I arrest them?" Brian put his arm around Heather. "Heather's my girlfriend."

"Your girlfriend is a thief?" Clay asked.

"Thief?" Brian glanced at Heather and back to Clay.

Heather rolled her eyes and said, "It is a long and very stupid story. Ask Cherry at the pharmacy. She thinks he's an ass, too."

Chris got out of the car and walked over to Brian and Heather, leaving Hunny in the back seat. Hunny started barking. "I have to leave Hunny in the car so your new boss doesn't shoot her. He's already threatened to once," Chris said.

Brian looked at Clay. "I'm the one who needs to know what's going on. You call my girlfriend a thief, threaten to shoot Chris's dog. You're really scoring points on your first day in town. Oh, I forgot, you also wanted to arrest Danielle and Walt."

"He wanted to arrest Little Mama?" Heather gasped. She turned to Clay and hissed, "Oh, you are a wicked man!"

Clay stood in silence, attempting to process all that had been said. Finally, he began shaking his head. "This town has problems. I suspect it has one of the highest capital crime rates in Oregon. We've got people wandering into the police station as if they own the place. We have an officer who doesn't seem to have a problem dating a thief who looks like she should be dating a gang member. Expect some changes. They didn't hire me just to cover for MacDonald. I'm here to fix the police department. Henderson, consider an early retirement. That way you can spend more time hanging with your skanky girlfriend."

Clay turned his back to Brian and the others. Brian lunged forward as if he were about to punch out his new boss for his last crack about Heather, but both Chris and Heather pulled him back, and Heather mouthed, *Not now.*

Missing the silent drama going on behind his back, Clay got into the police car, backed out of the driveway, and drove down the alley, out of sight.

FIFTEEN MINUTES LATER, the three sat around Heather's kitchen table, eating tacos, and drinking beer while Hunny napped at Chris's feet and Bella disappeared upstairs. Chris told his story first, about Bowman threatening to shoot Hunny. Heather followed with her story of being accused of shoplifting. Brian then told about the incident with Walt and Danielle down at the station. He ended up saying he wished he had ignored Chris and Heather's plea to let Bowman go, and he should have flattened the man.

"While I appreciate you wanting to knock that jerk's head off, jeopardizing your career over that idiot isn't worth it," Heather told Brian.

"And I'm supposed to just let him talk about you that way?" Brian asked. "Do nothing?"

Heather smiled at Brian, leaned over and kissed his cheek, and then said, "I never said do nothing. But there are more efficient ways to deal with someone like Bowman."

"I agree with Heather. And I'm sure we can work out something with Walt or Marie to knock that jerk off his feet," Chris said. "There is something satisfying when a bully like Bowman not only doesn't see it coming but can't figure out where the hell it came from."

"You have a point." Brian chuckled.

Before taking another drink of beer, Chris said, "I can't believe Bowman didn't know you can't arrest someone for shoplifting if they haven't left the store."

"Oh, Clay knows he didn't have grounds to arrest Heather, even if she had intended to steal the medicine. He just enjoys playing the tough guy," Brian grumbled.

"Then why did they hire him to cover for the chief?" Chris asked.

"And is that really true about him being hired to clean up the police department?" Heather added.

"Bowman is the city manager's brother-in-law," Brian said. "I suspect that's the only reason they hired him, because Clay and his family want to move back to town. I doubt they hired him to clean up Dodge. And frankly, if they were going to hire someone to do that—if we needed to be cleaned up—it wouldn't be Clay Bowman. Bowman has always had a high opinion of himself. Much higher than those around him."

"What was he like back then?" Heather asked.

"You mean when I worked with him?" Brian asked.

Heather nodded.

Brian considered the question a moment before answering, "I remember one woman who worked up front said Bowman thought he was real macho."

"Macho?" Heather frowned.

Brian nodded. "I wouldn't have used macho. I would have used hard-ass. At least in his mind. His idea of policing was getting in people's faces. He made snap judgments, which often proved to be wrong."

Chris chuckled and took a sip of his drink.

Brian frowned at Chris. "What?"

Chris shrugged. "Well, you used to be a little like that."

Heather giggled. "You arrested Danielle for murder... several times."

"In my defense, I had some good reasons to believe what I did back then," Brian insisted.

"You also thought I was a murderer," Chris reminded him.

"I had some good reasons to believe that, too."

"There is some truth to that." Chris flashed Brian a grin and finished his drink.

Brian let out a sigh. "I never cared for Bowman. I was glad when he left."

"Why would the chief hire someone like that? He must have known how he was," Chris asked.

"I don't think the chief had much choice, considering who Bowman's brother-in-law is. And I think the chief figured Bowman wouldn't be able to accept the job if he had his surgery this week. Pretty short notice for someone to move. Supposedly, Bowman was already an assistant police chief. But he obviously didn't give two weeks' notice, not much different from when he quit here the last time."

"I don't imagine his previous place of employment was sad when he quit without giving a two-week notice," Heather said. "They probably threw a party after he left."

FIFTEEN

On Tuesday morning, the mediums of Beach Drive, along with some of their non-medium neighbors, met at Pier Café for breakfast. Heather came without Brian because he was already at work.

Connor sat on a booster seat in a chair at the end of the table, with his mother, Lily, to his left, and his father, Ian, sitting to his right. Chris and Heather sat on the same side of the table as Lily, with Chris sitting between the two women. Danielle sat across the table from Chris, between Ian and Walt.

They had been discussing yesterday's events involving Clay Bowman and debating if they should tell the chief what had happened at the pharmacy and later in Heather's driveway.

"After Walt and I left the chief's house yesterday, I started wondering if we shouldn't have said anything about what happened at the station," Danielle confessed.

"Why?" Lily asked.

Danielle shrugged. "He's got a lot on his mind right now. Going in for major surgery and he's got the boys to worry about. It's not like he has a wife to help him team parent and deal with all this. Now, he's worrying about his replacement."

"I don't need to say anything to the chief about it right now," Heather said. "Brian knows what happened, and I imagine he'll let everyone at the station know what's going on. It would be better not to stress him out before his surgery, any more than he already is."

While they continued to discuss the pros and cons of going to the chief, or waiting until after the surgery when he was on the mend, a young woman with two young boys walked into Pier Café. After sitting in a booth across the diner, Carla brought the woman some menus and chatted with her for a few minutes before leaving to pick up a food order.

THE DISCUSSION of Chief MacDonald's replacement came to a halt when Carla arrived at the table with their food. She returned to the kitchen one more time to pick up the rest of the order. After distributing all the food, she said, "I met the new police chief's wife."

Heather looked up from her food at Carla. "Please don't call him the police chief. Call him the chief's temporary replacement."

Carla shrugged. "He is the police chief right now. At least that's what he told me."

"When did he tell you that?" Chris asked.

"He stopped in here late yesterday afternoon, right when I was getting off work. Introduced himself, told us he was the new police chief. Of course, I already knew who he was. I mean, I didn't know he was going to be the acting police chief. But I used to wait on him when he was a cop here. The first time."

"He had his wife with him?" Lily asked.

"No. He was alone."

Lily frowned. "You said you met his wife."

"I didn't mean last night." Carla turned from the table and nodded across the diner. "The woman over there with the two boys? That's her." Everyone glanced over at the table and then back at Carla.

"You never met his wife when he lived here before?" Heather asked.

"I recognized her. But I never met her before," Carla explained. "Her older sister is married to the city manager, Fred Lyons. She always kept to herself. I remember she wasn't particularly friendly. When she came in a few minutes ago, I thought that was her. I asked her if she was the new police chief's wife. Did you know they have twins?" Carla looked at Danielle. "You should talk to her. I bet she might have some good twin tips."

Danielle smiled at Carla. "Umm, we'll see."

ZACK LOOKED AT HIS MOTHER. "I want to see if they're catching anything."

"Mom, let us go," Eric said. "Dad's not even here yet."

Debbie frowned. "I don't want you boys out on the pier without me."

"Aww, come on, Mom, we're on the pier right now. We're not babies. We're not gonna fall off," Zack nagged.

"Okay, but keep an eye out for your father, and when he gets here, I want you both to come in."

The twins jumped up from the booth and raced off. Debbie watched as they hurried outside. Just as she was about to turn her attention back to the menu in her hands, Camilla Henderson entered the diner.

Debbie quickly raised her menu, concealing her face, while slouching down in the booth. *This can't be happening*, she thought. To Debbie's horror, Camilla joined a woman sitting in a booth behind her. Debbie crouched down even farther, hoping Camilla wouldn't notice her. As Debbie sat quietly in the booth, she soon discovered it wasn't difficult to overhear the women's conversation, considering they both spoke loudly.

"ARE you sure you want to eat here, Cam?" Lucy asked her sister.

"Why?" Camilla picked up the menu. "They used to have good food here. Have you seen something to the contrary?"

"I was speaking more of the company. Check out who's sitting on the other side of the diner. At the table with the little kid."

Camilla looked across the diner. "Oh gawd, is that the little savage who's latched onto Brian?"

"I doubt there are two of them."

"What's her name, Heather? She looks like a Transylvania street walker."

"Where do you come up with stuff like that? First, you call her a savage and now a Transylvania street walker." Lucy giggled.

"What I should do is file charges on that little tramp. She assaulted me. I should have her arrested."

"Unfortunately, no one saw her hit you. They only saw you slap her."

"Yeah, I slapped her. I would slap her again. Someone comes at me; I'll go after them."

"Do you want to stay?" Lucy asked.

"No. But you know what's funny?"

"What?"

"She's with that guy again. He's hot. No idea what he sees in her. And I certainly don't understand what Brian sees in her. I wonder if Brian knows she's not exclusive."

Lucy glanced over at Heather's table and back at her sister. "Maybe they're only friends. She's at the table with two other couples and a kid."

"Yeah, two other couples. Couples. There are three couples at that table. Yet she claims to be Brian's girlfriend. She's playing him for a fool. I bet she only attacked me because she was trying to convince him she was crazy jealous of him." Camilla let out a snort.

"You said Brian hired her to pretend to be his girlfriend. If that's the case, you can't really say she's playing him for a fool. He knows exactly what is what."

Camilla shrugged. "Either way, it makes Brian look ridiculous."

"Do you want to go? We haven't ordered yet. We could just go."

Camilla considered the suggestion a moment before standing up. "Yeah, let's get out of here. We can go to Lucy's. They serve breakfast."

DEBBIE PEEKED over her menu and watched as the two women exited the restaurant. Would her husband run into Camilla on the pier? The possibility made her nauseous.

"OH CRAP, look who just walked into the restaurant," Heather groaned as she stopped eating. Everyone at her table, except for Connor, turned to the front of the restaurant.

"It's the new police chief," Chris said.

"So that's him?" Lily murmured.

"I guess we shouldn't be surprised, considering his wife is here," Danielle said.

"You want to go over there now and ask her for some twin tips?" Chris teased.

"Oh, shut up." Danielle stabbed a piece of scrambled egg with her fork.

Chris chuckled and looked at Walt. "Hey, Walt, Brian wanted to slug our new police chief for the crap he was saying about Heather. But Heather and I convinced him it wasn't a smart move for his career. Especially considering the chief is on leave and Lyons is his brother-in-law. We reminded him there are other ways to vent our frustration until the chief is back at work and can deal with him. We figured you or Marie might want to do something. If you get what I mean."

Walt looked over at the booth with Bowman and his wife.

"WHERE ARE THE BOYS? They were on the pier waiting for you," Debbie asked as her husband joined her at the table.

"They're watching someone pull in a fish."

"I told them to come in with you." She sounded annoyed.

"I told them to stay outside. I'll get them when they bring the food. Have you ordered yet?"

"No. I wasn't sure what you wanted."

Clay picked a menu up from the table and started reading it.

"Umm… I saw someone I recognized. She just left. Wondered if you ran into her outside."

Clay looked up from his menu with a frown. "I didn't see anyone I knew. Who?"

"Camilla Henderson. Brian Henderson's wife."

Clay frowned. "No. It must be someone who looks like her. They got divorced around the same time we moved. I heard she left Frederickport after the divorce. In fact, I met Henderson's current girlfriend. What a skank." Clay shook his head and looked back at the menu.

"No. It was her. In fact, she was talking about Brian's girlfriend. I overheard her talking. She and another woman were sitting in the booth behind me. Brian's new girlfriend is sitting across the restaurant right now."

Abruptly, Clay looked up from the menu and glanced across the restaurant and spied Heather. He looked back to his wife without noticing Walt Marlow looking his way.

"I guess Camilla just moved back to Frederickport." Debbie didn't mention she hadn't learned that tidbit by eavesdropping.

"Did you talk to her?"

Debbie shook her head. "No. It's not like we were friends back then. I said nothing, and I don't think she even noticed I was sitting here. I just heard her going on about Brian's new girlfriend. She doesn't like her."

"What was she saying about the girlfriend?" Clay asked.

"They said she attacked Camilla. Camilla slapped her back, but no one saw how the girlfriend hit her first. She said she wanted to press charges, but because no one witnessed the attack on her, only that she slapped the woman, she couldn't do anything."

Clay looked back at Heather's table. "I was right about her. I can always tell."

Carla walked up to their table and asked Clay if they wanted coffee and were ready to order. Clay wanted coffee, but they were not ready to order yet. After Carla filled Clay's mug with hot coffee, she left the table.

Just as Clay was about to take his first sip of the coffee, his hand holding the mug shook.

Debbie frowned at her husband. "Clay, what's wrong?"

The next moment, the mug turned upside down, spilling hot coffee onto his crotch.

SIXTEEN

Lucy felt underdressed next to her sister. When Camilla had asked her that morning if she wanted to go out to breakfast, Lucy had just thrown on a pair of denims and a pullover sweater. She didn't bother putting on makeup, and the only jewelry she wore were the same stud earrings she always wore, and her wedding ring.

Camilla came out dressed as if she were going to show property and she wanted to impress the clients. She had obviously taken extra time applying her makeup and fixing her hair. With her outfit, she wore a gold necklace and matching bracelet along with her gold earrings. Even if Lucy wanted to change her clothes, she had only brought casual clothes with her, aside from the outfit she had worn to her uncle's funeral. She hadn't brought extra jewelry along, and the only makeup she owned was a tube of lipstick.

"I wonder if they still have really good hamburgers here," Camilla said as she and her sister walked into the diner and looked for an open booth.

"I doubt they're serving lunch yet." Lucy stopped at an empty booth. "This okay?"

"Sure." Camilla sat down in the booth.

"When we were kids and visited Uncle Homer, I always liked coming here." Lucy slid into the booth across from her sister.

"I remember. You called it your restaurant." Camilla picked up a menu from the end of the table.

"Well, they named it after me," Lucy teased. She picked up a menu.

"Really? Didn't Uncle Homer tell us he used to come here when he was a kid, years before you were born? Maybe Mom and Dad named you after a restaurant?" Camilla teased.

"Oh hush."

Camilla's cellphone rang. She pulled it out of her purse and looked at it. "It's our brother."

"So he finally decided to wake up?"

"I guess." Camilla accepted the call and put the phone to her ear. "Hello, Ted."

"Where are you?" he asked.

"We just sat down at Lucy's Diner."

"I'm hungry. There's no food in this house."

"You can meet us here. I can put your order in," Camilla offered.

"No. I'll be there in a few minutes. I'd rather look at the menu."

"Okay." Camilla set her phone on the table and looked at her sister. "Our brother's joining us for breakfast."

The server showed up at the table with a coffeepot. After being told they were waiting for one more person, the server poured them each a cup of coffee and then left the table.

Camilla looked at her sister. "I'm really surprised you and Ted are staying for so long. I figured you'd both be leaving right after the funeral."

"We assumed we'd have to go through Uncle Homer's house, clean it up, put it on the market. Neither of us imagined you'd decide to stay in Frederickport and move into the house."

"You should have asked. You knew the terms of the will. We can only sell the house if we all agree. Otherwise, it's to be used as our family's vacation home."

"It's not exactly a family vacation home if you move in full time."

"Hey, you and Ted are welcome to move in, too." Camilla picked up her cup of coffee and took a sip.

"I don't get you. It's been ten years. Why do you want to move back here? Do you still have friends here? If so, I didn't see them at the funeral."

"It was time to move back."

"Is this about Brian?"

"What do you mean?"

"Come on, Cam. You seem upset that he has a girlfriend. You're the one who left him. Did you seriously think he'd stay single all this time?"

"I didn't expect him to start dating women young enough to be his daughter. Especially one who looks like she belongs to a cult."

Lucy fidgeted with the rim of her coffee cup, absently running a finger over its rim while staring down into the coffee. Without looking up at her sister, she said, "When you first told us you were leaving Brian, Ted and I wondered if you had a boyfriend."

"Maybe Brian had a girlfriend."

Lucy looked up to her sister. "Brian? Brian cheated on you?"

Camilla let out a sigh. "Not that I know of. I'm just saying, why did you wonder if I had been cheating and not Brian?"

"I never saw Brian as the cheating type. When I was around him, he never flirted with other women. He used to get really irritated with guys who disrespected their wives. It was one thing I always respected about him."

"And so you assumed I cheated?"

Lucy shrugged. "Admit it, you always liked to flirt. I often wondered if it bothered Brian."

"Brian never complained. Fact is Brian never complained about anything. He was always quite content. Too content." Camilla took a sip of her coffee.

"Is that a bad thing?"

Camilla let out a deep sigh. "No. When I look back on things, I have regrets. I admit I took Brian for granted. The grass is not always greener on the other side."

"When you told us you were leaving Brian and moving from Frederickport, we sorta figured the next time we heard from you, you'd be telling us you were living with someone. Ted and I figured that's why you left town. Knowing Uncle Homer, he would have cut you out of the will if he found out you left Brian for another guy."

"Uncle Homer was disappointed, to say the least, when I told him I didn't love Brian anymore, but he didn't think anyone should stay with someone they didn't love. Is that why you made me that surprise visit a month after I moved?"

Lucy shrugged sheepishly, no longer fidgeting with her coffee cup. "You were living in a little one-bedroom apartment. There was no sign of any man. In fact, you didn't get any calls while I was there. And you seemed genuinely happy to see me. So I figured, I guess there really wasn't another guy."

"I was lonely. I was happy to see you."

"I told Ted you weren't living with anyone. And I didn't think you had a boyfriend. You did seem a little lonely."

Camilla shrugged. "I guess I was trying to find myself."

"Ted didn't quite believe me. He had talked to Brian after you split up. Brian told him you left him for another guy."

"Yeah, I imagine he thought that. He asked me once if there was someone else, and I said no. He obviously didn't believe me. Not sure what he believes now."

"Hey, scoot over," a male voice said. Both women looked up and found their brother standing over them. Lucy scooted over, making room for Ted.

LUCY'S DINER was a short walk from Adam Nichols's office. Adam often walked there for a quick breakfast or lunch. This Tuesday morning, he assumed he was alone when he headed to the restaurant. He didn't know the spirit of his grandmother, Marie Nichols, had stopped by to check on him and decided to join him for breakfast.

Walking toward an empty booth, absently distracted by his cellphone, he heard someone call out, "Adam? Adam Nichols?"

Adam stopped walking, lowered his cellphone, and looked to the nearby booth. There were three people there, and only one looked familiar.

"Hi," the familiar-looking woman said. "I'm Camilla Henderson. I worked at the title company. We closed a lot of escrows together."

"Oh my. I smacked that woman the other day," Marie told deaf ears.

Adam's eyes widened with recognition. "Oh, yes, Camilla Henderson." He almost added Brian Henderson's ex, but said, "I heard your uncle Homer died. I'm sorry for your loss. I didn't know him, but my grandma was friends with him."

"Yes. She was more friends with my aunt. I heard she passed away. She was a nice lady," Camilla said.

"A nice lady who whacked you upside your head," Marie scoffed.

"Adam, this is my sister, Lucy, and my brother, Ted." Camilla looked at her siblings and added, "This is Adam Nichols. He's a real estate broker and owns Frederickport Vacation Properties, down the street."

Ted stood briefly, shook Adam's hand, and then sat back down as they all exchanged more pleasantries.

Camilla scooted down in the booth and said, "Would you like to join us, Adam?"

Adam smiled at Camilla and accepted her offer, taking a seat next to her.

Marie chuckled. "I know why you accepted her offer. You'd like a shot at listing Homer's house."

"Are you still working as an escrow officer?" Adam asked.

"No. Actually, I got my real estate license." Camilla smiled at Adam.

"How is the real estate market here?" Ted asked Adam.

"It's a seller's market. I understand Homer left his house to the three of you." He looked at Camilla. "If you decide to sell and want to use a local Realtor, I do referrals."

"Actually, I've moved back to Frederickport."

Adam arched his brows, wondering if Brian knew. He and Melony had been so busy the last couple of weeks working on their new house, they hadn't had an opportunity to visit with friends and catch up on the gossip. "Do you have an Oregon real estate license?"

Camilla shook her head. "Not yet. But we're not planning to sell the house. I intend to move into it."

"Adam, we're trying to convince Cam to sell Uncle Homer's house and buy something a little more manageable for just one person. Are there any good properties on the market right now that might be good for Cam?" Ted asked.

"Ted, I don't want to sell," Camilla snapped.

Adam ended up regretting accepting the invitation to join them for breakfast, which proved awkward. It was clear the brother and sister wanted to sell the uncle's house, but Camilla refused to budge. Adam did not know the terms of Homer's will, but it seemed Camilla called the shots. He finally diverted the conversation by telling Camilla of his recent marriage.

When they all finished breakfast, Adam told them he needed to get back to work. Marie decided not to follow him back to his office, but stayed to eavesdrop, curious about what the three might say about selling the property once Adam was gone. But Camilla and Lucy left right after Adam, leaving Ted alone at the table with Marie.

Marie was about to leave when Ted's cellphone rang. He answered the call by saying, "I could kill my sister."

SEVENTEEN

Until they could find a suitable rental, Clay and his family planned to stay in his brother-in-law's garage apartment. It didn't have a washing machine, and Debbie's sister had told them they could use hers while they stayed with them. Currently, he owned only two uniforms, and the one he'd worn yesterday was wadded up in the hamper. Debbie had planned to wash both uniforms tonight.

At the café he had tried to wipe up the coffee from his pants with a damp napkin and then dry it with another napkin, but it still looked like he had peed himself. He considered going back to the apartment with Debbie and having her hand-wash the pants and then drying them with a handheld hairdryer, but he worried that would take too long, and the last thing he wanted was his nosey sister-in-law telling her husband that he had been home for an hour when he was supposed to be at work. All he could do now was lock himself in his office until his pants dried and hope he'd wiped up enough coffee that it hadn't left a stain. He still didn't understand what had happened at the restaurant.

After parking the car, Clay removed his jacket. He got out of the vehicle and draped the jacket over his arm, using it to conceal the stain. What he didn't realize, the coffee hadn't confined itself to the front of his pants.

"GOOD MORNING, CHIEF BOWMAN," Colleen greeted.

"Good morning," Bowman said gruffly. "I don't want to be disturbed. You can put calls through, but I'm not accepting any visitors right now." Not waiting for a response, he hurried toward his office.

Ten minutes later, Brian and Joe showed up at Colleen's desk. "Have you seen Chief Bowman?" Brian asked. "We stopped by his office, but no one's there. And his car's out front."

"Oh, he's there," Colleen whispered as she looked down the hall, making sure Bowman wouldn't suddenly appear and catch her talking about him.

"He didn't answer the door," Joe said. "And he wasn't in the break room."

"Maybe he went to the restroom," Brian suggested.

"I think he wet his pants," Colleen whispered.

Brian arched his brows. "Excuse me?"

"He came in and was holding his jacket in front of him, like he was trying to cover himself. It looked super awkward. Not how a guy holds a jacket. And he told me he didn't want to be disturbed, but I could put calls through. Which is weird. I mean, if you don't want to be disturbed, why would you be okay with putting calls through?"

"And that's why you think he wet his pants?" Joe asked.

"No. When he walked away, the back of his pants looked all wet. Not like he sat on something, but like he... well..." Colleen cringed and added, "But please, don't tell him I told you that."

"Don't worry, we won't say anything," Brian said.

They all stopped talking when someone entered the front waiting area. Through the window, Colleen could see it was the city manager, so she buzzed him in without waiting for him to request entry.

"I'm here to see Chief Bowman," Fred told Colleen when he

stepped into the front office. He gave both Joe and Brian a nod of greeting.

"Umm... he's in his office, but he said he didn't want to be disturbed," Colleen said.

Fred smiled. "I'm sure that doesn't apply to me." Not waiting for a name tag, Fred started toward the chief's office. Colleen immediately picked up the phone to call Bowman and inform him Fred was on his way.

AFTER GETTING off the phone with Colleen, Clay rushed to unlock the office door. He wanted to be sitting behind the desk when Fred walked in, unfortunately he didn't make it to his desk in time, and he reluctantly turned around and greeted his brother-in-law, who immediately noticed the stain.

Fred arched his brows. "Did we have a problem?"

Bowman laughed nervously, shook Fred's hand, and said, "I had breakfast with Debbie and the boys, and you know how kids are. Always spilling something. Unfortunately, I don't have an extra pair of clean pants. Figured they can dry here while I get some work done." Bowman pointed to an empty chair before taking a seat behind the chief's desk.

"I don't know how you and Deb do it with twins. Double trouble." Fred laughed and sat down. "So, tell me, how are you settling in?"

"Good. Good. Yesterday I walked around town, visited some businesses, introduced myself."

Fred nodded. "How are you doing with everyone here? Was it strange coming back, this time as the boss?"

"It's been okay, so far. The only one who seems problematic is Brian Henderson."

Fred shrugged. "Henderson has been working for the police department longer than anyone else."

"And he has never really advanced, has he?"

"In fairness to Henderson, it's my understanding he turned

down several promotions over the years. He's not interested in moving up the ladder."

"Then he should be more receptive to submitting to my leadership, shouldn't he?"

Before Fred responded, the office door opened. Bowman was about to reprimand the person barging into his office without first knocking but swallowed his words when Chief MacDonald walked into the room.

Fred stood up and faced MacDonald. "Chief, you're supposed to be at home, getting ready for your surgery."

MacDonald absently shook Fred's hand, gave Bowman a nod of greeting, and glanced around his office. He noticed the missing photos, nameplate, and other items out of place. "My surgery's not until Friday. I just thought I'd stop in and see how everything is going."

Fred sat back down, and MacDonald took the empty chair next to him while Bowman remained sitting at the desk.

"Everything is fine," Bowman said.

Leaning back in the chair, the chief crossed one leg over the opposing knee while focusing his attention on Bowman. "I understand there was an incident with the Marlows yesterday."

"What kind of incident?" Fred asked.

Bowman shrugged. "It was more of a misunderstanding. Mrs. Marlow was wandering around in the back offices without proper identification, and when I asked who she was, she refused to tell me."

"From what I understand, you grabbed her by the wrist, a little too tight. And she asked you to let her go because you were hurting her, and you wanted to arrest her," the chief said. "I might add, she is eight months pregnant."

"The woman just walked into this office without so much as knocking. I didn't know who she was," Bowman insisted.

"I think Clay's right. It sounds like a misunderstanding," Fred said.

COLLEEN SAT ALONE at the front desk when a woman she didn't recognize walked up to the window separating the offices from the front waiting area. "Can I help you?"

"Is Brian Henderson here?" the woman asked.

"Yes. You want me to call him?"

The woman nodded.

Colleen picked up the phone. "Who should I say is calling?"

"Tell him it's Camilla Henderson."

Colleen smiled. "Oh, are you Brian's sister?"

Camilla shook her head. "No. I'm Brian's ex-wife."

BRIAN WAS TEMPTED to tell Colleen he didn't want to speak with his ex-wife, but he was curious about what she had to say. Plus, if she was really planning to stay in town, there was no way he could avoid seeing her, and he had also been married to the woman for a quarter of a century.

After being buzzed through the door and issued a name tag, Brian led Camilla to the break room, passing the chief's office, its door still closed. Once in the break room, Brian shut the door and then asked Camilla what she wanted.

Still standing, Camilla smiled at Brian and glanced around the room. "Can we sit down and talk?"

Brian shrugged and then motioned to the table and chairs. They each sat down.

"I'm sorry about how I acted when I saw you the other day," Camilla began.

Brian wanted to ask her if she was sorry that she had hit Heather, but he realized that wasn't fair, since he understood Camilla sincerely believed Heather had hit her first. "I imagine it was a tough day for you. I know you were close to Homer."

Camilla nodded. "I also feel guilty that I haven't been back for so long. But I didn't want to see him like that."

"I hadn't seen him for a long time myself."

"I'm also sorry I was such a bitch when you'd go over to play cribbage with him. I think I was just jealous."

Brian shrugged. "Water under the bridge, as they say."

"You know, you look great, Brian."

"Thanks." Brian knew Camilla wanted him to extend the same compliment. After all, she looked good. She looked younger than the last time he had seen her. Instead, he asked, "Why did you want to talk to me?"

"Like I said, I just wanted to apologize for the other day. Now that I'm moving back, I figure we'll run into each other from time to time. No reason for it to be awkward or a bunch of drama like the other day. Thought we could come to a truce of sorts. Perhaps someday get to the place we can be friends again."

"No drama would be nice." Brian smiled.

"I haven't seen many people since I got back. Is Joe still here?"

"Yeah. He got married last month."

"Really? What about the chief? I heard about his wife. Did he ever get remarried?"

"No. In fact, he's out on medical leave. He's having a knee replacement surgery. He'll be out for a few months, at least."

"Does that mean you're the acting chief?"

Brian shook his head.

"Did you turn it down?"

Brian smiled. "No. I would have filled in for the chief. In fact, I've been acting chief several times since you left. But the powers-that-be decided to bring in someone else. Do you remember Clay Bowman?"

Camilla stared dumbly at Brian. "Who?"

"Clay Bowman. He used to work here."

AFTER THEY FINISHED THEIR DISCUSSION, Camilla told Brian he didn't need to escort her back to the front office. Alone, Camilla walked down the hallway until she came to the chief's office, its door still closed. She glanced up and down the hallway, wanting to make sure no one was coming. Camilla reached for the doorknob, turned it, found it unlocked. She swung the door open.

Had Camilla arrived ten minutes earlier, she would have found Chief MacDonald and Fred Lyons with Clay, but they had both left, and Bowman remained, sitting behind the desk. Bowman looked up the moment the door opened, and once again he was prepared to reprimand whoever had entered his office without knocking, but he was not prepared to see Camilla Henderson standing in the doorway.

"Hello, Clay," Camilla purred. She stepped all the way into the office, closed the door behind her, and said, "We need to talk."

EIGHTEEN

Debbie Bowman's only family was her older sister, Robyn. Their father had died when they were in elementary school, and their mother had passed away not long after Debbie married Clay. It was difficult leaving her sister when moving from Frederickport ten years earlier, especially with the twins on the way. But Debbie understood moving was the best thing for her marriage and for Clay's career.

One advantage in moving back to Frederickport, Debbie now had someone willing to babysit, and Robyn had agreed to watch the boys while she drove to the police station to take Clay his lunch.

After the incident in the diner at breakfast, Clay had asked Debbie to bring him a sack lunch that afternoon. Initially, he'd intended to visit more businesses and grab lunch then, but after spilling coffee all over his pants, he decided he would stay in his office.

Debbie still couldn't get the image of Clay's shaking hand out of her mind, before he dumped hot coffee in his lap, or the way he leapt from the chair, cursing, while grabbing the napkin off the table to wipe up the spill. She had foolishly asked if he was alright, to which he responded, "Hell no, I'm not alright; the coffee was hot!"

When she'd tried to ask him what had happened, he'd shut her down and said he didn't want to talk about it. She couldn't help but wonder if he'd had a seizure or something. She wanted to broach the subject with him again, but she didn't want him to get mad.

Debbie parked in front of the Frederickport police station and looked at the building for a moment. She hadn't stepped foot in the station since moving. But they had driven by the place many times over the years when visiting Fred and Robyn. Once, Debbie had asked if Clay wanted to stop in and say hi to some people he had once worked with. He'd declined the offer, telling her there was no one who worked there he cared to see.

After getting out of the car, Debbie walked up to the station, sack lunch in hand.

"I'm Chief Bowman's wife," she told the woman at the front desk, who sat behind a glass window. A few moments later, the woman buzzed her in and handed her a name tag.

While Debbie hadn't been in the Frederickport police station for a decade, she remembered where the police chief's office was located. Walking down the hallway, she spied the nameplate on the door. She remembered it originally said, "Police Chief MacDonald," but someone had taped a piece of paper over MacDonald, with "Bowman" written across it in felt-tip pen.

Debbie was about ten feet from the door when it opened, and a woman stepped out of the office, closing the door behind her. Debbie froze. It was Camilla Henderson.

BRIAN TURNED down the hallway leading to the front entrance and saw Camilla hadn't left yet. She stood in the middle of the hallway, her back to him. Ten feet from Camilla stood another woman he did not recognize. The two women stared at each other, neither of them moving. While he couldn't see Camilla's face, the other woman looked as if she were staring down a grizzly bear who was about to pounce and because of that she was too terrified to move.

Confused, Brian called out Camilla's name. She turned to him.

"Oh, Brian," Camilla started walking toward him.

With Camilla's attention diverted, the other woman continued down the hallway, hastily entering the police chief's office.

When Brian reached Camilla, he asked, "You're still here?"

"I was just looking around. It's been a long time since I've been here. I wondered what had changed."

He motioned behind Camilla. "Do you know who that woman is? The one who walked into the chief's office."

Camilla glanced from the closed door leading to the chief's office back to Brian. "I think that was Clay Bowman's wife."

"Speaking of Bowman, he's not fond of people wandering around in the station. He jumped all over a friend of mine who stopped by. He even wanted to arrest her."

Camilla smiled. "Really? Well, I'm not too worried about it."

ACROSS TOWN at Homer Carter's house, Ted and Lucy stood in the kitchen, whispering, while Flora was in her room down the hall, with the door shut.

"I guess she's really staying." Lucy glanced toward Flora's bedroom. "Cam wanted her out two days ago."

"Serves our sister right," Ted grumbled. "Now she can have a roommate."

Lucy groaned. "This is just so wrong. I don't know what Uncle Homer was thinking, making a provision that we couldn't sell the house unless we all agreed."

"I never thought it would be an issue. Although, back then, I never realized how much I'd count on this inheritance to pull us through some tight times."

"You and me both." Lucy started to say more, but stopped when she heard the door to Flora's bedroom open. Both she and Ted stayed quiet, looking toward the bedroom.

"I need to talk to you both," Flora announced when she stepped into the kitchen a few moments later. "Before your sister comes back." Lucy and Ted exchanged quick glances and looked back at Flora.

"What about?" Ted asked.

"On Friday, I received my last paycheck from your uncle's estate. But it was significantly short. I tried bringing it up with your sister, but she keeps blowing me off."

Lucy frowned. "Short?"

"What days didn't she pay you for?" Ted asked.

"I was paid for all the days I worked. I wasn't talking about that."

"Then what are you talking about?" Ted asked.

"When your sister first hired me, I told her I had a job offer at a care home in Portland. Admittedly, the pay was not as good as what she was offering, but the care home offered medical and retirement. That's when she told me that while she couldn't offer the same benefits as the care home, she would give me something like a severance package after Mr. Carter passed, which would come out of the estate. She would calculate it on how long he lived. If I left before Mr. Carter passed, forcing the family to arrange other care for your uncle, I wouldn't get anything."

"I assume you have this in writing?" Ted asked.

Flora shook her head. "No. Your sister said her duties as his trustee didn't give her the rights to make a legal, binding contract like that. But she said once he passed away, she would make sure the heirs would compensate me for the money from his estate. It would basically be a retirement package for all the years I cared for your uncle, and you didn't have to worry about him. She said, if I expect her to trust me to care for Mr. Carter, I should trust her to care for me after he passes away."

Ted arched his brows. "Trust her?"

Flora nodded. "I just figured it sort of made sense. And like I said, the pay was better than what the care home offered, and I would only have to care for one person. And she offered room and board. I assumed the extra compensation she promised would be included in my final paycheck. It wasn't."

IT WAS noisy over at Lily and Ian's house with all the construction going on. They were adding a second floor to their house and hoped to have the project finished at least a month before their baby arrived. Ian was over at Marlow House, where he and Walt were on a Zoom call with their agent. Danielle and Lily had taken Connor over to Heather's, where they brainstormed baby names for both Danielle and Lily.

Heather had gotten home from work twenty minutes earlier and had already changed out of her work clothes into stretch pants and a baggy peasant dress. The three women gathered around the kitchen table while Connor sat on the floor, playing with Bella.

"Are they still working over at your house?" Heather asked Lily.

"Yeah. John's over there with a couple of guys. They should be leaving pretty soon."

"It's coming along a lot faster than I thought it would," Danielle said.

Lily shrugged. "Not fast enough for me. Okay, back to names!"

"Well, I love Addison Marie," Heather said.

"Walt does too." Danielle smiled. "But remember, say nothing to Marie. We want it to be a surprise."

Heather looked at Danielle. "Which also means don't say anything to Mel or Adam. Because if they start talking about it, little nosy eavesdropping Marie will hear."

"Which also means I can't tell Ian," Lily said. "While Marie's pretty good at letting us know when she's around, we never know for sure."

Heather leaned back in her chair and crossed her arms across her chest. "I used to think seeing and hearing spirits might be scary —or at the very least, creepy. But you know, I'm glad I can see spirits now. Because it would kinda freak me out to know they might be around, but not knowing for sure."

"Gee, thanks," Lily grumbled.

Heather gave a shrug, and the next moment her kitchen door

opened. The women turned to the now open door and watched as Brian Henderson walked into the house.

"You guys having a party?" Brian asked as he closed the door behind him.

"Just hanging out. Walt and Ian are doing writer stuff, and guys with hammers are over at Lily's," Heather explained.

Brian greeted Danielle and Lily, gave Heather a quick kiss, and then helped himself to a beer from the fridge before joining the women at the table. After sitting down, he glanced over to Connor, who rolled around on the kitchen floor with Bella while the cat batted the toddler's face. Brian cringed. "I still can't believe that." The women laughed.

The first time Brian had seen Connor play with Bella, he'd expressed his concern that the cat could scratch the boy. Heather had explained Walt had had a long talk with Bella, and the cat understood that if she did not want to play with Connor, all she needed to do was walk away. But if she wanted to play with him, she could never use her teeth or claws. However, if Connor hurt the cat, hissing and then leaving was acceptable. Fortunately, Bella had never had a reason to hiss at Connor.

Danielle asked Brian how he was getting along with his new boss.

"I haven't seen that much of him. But the chief stopped in today —the real chief."

"How did that go?" Heather asked. "Did he say anything about Bowman's behavior with our little mama?"

"Hey. I'm a little mama too," Lily reminded her with an exaggerated pout.

Heather flashed Lily a smile and said, "You are the Head Mama."

"Okay, I accept that." Lily beamed.

Brian chuckled before saying, "I didn't see the chief. I only knew he was there because Colleen told me. From what she said, he planned to stay and talk to us, but he got a call from his doctor and had to leave."

"I hope there's not a problem," Danielle said.

"I don't think so. He said something to Colleen about him forgetting to set up some pre-op test, and he needed to do that. But to tell us hi when she saw us."

"When we were out to breakfast this morning, we saw Bowman," Heather began. She then told him about Walt dumping hot coffee on the unsuspecting lawman.

Brian cringed. "That sounds very adolescent and painful. I love it."

"Actually, Walt felt a little guilty. He said he should have done it when he was drinking water, not hot coffee," Danielle said. "I don't like him, but I hope he's okay."

"And he let out a wail," Heather added.

"That explains something Colleen told us. But when I saw him later this afternoon, he seemed to be walking okay." Brian then told them about his discussion with his ex-wife Camilla.

When Brian finished his telling, Heather asked, "So she wants to be friends?"

Brian gave a shrug, and before taking a swig of beer, he said, "That's what she claims."

NINETEEN

Millie Samson wasn't just a docent at the Frederickport Museum, the elderly woman had been a member of the Frederickport Historical Society's board of directors since its inception. While she didn't docent at the museum on Wednesdays this month, she came in to restock the museum gift shop. Next week, the local schools were off for spring break, which often meant more museum visitors.

The docent scheduled for Wednesday morning was one of the newer docents, Trish Bean. Trish and Millie attended church together, and Millie had been trying to get Trish to docent since her husband had passed away several years earlier. Not only was Trish well versed in Frederickport history, she loved talking to people. Albeit, Trish could be a gossip.

While Trish talked to visitors in the main section of the museum, Millie busily attended to the museum store, sorting through boxes behind the counter. She looked up when someone walked into the gift shop. Millie immediately recognized him—Clay Bowman. She had known his brother-in-law, Fred, and his wife for years. She remembered when Fred had helped Clay get a job at the local police department. It had surprised her when Clay took a job in another state, moving his young wife far away from her sister, considering how close the two had always been. Then someone had told Millie she was expecting twins. Millie always thought it a pity that Debbie no longer lived close to her sister, which could have been a tremendous help when dealing with twins. While she had never seen Clay since he left town, she had seen Debbie a few times when she had visited her sister and brought her sons into the museum. But it had been a few years since she had seen Debbie or her boys.

"Well, Clay Bowman. Welcome back to Frederickport. I understand you're acting chief while Chief MacDonald has his knee surgery and recovers," Millie greeted.

"Thank you. Nice to see you again, Mrs. Samson." Clay smiled.

"I suppose I should call you Chief Bowman now." Millie grinned. "So what brings you into the museum?"

"I'm just trying to get around to all the businesses in town. Introduce myself—or in your case, reintroduce myself." Clay glanced around the museum store.

"Your wife must be thrilled to be living close to her sister again. Someone mentioned you're staying in Fred's garage apartment. I imagine it must be a little crowded for all four of you."

"It's only temporary."

"I understand you may stay on at the department after Chief MacDonald returns."

"That's the plan."

"You and your wife aren't the only former Frederickport residents who've recently moved back to town. Camilla Henderson also returned. I believe she left Frederickport about the same time that you moved. You must know her. She used to be married to Brian Henderson."

"I remember her."

"Oh, it's our new police chief!" Trish Bean said as she walked into the gift store.

"Mrs. Bean, hello. Nice to see you again," Clay greeted.

"Thank you. You two were talking about Camilla. Oh my, it was quite the scandal at poor Homer Carter's funeral. What a home-

THE GHOST AND THE TWINS

coming for that poor girl." Trish shook her head and gave several tsk-tsks.

"What happened?" Clay asked.

"Oh, Trish, I wouldn't call it a scandal," Millie said.

Ignoring Millie, Trish looked at Clay. "Camilla's ex-husband showed up at Camilla's uncle's funeral, and he had the audacity to bring his girlfriend along. His much younger girlfriend, who then attacks Camilla. Physically attacks her!"

"Oh, Trish, that's not true. No one saw Heather hit Camilla."

"Just because no one saw Heather hit her doesn't mean it's not true," Trish said. "And why else would Camilla slap her like that in front of everyone?"

"Brian's girlfriend physically attacked Camilla?" Bowman asked.

Trish said, "Yes," at the same time Millie said, "No."

The museum phone rang, interrupting the debate. Millie answered the phone call and, a moment later, hung up and said, "I have to go back to the office and do something." Millie looked at Clay and said, "And no, I don't believe Heather hit Camilla. It was some sort of misunderstanding." Millie flashed Trish a reprimanding glance before telling Clay it was nice seeing him again, and then she left the gift shop and headed for the office in the back of the museum.

"Frederickport seems to have changed since I lived here," Bowman said. "Women brawling at funerals."

"I think Millie has a soft spot for that Heather Donovan. Not sure why. Although, one of the other docents said Millie was relieved when Heather stopped volunteering. She was a docent for a while. They say Millie was nervous Heather might slap one of our visitors."

"Why would she do that?"

Trish shrugged. "She would get irritated if anyone touched a display. Which I can understand, but we can't go around slapping hands. Heather's a little volatile. Some people say she practices witchcraft. Which might explain how someone like Brian Henderson got hooked up with her. She cast a spell on him!"

"I understand she lives near Marlow House," Bowman said.

"Yes. They're friends too. She and Danielle Marlow."

"What is Danielle Marlow like?" Bowman asked. "She moved here after I left, and I understand there have been several murders in and around Marlow House since that time."

Trish nodded. "I know, right? Very odd, if you ask me. I don't really know her. She used to be involved with the museum but stepped back for some reason. I think there was a disagreement between her and the board members. Jolene Carmichael, in particular. Do you remember her?"

Clay nodded. "Wasn't she murdered?"

Trish grinned. "Yes. And you know who found the body? Heather Donovan."

"Really?"

"Yes. Oh, another thing about Danielle Marlow, her husband. That is the oddest thing. He's not from here. But he's related to Frederick Marlow. And he has this uncanny likeness to Frederick Marlow's grandson, who he apparently was named after. From what I heard, he and his fiancée—not his wife now—stayed at Marlow House. It's a B and B, you know. And after they left, they were in a car accident. She was killed in the accident, and he came back to Marlow House after he got out of the hospital. And he ended up marrying Danielle Marlow. Of course, she was Danielle Boatman then."

"I read online that he has amnesia," Bowman said.

"He supposedly got amnesia after the accident and never regained his memory. After that, he wrote a book that became a bestseller. And I heard, before the accident, he wasn't even interested in writing. He was a real estate agent. And I've also heard, from someone I know who's a friend of the woman who's the housekeeper at Marlow House, that he dabbles in magic."

Bowman arched his brows. "Magic?"

Trish nodded again, this time vigorously. "Yes. He can make things fly across the room." Trish paused a moment, considering what she had just said before adding, "Which might explain why the Marlows are such good friends with Heather Donovan. Did I mention Heather is a witch?"

ON WEDNESDAY AFTERNOON, Heather, Danielle, and Lily met up for lunch at Beach Taco. After placing their orders and getting their beverages, they found a table and sat down.

"Who's watching Connor, Marie or his dad?" Heather asked Lily.

"With the construction going on, and John always around, Marie's not doing that much babysitting," Lily explained. "And I hate leaving him at home with Ian right now. Too much to get into with the construction going on. Not saying Ian doesn't watch him, but..."

"Yeah, I get it," Heather said.

"I was going to bring him, but his grandma wanted him to come over today, so I took her up on the offer. I'm going to take advantage of this personal time for as long as I can. Before I know it, I won't have any time for myself," Lily said.

"Amen to that." Danielle glanced down to her own full belly.

Children's voices caught their attention. They glanced to the front door and watched as two boys, about the age of Evan, ran into the restaurant, followed by a young woman.

"They look like twins." Lily looked at Danielle and added, "That's going to be you."

"That's the wife of the chief's replacement," Danielle said. "She's the woman who was with him when he had that unfortunate accident with the coffee. Remember?"

Lily took another look at the woman. "Oh, it is."

Heather studied Bowman's wife and sons. "Those boys look like miniatures of their father. I hope that's the only way they're like him."

They watched as Mrs. Bowman stood at the order counter, reading the menu posted on the wall over the counter, seemingly oblivious to her sons, who started wrestling behind her after one boy poked the other.

"Well-behaved children," Heather snarked. "I understand they're homeschooled."

Lily, who had stopped looking at the Bowmans, glanced back over to the boys, who were now running around an empty table, with one chasing the other and shouting, the mother still ignoring their behavior. "Homeschooled? She's clearly doing my fellow teachers a favor. If she can't make her own children behave when she's with them, then I doubt she'd be supportive of a teacher trying to make her boys behave in class."

Heather chuckled. "I can see Walt now if your twins—when they are those boys' age—started acting that way."

Both Lily and Danielle looked at Heather. "What do you mean?" Danielle asked.

"He'd probably use his energy to sit their butts on the bench, and they'd be stuck there." Heather snickered.

"Or he could promise to send them flying around the living room when they get home, if they behaved," Lily suggested. "Evan sure enjoys flying around the living room."

"So does Chris." Danielle picked up her drink and took a sip.

"That's because Chris hasn't really grown up," Heather snarked. They all laughed.

Someone behind the order counter called out their number.

"I'll get it." Heather stood up. "You don't need one of those brats knocking you down."

Fortunately for Heather, Mrs. Bowman had finished placing her order and had just turned around to her boys when Heather stood up. She ushered the twins to a table, and they all sat down. A few minutes later, Heather returned to her table with the food.

Just as Heather sat down, a man joined them, sitting in the empty chair. "I finally found you!" he told Heather.

Both Heather and Danielle turned to the new arrival, but Lily looked at Heather, waiting for her food.

"Homer Carter?" Heather blurted.

Lily frowned and looked at the empty chair, which had both Heather's and Danielle's attention. "Don't tell me, there is a ghost sitting with us, right?"

"You don't see him?" Danielle asked Lily.

Homer turned to Danielle. "Do you?"

"This is my friend Danielle Marlow. She can see spirits, too," Heather explained.

Homer grinned at Danielle. "Marie told me about you. Nice to meet you."

"Nice to meet you too," Danielle said.

"Okay, guys, while you two have a nice conversation with your ghost, can I please have my food? I'm hungry. My baby's hungry too," Lily said.

"She can't see me, right? But she knows about all this?" Homer asked.

Heather gave a nod as she handed out the food. A few minutes later, after Lily started eating her lunch, Homer told Heather, "I was hoping to find you. It's time I move on. I was wondering if you could tell Brian goodbye for me, and let him know how much I've appreciated his friendship."

"Certainly. I'm curious; where have you been spending all your time since your funeral?" Heather asked.

"I've been hanging around my house. Regretting even more how I wrote my will. So much contention. Ted and Lucy want to sell the house, and by some of the phone conversations I overheard them making to their spouses, I have a feeling both of them are having money issues. And then Flora is angry, claims Camilla offered her a pension after I died. Anyway, I don't need all this drama. I've lived my life. Time to move on."

TWENTY

Brian Henderson, with his shortly cropped gray hair and stocky build, wasn't someone you'd expect to find wearing a woman's dark purple silk robe. When ordering the robe online, Heather had accidentally selected the wrong size. She didn't bother sending it back because she could still wear it, even though it was several sizes too large. On Brian, it was a little snug.

Brian had stopped over at Heather's on Wednesday night and had stayed over. Early Thursday morning, Brian, wearing the purple robe, sat with Heather at her kitchen table, drinking coffee while his uniform finished drying. He had intended to go home and change into a clean uniform before work but stayed for breakfast while washing his uniform at Heather's house.

"Sorry I messed up your jogging routine." Brian took a drink of his coffee.

"You didn't. I intended to run later this morning, anyway."

"What about work?" Brian set his cup on the table.

"I don't have to go in until eleven this morning." Heather grinned.

Brian arched his brows. "Wow. Cushy job."

Heather let out a sigh. "I know. I love my job." She leaned back in the chair and sipped her coffee.

"I used to love my job, too." Brian absently fidgeted with the handle of his coffee mug.

Heather frowned. "Is it that bad now?"

Brian looked up at Heather. "Bowman's a jerk."

"Yeah. I know. But it's not forever. The chief should be back in a few months."

"Yesterday, when someone mentioned the chief would only be gone a couple of months, Bowman told them not to expect the chief back for at least six months, or longer. I swear, he acts like the chief retired and isn't coming back. He's not running the place like someone who's simply holding down the fort—maintaining the status quo. He's actively making changes."

"Like the name tags and checking IDs of all visitors?" Heather asked.

Brian nodded and picked up his mug, finishing the last of his coffee.

"Oh my!" A familiar voice entered the room. One that only Heather could hear. The ghost of Marie Nichols now stood by Heather's table, curiously looking Brian up and down while suppressing laughter.

"Ghost warning," Heather said dryly. "Marie's here. Morning, Marie."

BRIAN DRESSED and left for work not long after Marie's arrival.

"I probably shouldn't have told Brian you were here," Heather said as she straightened up the kitchen before going upstairs to change her clothes.

"Why?" Marie asked.

"He looked embarrassed."

"It was cute, both of you wearing robes and playing house. So, tell me, dear, when is he going to make an honest woman of you?"

"I thought you said he was too old for me?" Heather started for her bedroom, Marie following alongside.

"Yes, he is much older. But you two do seem to get along well."

Now walking up the stairs, Heather paused a moment and looked over at Marie. "I already told you I don't want to get married. Ever."

"I am a little surprised he doesn't keep some of his clothes here," Marie said. "Or a shaving kit, at least."

"I bought him a toothbrush. I don't want to be responsible for his teeth decaying because he sleeps over." Now on the second floor, Heather continued to her bedroom.

"There was a time I didn't approve of unmarried people cohabitating, but I know the world has changed. And if two people care about each other, like you and Brian, I suppose I can understand when they move in together."

"We're not moving in together." Heather walked into her bedroom. "He simply stays over some nights."

"I imagine you eventually will. Or do you want to wait until you get married?"

Heather let out a sigh and turned to Marie. "You are not listening. I told you, Brian and I, we're not getting married. Never. Ever. Brian has already been married twice. Didn't work out too well for him. Personally, I don't have a desire to get married. Maybe, if I wanted kids, I'd consider it. But I don't."

"Really? Never?"

Heather shook her head.

"You want to live alone forever?"

Heather looked at Marie. "You lived alone for years after your husband died. Why didn't you remarry? Was it because the love of your life died, and you couldn't replace what you had?"

Marie rolled her eyes. "Okay. Point taken. My husband was a putz. And I did rather enjoy living alone after he died. Being able to do what I wanted. Of course, I had Adam, who was always there when I needed him."

Heather grinned and then walked to her dresser and took out a pair of jogging pants. "I also enjoy living alone and having my own space. And I told Brian, when we first got together, that I'm not looking to marry anyone—or live with anyone."

"But he does spend the night here frequently," Marie reminded her.

Heather looked at Marie and grinned. "I like sleepovers."

CAMILLA SAT with her siblings at Pier Café, waiting for their breakfast order to arrive. Instead of feeling sad that Ted and Lucy planned to head home on Saturday, she counted down the hours. After they left, she would no longer have to endure their constant badgering, trying to get her to change her mind about selling Uncle Homer's house. Although she imagined she would receive constant phone calls and letters, but calls could go unanswered and letters unread. She silently sipped her coffee while Ted again recounted all the benefits of selling the house now and buying something smaller. All the while, Lucy interjected her opinions, supporting Ted's perspective. Camilla felt a brief sense of relief when her cellphone rang, but when she picked it up and saw who was calling, she momentarily considered ignoring the call.

"Good morning, Flora," Camilla eventually answered. Ted and Lucy sat quietly, listening to Camilla's side of the conversation. "We went out to breakfast... Your door was closed... I'm not sure when I'll be back... We've already ordered our food. We're waiting for it... No, I'll be coming directly home... I don't know what we need to talk about... Don't bother waiting. I'm sure you have things you need to do. Not sure when I'll be there... I'm walking... Along the beach, of course. It's only a couple of miles... Yes. I know... it's a nice day..." After a few more minutes of conversation, the phone call ended.

"Lord, that woman is persistent," Camilla muttered as she set her cellphone on the tabletop.

"She claims you offered her some sort of pension," Ted said.

Camilla arched her brows. "Did she? The woman only took care of Uncle Homer for... what was it... six years? Pensions are something people get after maybe twenty years."

"So she was lying?" Lucy asked.

Camilla shrugged. "We discussed a lot of things when I hired her. But I certainly did not promise to give her a share of Uncle Homer's estate. I wouldn't have the right to do that, now, would I?"

"What is this about you walking home? Were you just saying that?" Lucy asked.

"No. It's a lovely day. I thought after we have breakfast, you can take my car back to the house, and I'll walk home. I've missed walking along the beach." Homer's house was a block from the ocean and about two miles down the coast from the pier.

MARIE TOLD Heather that one reason she had stopped by her house was to check on her, because she had looked down the beach early that morning and didn't see Heather jogging, which was her routine. When she arrived at Heather's house, she saw Brian's car and decided there was no reason to check on Heather. She didn't intend to go inside. But before leaving, she peeked in the kitchen window, and after seeing Brian sitting at the table in Heather's robe, she couldn't resist popping in.

Marie ended up joining Heather on her run, as she wanted to discuss Danielle's upcoming baby shower. With Heather wearing her dark green jogging pants and sweatshirt, they headed down to the beach, and Heather ran south toward the pier. Yet, once they reached the pier, Heather grumbled something about drinking too much coffee, and then told Marie they needed to stop at Pier Café so she could use the bathroom. While there were other public bathrooms on the pier, Heather said they all smelled like fish and were disgusting.

AFTER HEATHER ENTERED PIER CAFÉ, she walked straight to the restroom without paying attention to who sat at the tables and booths in the diner. She didn't notice Carla, the server, who looked her way.

Inside the women's restroom, someone was in the first stall, and the second was empty. Heather entered the empty stall while Marie stood by the sink, waiting and looking into the mirror while thinking how odd it was that she no longer had a reflection.

A few minutes later, Heather stepped out of the stall at the same time as the woman in the other stall walked out. To Heather's surprise, it was Camilla Henderson.

Upon seeing Heather, Camilla stopped abruptly and demanded, "What are you doing in here?"

"What do people usually do in bathrooms?" Heather turned her back to Camilla, walked to the sink, and started washing her hands.

"You're following me!" Camilla accused.

Marie looked at Camilla and shook her head. "Don't be a twit. You're lucky I can't smack you again."

"Why would I follow you?" Heather asked. "I don't even know you."

"But I know all about you. Typical opportunist, preying on vulnerable older men. But your time taking advantage of Brian is over!"

"WHAT TOOK YOU SO LONG?" Lucy asked her sister when she returned to the table.

"You'll never believe who I ran into in the bathroom." Camilla scooted onto the bench seat and picked up the napkin she had left on the table. "That ridiculous little tramp Brian has been seeing."

"The vampire?" Ted grinned.

Camilla glared at her brother. "Whatever she is, I told her she might as well pack it up. I'm going to make sure Brian sees how foolish he's behaving."

"Why do you care?" Ted asked. "If Brian's happy, let him be."

"He's not happy," Camilla insisted. "He never remarried, and Brian is the type of man who needs to be married. But he's remained single since the divorce. Which can only mean one thing. He's never gotten over me. And now this little opportunist has gotten her claws into him, well, there is only one thing I can do."

"Which is it?" Ted asked. "Is she Brian's girlfriend or someone he paid to pretend to be his girlfriend? Because if it's someone he hired, then she doesn't have her claws into him. You need to make up your mind."

CAMILLA LEFT her brother and sister to drive home in her car, while she walked south down the beach. She breathed in the fresh ocean air and was grateful for the jacket she had brought along, considering April's cool air. Overhead, there wasn't a cloud in the sky, nor had there been any clouds when they had first arrived at Pier Café, which was one reason she had decided she would walk home after breakfast.

THE DRIVER HAD PULLED up to one of the parking lots along Beach Drive and noticed someone jogging north along the beach. Aside from the driver's vehicle and the jogger, both the beach and parking lot were empty. The driver pulled out a pair of binoculars and had a closer look. Heather Donovan. The driver put away the binoculars and headed toward the pier. A few minutes later, the driver noticed Camilla Henderson's car pulling out of the pier parking lot. But Camilla was not in the vehicle.

The driver pulled into the parking lot and parked. Walking down the pier, binoculars in hand, the driver looked north. He spied Heather Donovan in the distance. She had turned around and now headed his way. He then looked south and spied a familiar person, Camilla Henderson. No one else was along that section of the beach. Getting back into the car, the driver drove out of the parking lot and headed south.

CAMILLA HAD BEEN WALKING for about thirty minutes when she realized she needed to go to the bathroom, and there was no way she would make it all the way back to the house. Fortunately, she remembered there was a public restroom up ahead.

When Camilla reached the public restroom, she had the uncanny feeling someone was watching her. But the parking lot was empty, and there was no one else on the beach. There were houses along this section of the shoreline, but all their blinds were shut, and there were no people or vehicles in sight. She stepped into the women's bathroom and found it empty. When she was done, Camilla walked to the sink, washed her hands, and headed outside. She took a few steps and then felt a sharp pain hit the center of her back. Camilla cried out and lunged forward. She fell to the ground before all went black.

The person wielding the knife leaned over Camilla and checked her pulse. The killer pulled the knife from Camilla's back, removed Camilla's cellphone from her purse, and wrapped both items in a handkerchief before dragging Camilla's body into the women's bathroom.

After returning to the hiding space, the killer used the binoculars to look up the beach. The killer smiled when Heather Donovan came into view, jogging toward the public restroom. But a few seconds later, instead of continuing all the way to the restrooms, Heather turned and started back toward the pier.

TWENTY-ONE

Danielle rolled over on the mattress and sleepily opened her eyes. She was alone in bed and heard rustling in the nearby closet.

"Walt?" she called out.

"Shh… go back to sleep." Walt stepped out of the closet, walked to the bed, leaned down, and kissed Danielle's forehead.

She groaned. "Is it morning already?"

"Yes. Go back to sleep. I should be back in a couple of hours."

Danielle knew where Walt was going so early—to pick up Edward MacDonald and take him to the surgery center for his operation.

Danielle yawned and stretched. "Let me go make you coffee." She started to sit up in bed, but Walt gently pushed her down and gave her another kiss. "Go back to sleep, love. You need your rest."

"Okay," she mumbled, too tired to argue. Danielle rolled over on her side, grabbed one of Walt's pillows, and pulled it to her chest. Closing her eyes, she said, "Tell the chief I love him."

Walt chuckled. "I will."

EARLY FRIDAY MORNING Chief MacDonald opened his front door for Walt Marlow and was greeted with, "My wife says she loves you."

Holding the door open for Walt, MacDonald smiled as Walt entered the house. "Really?"

Walt shrugged. "I suspect it was her way of sending her well-wishes for the surgery."

"Tell Danielle I love her too." The chief shut the door.

"Hmm… should I be jealous?" Walt teased.

MacDonald chuckled. "I seriously doubt it." The two men stood in the MacDonald living room. "I'm almost ready."

"Did the boys stay with Sissy? Danielle mentioned they might."

"They spent the night there. She's taking them to school this morning before she goes to work. By the way, I really appreciate this."

ACROSS TOWN A FEW HOURS LATER, Ted and Lucy sat at the kitchen table, discussing their sister's whereabouts while Flora stood at the counter, pouring herself a cup of coffee.

"She didn't come home last night?" Flora asked.

"No. And it's so typical of her to not call," Lucy grumbled.

"Aren't you worried?" Flora asked.

Ted looked at Flora. "This is Frederickport; what could happen?"

Ted's comment made Flora choke on her coffee. She sputtered.

Ted frowned at Flora. "Are you okay?"

Flora grabbed a paper towel and wiped her mouth. She looked at Ted. "While I'm sure your sister is fine, you're not serious about Frederickport?"

"What do you mean?" Lucy asked.

Flora shook her head and muttered, "Never mind."

HEATHER STEPPED out onto her front porch with Bella in her arms and locked her door. With her purse draped over her right shoulder and her cat in her arms, she made her way to the front sidewalk, where Chris would pick her up for work. When she stepped onto the sidewalk, it surprised her to find Camilla standing there, looking up at her house.

"What are you doing?" Heather asked.

Camilla looked to Heather. "Is this where you live?"

"Are you stalking me?" Heather asked.

Instead of answering, Camilla hurried away. The next moment, Chris pulled up in front of Heather's house and parked.

"Who is that you were talking to?" Chris asked when Heather climbed into his car a minute later with Bella.

"That was Brian's ex. She was standing there staring at my house."

"Why?"

"I don't know. But the woman is creeping me out. What is she doing this early in the morning, stalking the girlfriend of her ex-husband?" After closing the car door, Heather tossed her cat in the back seat with Hunny. Hunny immediately jumped from the seat to the floor, trying to get as far away from the cat as possible.

"Is she stalking you?" Chris asked.

Now buckling her seatbelt, Heather shrugged. "I'm not sure what it is. But the woman acts like I broke up their marriage or something. They've been divorced for ten years, a good five years before I ever met Brian. It's just weird."

BRIAN HENDERSON and Joe Morelli sat in the break room of the Frederickport police station on Friday morning, each drinking a cup of coffee before their shift started. Brian was about to take another drink of coffee when his phone rang. He set the mug on the table, picked up his cellphone, and looked to see who was calling. It was Heather.

Joe silently drank his coffee while listening to Brian's side of the conversation. When the call ended, Joe asked, "What was that all about?"

"When Heather was going to work this morning, she found Camilla standing in front of her house, staring at it. After Camilla asked Heather if that was her house, Heather asked if she was stalking her. But Camilla just ran away."

"Camilla, as in your ex?" Joe asked.

Brian nodded. "I don't know what Camilla's deal is. One minute she's telling me she wants to be friends, and the next she's harassing my girlfriend. I guess they ran in to each other in the bathroom at Pier Café yesterday. Camilla got all in Heather's face and pretty much told her she needed to stay away from me."

"Camilla obviously wants to be friends with you—but not Heather."

Brian let out a snort at Joe's comment.

"Here you are," Bowman said as he walked into the break room. "I've been looking all over for you two."

Brian glanced at his watch and then looked back to Bowman. "Our shift doesn't start for another fifteen minutes. Joe and I like to come in early before we have to start."

Bowman looked to Brian. "I assumed you would want to know your ex-wife's sister just called the station to report a missing person—your ex-wife."

"Camilla's missing?" Brian frowned.

"Her sister said they had breakfast yesterday morning at Pier Café, and Camilla decided to walk home. She never made it. They didn't call right away, because they assumed she had met up with some friends and just didn't bother checking in. But this morning, they figured they'd better call since she's not answering her phone, and they have her car."

"I don't think we have much to worry about," Joe said. "Camilla was over on Beach Drive this morning."

Bowman frowned. "How do you know that?"

Joe glanced at Brian, waiting for him to explain.

Brian looked from Joe to Bowman, who now stared at him. Brian shrugged. "I talked to Heather a few minutes ago, and she said something about seeing Camilla in front of her house a little while ago."

Bowman arched his brows. "Really?"

"You say Camilla has been missing since yesterday morning? And no one has seen her?" Brian asked.

"Apparently your girlfriend has," Bowman said.

Brian shrugged again. "Heather just said she looked like Camilla. Maybe it was someone who looks like her."

Joe frowned at Brian yet said nothing.

"If that's the case, I think we should investigate." Bowman looked to Joe. "I'd like you to go with me to Pier Café so we can ask them a few questions."

"Joe and I can do it," Brian offered.

Bowman looked back at Brian and shook his head. "No. I think it best if you recuse yourself from this case."

"Case? We have a case?" Brian asked.

"If your ex-wife is truly missing, I think it would be inappropriate for you to be involved in the investigation," Bowman said.

JOE AND BOWMAN sat together at Pier Café's lunch counter, talking to Carla, who stood on the other side. She had just poured the police officers each a cup of coffee.

"Yes, I saw them. Camilla and her brother and sister," Carla told them. "They had breakfast."

"I understand Camilla had some sort of altercation with Heather Donovan?" Bowman said.

Joe turned to Bowman and frowned. Although Brian had mentioned that to Joe after Heather's phone call, Joe hadn't shared that information with Bowman. But obviously someone had, perhaps Camilla's sister when calling in the missing person report.

"I know nothing about that," Carla said.

"You didn't see Heather Donovan here around the same time as Camilla?" Bowman asked.

"Well, yes. Heather came in to use our bathroom. Later, I saw both Heather and Camilla come out of the bathroom. It didn't look like they were even talking to each other. Camilla returned to her table, and Heather left." Carla shrugged.

"You're saying Donovan came in just to use the bathroom?" Bowman asked.

"Yes. She didn't order anything," Carla said.

"She lives down the street. Why would she come here to use your bathroom?" Bowman asked.

"Heather runs about every morning along the beach," Joe interjected.

Bowman turned to look at Joe.

"It's common knowledge. She probably was on her run, had to use the bathroom, and stopped here," Joe explained.

"There are public restrooms on the pier. Why come in here?" Bowman asked. When Joe did not respond, he looked at Carla, who only shrugged.

"I THINK we need to retrace her steps," Bowman told Joe after the two left the diner and stood on the pier.

Joe frowned. "How so?"

"From what the sister says, the house they're staying at is about two miles from here and about a block from the ocean. We should start walking down the beach in that direction. See what we find."

"I seriously doubt there's a problem. There's no reason to walk two miles," Joe said. "This morning Heather called Brian and told him when she was going to work, she saw Camilla standing in front of her house. That wasn't even an hour ago."

"I thought Brian said he wasn't sure it was Camilla. That it might be someone who looked like her?"

Joe started to say Heather had talked to Camilla, but decided not to, since Brian had obviously withheld that information from Bowman for some reason.

Bowman turned and said, "Come on. We're going to take a walk."

Joe stifled a groan and fell alongside Bowman as they made their way from the pier to the beach below.

"What was this about an altercation between Heather and Camilla?" Joe asked Bowman after the two had been walking in silence for about ten minutes along the beach.

"From what the sister told me, Camilla Henderson went to the women's restroom at Pier Café, and when she stepped out of the stall, she found Heather Donovan standing there. Mrs. Henderson felt the woman was stalking her."

"I think it would be more Ms. than Mrs.," Joe said. "Brian and Camilla have been divorced for a decade."

"From what Camilla's sister said, Camilla talked about her and Brian getting back together. But Heather Donovan was determined not to let that happen."

"No way," Joe scoffed. "While I don't get Heather and Brian, I don't believe for a minute Brian has any interest in getting back with his ex."

"You and Brian are pretty close?" Bowman asked.

"He was the best man at my wedding."

"I heard something around the office that Brian had been dating Donovan for quite a while before you found out. That you didn't know. And that you were quite shocked. Which I can understand, after seeing Donovan."

Joe shrugged. "Yeah. That's true. I must admit, it surprised me."

"So why would it be so implausible that Brian might surprise you again?"

Joe didn't answer. Instead, he silently walked along the beach with Bowman.

They had been walking for about thirty minutes when Bowman spied the public restrooms. He stopped and pointed to the building. "Let's stop there. If Camilla came this way, it's possible she stopped at the bathrooms."

Trailing alongside Bowman, Joe followed his boss. They stopped in front of the women's restroom. Hands on hips, Bowman looked at the concrete around the door leading into the bathroom. He frowned. "That looks like blood." Bowman pointed to the spot and then turned and walked into the women's bathroom. Joe knelt by the red stain to have a closer look when Bowman shouted, "Morelli, get in here!" Joe jumped up and ran into the bathroom.

Once inside the doorway, Joe froze. Sprawled on the concrete floor was the body of Camilla Henderson. Chief Bowman knelt at her side, taking her vitals.

Bowman looked up to Joe. "She's dead."

TWENTY-TWO

B rian sat across from Chief Bowman in the interrogation room. He glanced to the one-way mirror, certain Joe stood on the other side, listening. While Brian disliked being on this side of the interrogation table, he understood why Bowman needed to question him.

"When was the last time you spoke to your wife?" Bowman asked.

"You mean ex-wife?" Brian corrected. "We've been divorced for ten years."

"Okay. Ex-wife. When was the last time you saw her?"

Brian considered the question for a moment, trying to figure out what day that had been. Finally, he said, "It was Tuesday. She stopped at the station, wanted to talk to me. You can ask Colleen. Camilla signed in up front."

"What did she want to talk to you about?"

Brian shrugged. "You probably already know, but her uncle passed away. That's why she and her brother and sister came to town. There was the funeral last week. Camilla decided to stay in Frederickport and move into her uncle's house. She was hoping we could come to friendly terms, since we would likely run into each other from time to time. You might say she was extending an olive branch."

"So you and your ex had been on bad terms?"

Brian leaned back in his chair, his arms now folded across his chest. "Not bad terms. Not good terms. I hadn't seen Camilla since she left town during our divorce. That was ten years ago. Frankly, it's been years since I gave her much thought. A more apt description, it was awkward."

"But you attended her uncle's funeral? Took your current girl-friend with you?"

"Her uncle, Homer Carter, we were good friends. In fact, he's the one who introduced us. We remained friends after the divorce. I used to go over to his house each week to play cribbage. But then he got Alzheimer's, and, well, cribbage stopped."

"I understand there was some sort of altercation at Mr. Carter's funeral, between Heather and Camilla. Heather hit your ex-wife?"

Brian sat up abruptly in the chair, his arms no longer folded across his chest. "Heather didn't touch Camilla. I was right there. But Camilla slapped Heather."

"Why would she do that?"

Brian shrugged. "I'm not sure. But from things Camilla said, it bothered her seeing me with Heather."

"You mentioned Heather claimed to have seen Camilla this morning, in front of her house."

Brian inwardly groaned. The coroner had already determined Camilla had been dead for hours before Bowman and Joe discovered her—hours before Heather claimed to have seen her. When Brian had first recounted Heather's phone conversation with Joe, he did not know his ex-wife was no longer alive. But when Bowman had walked into the break room and announced she had been missing over twenty-four hours, Brian's gut feeling had kicked in that something was wrong, which was why he'd tried backpedaling what he had told Joe. "She was obviously mistaken."

"I'd like you to tell me exactly what Heather told you this morn-ing," Bowman said.

Brian glanced at the mirror. If he wasn't sure Joe was watching, he'd be tempted to give Bowman the abbreviated version of the conversation. Reluctantly, Brian repeated Heather's phone conversation.

"Why would Heather say that? Obviously, she didn't see or talk to Camilla this morning. Not unless the coroner is mistaken about the time of death."

Sitting up straight and folding his hands on the table, Brian glanced at the mirror and then back to Bowman. He shrugged. "It was probably someone who looked like Camilla. After all, Heather's only seen her a few times. After the woman asked if that was Heather's house, Heather, believing it was my ex, asked if she was stalking her. That question probably freaked out the poor woman, so she just ran off. That's obviously what happened."

"When was the last time you saw Heather?"

"Yesterday morning, before work."

"Where was this?"

"Her house. I had spent the night. I left there and came to work."

"What time was that?"

Brian gave the time.

"I understand Heather ran into Camilla at Pier Café later that morning."

"Yeah, she mentioned it. Heather likes to jog in the morning, and she stopped at the restaurant to use the bathroom, where she ran into Camilla. Afterwards, Heather finished her jog and went to work."

"What was said between Camilla and Heather when they ran into each other?"

Brian shrugged. "You'll have to ask Heather."

"I will." Bowman glanced down at the notebook in his hand and then back to Brian. "I'm curious about one thing. I understand Heather works for some nonprofit organization."

"Yes."

"When does she go into work?"

"She typically works from eight to five."

"But she didn't yesterday? It was after eight when she was using the bathroom at Pier Café."

"Heather's schedule can change. Yesterday, she didn't have to go in until eleven."

BRIAN STOOD with Joe in the office next to the interrogation room, watching as Bowman prepared to interview Camilla's sister.

"It's obvious Bowman intends to take over this case," Joe said.

"I assume I'll be a suspect, considering Camilla was my ex. Bowman probably feels you can't be impartial since we're friends."

"I know you didn't kill her."

Brian reached over and gave Joe's shoulder a quick pat. "No, I didn't. But I'd like to find out who did. Why would someone want to kill Camilla? It makes little sense, and I refuse to believe we have some psycho out there randomly killing women. But I really don't know what her life's been like these last ten years. I don't even know if she has a boyfriend out there."

"I heard him tell you not to discuss this case with anyone outside the department," Joe said, "and not to call Heather and tell her about the murder."

"Yeah."

"If it makes you feel any better, he told me the same thing, specifically mentioning my wife."

Brian chuckled. "Yeah, he said it could jeopardize the case. I guess he forgot what Frederickport's like. You and I not talking won't stop the gossip, and he already interviewed Carla."

LUCY DABBED her red-rimmed eyes with the tissue as she sat across the table from Chief Bowman in the interrogation room.

"I can't believe she's dead. Why would someone do this?"

"Can you think of anyone who'd want to hurt your sister?"

Absently chewing her upper lip, Lucy shook her head for a

moment and then looked up to Bowman. "I bet it's that woman Brian's been seeing."

"Are you talking about Heather Donovan?"

"I think that's her name. She's a weirdo. Dresses all dark and creepy. I can't even believe Brian is seeing her. What is he thinking?"

"I understand your sister claimed Heather struck her—unprovoked—at your uncle's funeral, which made your sister slap her. But from what Brian says, Heather never touched her. Apparently, no one actually saw Heather hit Camilla, but some saw your sister slap Heather."

Lucy stared at Bowman for a minute, not responding. Finally, she blurted, "I saw her. I saw Heather hit Cam."

"You did? Did you tell anyone?"

Now biting down on her lower lip, Lucy shook her head. "No... should have. But I didn't. I was hoping it would all blow over. I didn't want all the drama."

TED SAT ACROSS FROM BOWMAN, who had just asked if he had seen Heather hit Camilla. Ted shook his head. "No. But I believe my sister when she said the woman hit her. Cam isn't the type to just walk up to someone and slap them. And I don't understand why this Heather person would have such an issue with my sister. After all, Cam's the one who ended the marriage, not Brian. And it's been years. But it's obvious the woman felt threatened by my sister, which is why she attacked her."

"Other than Heather Donovan, do you know of anyone else who had an issue with your sister?"

Ted considered the question for a moment. "The only one I can think of is Flora. She was my uncle's caretaker. She was living in my uncle's house with him. Cam wanted Flora to move out by last Sunday, but Flora refused and told Cam she would have to evict her before she would leave. She wanted to stay until she could find a place to live and a new job. I can't say I really blame her. She also claimed Cam promised her some sort of pension after my uncle died, if she was still taking care of him. Cam claims Flora misunderstood."

"Who inherited your uncle's estate?" Bowman asked.

"It's divided equally between me and my sisters. But now, with Cam gone, I assume her share will go to her heir."

"Who would that be?" Bowman asked.

Ted shrugged. "I don't really know."

After Bowman finished interviewing Ted and Lucy, he asked Joe to go somewhere with him. Brian assumed he was taking Joe to Homer's house to interview Flora. But Brian was wrong.

CHRIS JOHNSON, aka Chris Glandon, initially purchased the Gusarov Estate to house the Glandon Foundation offices. He soon realized there was enough room on the property to relocate Glandon's commercial ventures to Frederickport. Yet this didn't mean the former Gusarov estate was suddenly teeming with people. Since the neighborhood was primarily residential, even with Chris's finances and clout, that would not have been possible. However, many of the Glandon employees worked remotely. Aside from Heather and Chris, there were about a dozen full-time employees who worked at the site. They all parked on the property, behind a privacy wall, and most casual observers would have no idea an empire worth billions operated from what had once been the Gusarov Estate.

HEATHER SAT AT HER DESK, updating Chris's calendar, when her office door opened, and the receptionist walked in. The woman looked frazzled. "There are two police officers asking for you."

Heather smiled. The receptionist was new and probably didn't know she dated a local cop. "Tell them to come in."

The next moment, Chief Bowman marched into Heather's office, Joe trailing behind him, and the receptionist lingering in the background, watching. Heather's smile vanished as she tried comprehending why Bowman stood in her office glaring down at her, while Joe stood off to the side, his expression she could only describe as apologetic.

"Stand up, Ms. Donovan," Bowman barked.

"Excuse me?" Heather remained sitting. She glanced at Joe, who motioned for her to stand, his expression pleading. Before she could comply, Bowman grabbed her by the wrist and jerked her to her feet while saying, "Heather Donovan, you are under arrest for the murder of Camilla Henderson…"

Startled by the assault, Heather let out a loud cry as Bowman read her Miranda rights. The next moment Hunny, Chris's pit bull, charged into the room, barking. Bowman pushed Heather to the side and reached for his gun. Joe immediately grabbed Hunny by the collar and put himself between the dog and the police chief, who now pointed the gun in his direction.

Chris charged into Heather's office next, yelling, "What the hell is going on?" and then froze in his tracks when he saw Bowman pointing the gun at Joe, who had pushed Hunny behind him, still holding her collar.

Bowman aimed the gun at Joe. "Get out of the way, Morelli."

"I won't let you shoot Hunny," Joe snapped.

"The dog was going to attack me."

"Because you grabbed Heather," Joe argued. "She was naturally protecting her."

With Bowman distracted by his conversation with Joe, and his gun now lowered, Chris quietly grabbed hold of Hunny's collar, led her from the room, and locked her in his office. Chris returned a moment later and found Bowman handcuffing Heather. "What is going on?" Chris again demanded.

"We're arresting Miss Donovan for the murder of Camilla Henderson." Bowman shoved Heather toward the door, her hands secured behind her back.

Chris looked at Heather. "I'm calling Mel. Don't say a word."

Heather gave Chris a nod while tears streamed down her face. As Bowman led Heather from the office, Joe looked back to Chris and mouthed, *I'm sorry.*

TWENTY-THREE

"**N**ot sure who Mel is, but I doubt he'll be able to help you." Bowman snickered as he shoved Heather into the back seat and slammed the door shut. Joe stood silently by the passenger door and watched Bowman walk toward him, en route to the driver's side of the car.

Bowman paused a moment and looked at Joe. "Never get between me and my gun again, because the next time, you'll either be shot or out of a job."

Joe didn't respond. He stood silently and watched Bowman walk around the front of the vehicle. As Bowman climbed into the driver's seat, Joe reached for the handle of the front passenger door. He glanced in the back seat to Heather before getting into the car.

"WHAT THE HELL IS GOING ON?" Brian demanded as Bowman brought Heather into the station to be booked. Heather silently looked at Brian, her eyes wide and terror filled, and her hands still secured behind her back.

"Remember what I told you, Morelli. Put a muzzle on your buddy." Bowman shoved past Brian and kept walking with Heather.

Joe grabbed hold of Brian's arm, stopping him from following Bowman and Heather. Frantic, Brian turned to Joe. "What's going on?"

"Bowman arrested Heather for Camilla's murder," Joe explained.

Brian's heart raced. "She didn't murder Camilla. No way."

"I agree. Whatever I might have thought about Heather in the past, I don't see her as a killer. Especially not someone she barely knows. Heather is too concerned about karma to murder anyone."

"Why didn't you tell me you guys were going to arrest her?"

Joe shook his head. "I didn't know. At least, not until we pulled up in front of the Glandon Foundation."

"Damn," Brian cursed.

"Bowman told me you have to stay away from Heather while she's being booked, and he doesn't want you talking to her at all while she's being held."

"He can't do that."

"He says you'll interfere with the case, and if you don't follow his instructions, he'll suspend you without pay."

Exasperated, Brian combed his fingers through his hair and looked down the hallway where Bowman had taken Heather. "What am I going to do?"

Smiling, Joe reached out and touched Brian's arm. "The last thing Chris said as Bowman led Heather out of her office, he told her not to say anything and that he was calling Mel."

Brian visibly relaxed. He turned to Joe and smiled.

HEATHER HAD STOPPED CRYING and had pulled herself together. She sat quietly in the interrogation room, her hands folded before her on the table. She glanced around the room and then stared at the one-way mirror, wondering if Brian was on the other side. When driving over from her office, Heather had sat quietly in the back seat of the police car and listened to Bowman laying down the rules to Joe regarding her future interactions with Brian. If Brian wanted to keep his job, he couldn't interfere with the case against her, and according to Bowman, that meant he needed to keep his distance. Bowman didn't want Brian doing anything that might help Heather's case. Heather wasn't sure if that was legal, but she had since calmed down and was no longer afraid. After all, Chris had promised to call Mel.

Heather sat back in the chair and wiped away any remaining tears. At least he had finally removed the damn handcuffs. While silently rehashing all that had happened since Chief Bowman and Joe had walked into her office to arrest her, she had to admit, Joe did not look happy about the arrest.

Heather had a new respect for Joe Morelli. It wasn't because of his attitude regarding her arrest. But she believed Joe had probably saved Hunny's life this afternoon. Had he not intervened when he had, Heather had no doubt Bowman would have shot Hunny. She didn't even want to consider the series of events that would have followed.

The door to the interrogation room opened, and Heather looked to the doorway and watched as Bowman strutted into the room—he didn't walk; Heather thought he looked like an overconfident rooster. She reminded herself of what Chris had told her. *Say nothing.*

Bowman sat at the table across from Heather and smiled. She said nothing.

"Well, Miss Donovan, you've got yourself into a heap of trouble."

Heap of trouble? What do you think you are now, a cowboy? Heather thought.

Bowman leaned back in the chair and crossed his arms over his chest. "I don't believe you meant to kill Camilla Henderson. It was a crime of passion. You were jogging; you stopped at the bathroom along the beach. Encountered Camilla for the second time that morning. She was all in your face, threatening to break up you and Brian, and you just snapped."

Heather said nothing; she just stared.

"I can help you out. We can show it wasn't premeditated; you were provoked. After all, Camilla attacked you at the funeral. People saw. This is your first offense; I would recommend just a few years. You're a young woman and will be out before you know it." Bowman leaned forward, now resting his elbows on the table. "But if you don't plead out, I can guarantee you are going to spend the rest of your life behind bars. And Miss Donovan, that is going to be a really long time."

Heather remained silent.

"Come on, what do you say? Don't you want to make it easy on yourself? We all know you did it."

"I don't recall waiving my right to an attorney. I wish to see my attorney."

Bowman leaned back in the chair again and smiled at Heather. "Okay. You can call your attorney." Bowman slapped his cellphone on the table and slid it over to Heather. "Do you need a phonebook to find one? Or should we see if you qualify for a public defender? I doubt you do. You own a house, but I imagine you'll have to take a loan out on that to get bail. If you're even granted bail. And then there are the attorney fees. You'd be better off pleading out, and then when you get out in a couple of years, you'll still have a home. But if you decide to take this to trial, you'll probably still end up behind bars, and when you get out, you'll be on the streets. Even if your attorney somehow gets you off, you'll probably lose your house to pay for legal fees. Wouldn't it be easier to be a guest of the state for a few years and have a home when you get out?"

The door to the interrogation room opened, and Melony Carmichael Nichols walked in, reminding Heather for a moment of *Legally Blonde*'s Elle Woods. A tall Elle Woods.

"Who are you?" Bowman demanded without bothering to look at her name tag. "How did you get in here?"

"I'm Ms. Donovan's attorney, Melony Carmichael. I hope you aren't questioning my client without her attorney present."

Heather let out a sigh of relief and smiled up at Melony while remaining silent.

Bowman frowned. "Mel?"

"My friends call me Mel. You can call me Ms. Carmichael." She turned to Heather and smiled. "Heather, don't worry. I'll have you out of here before you know it."

"Maybe Ms. Donovan has an attorney, but she is being charged with murder, and if I have my way, there won't be bail."

Melony smiled at Bowman. "I doubt you'll get your way. My client has never been arrested. She is a respected member of this community, and your case is very flimsy. She didn't even know the victim."

"If bail is set, it won't be under a million dollars. I don't think your client can afford you and her bail. Ms. Donovan would be better off to plead out, and instead of sacrificing her home to pay your legal fees and bail, she'll be out in a couple of years and have a home to come back to."

Melony walked to Heather and placed a hand on one of Heather's shoulders while she looked across the table to Bowman. "Actually, I'm taking Heather's case pro bono, because not only am I convinced of her innocence, she's a dear friend of mine. As for bail, I've already heard from Chris Glandon. He told me he'll cover Heather's bail, no matter what the price—one million or ten million."

Bowman stared blankly at Melony.

"Now, I would like to speak to my client. Alone."

———

BOWMAN STORMED out of the interrogation room, slamming the door behind him. He marched over to the adjacent office and reached for the doorknob.

"You can't go in there," a voice called out.

Bowman spun around and found himself facing Joe Morelli.

"Heather is in the interrogation room with her attorney," Joe reminded him. "If you go into that office, you'll be able to hear everything they say. None of us can be in there when a client is with their attorney."

"Who is this woman who claims she's an attorney?" Bowman demanded.

Joe frowned. "You don't know?"

"She says she's Melony Carmichael. I remember an attorney who used to be in town named Carmichael, but that was an old man."

"That was her father," Joe explained. "But she's never been a member of his firm. She moved back to town a couple of years ago from New York. Melony is probably one of the top criminal attorneys in the state."

"I've never heard of her," Bowman grumbled. "She said something about a Chris Glandon paying Heather's bail. Who is that?"

Joe smiled. "Glandon—Glandon Foundation. Where she works. Chris Glandon is the head of the Glandon Foundation. He's worth, like, billions."

Bowman frowned. "That guy who's her boss. His name is Chris. But I thought it was Chris Johnson. The one with the pit bull."

"Yeah, well, Chris Johnson works there too. Heather is his assistant."

"What is this Glandon Foundation, anyway?" Bowman asked.

Joe frowned. "I assumed you knew."

"Fred just mentioned something about the Glandon charity that moved to town. They've been working with the museum, the local humane society, and some other charities. What I don't understand, why would a nonprofit pay the bail of one of their employees who has been accused of murder? I doubt that's even legal. It would probably violate their nonprofit status. I would think it would be more prudent to terminate the employment so the employee doesn't tarnish their reputation. Her bail is going to be a million dollars, at least. That money could be better spent elsewhere."

Joe shrugged. "I doubt Mr. Glandon would agree. Anyway, the bail money is probably not coming from the Glandon Foundation, but from his private funds. From what I understand, Mr. Glandon is quite fond of Heather Donovan, and to a multibillionaire, a million dollars isn't that much money."

"Does this Chris Glandon live in Frederickport? I'd like to talk to him."

Joe didn't answer immediately. Finally, he said, "According to the tabloids, Chris Glandon travels the world. But I suppose you could Google it."

TWENTY-FOUR

After being reminded he couldn't enter the office next to the interrogation room because he could overhear the conversation between Heather and her attorney, Bowman instructed Joe to stand guard outside the interrogation room and stay there after the attorney left. He explained he had a few things to do, and he would personally escort Ms. Donovan to lockup when he returned. She was to remain in the interrogation room with Joe guarding the door until he returned. Under no circumstances was Brian to be allowed to talk to her.

Bowman went back to his office and retrieved a small voice-activated recorder he had purchased some time ago and had brought to his new office. After checking the recorder's batteries, Bowman slipped it in his pocket and headed to lockup.

WALT AND DANIELLE sat together on the parlor sofa Friday afternoon, discussing boys' names to consider, when pounding came at the front door. Instead of immediately answering the door, Walt got up from the sofa and peeked out the parlor window. Chris stood on the front porch with Bella in his arms and Hunny by his side.

"It's Chris." Walt walked from the window to the door leading to the entry hall. A moment later, he opened the front door and stood to one side as Chris walked in without a greeting.

"Where's Danielle?" Chris asked.

"She's in the parlor. I'm surprised you knocked." Walt grinned.

Chris looked at Walt, his face unsmiling. "I didn't have my key. But we need to talk." He handed Bella to Walt and headed to the parlor.

"Bowman arrested Heather," Chris announced when he walked into the parlor. Walt and Hunny trailed behind him.

Danielle turned around on the sofa and looked at Chris. "Arrested?"

"What for?" Walt asked.

"Did that stupid Bowman accuse her of shoplifting again?" Danielle asked.

"No. For the murder of Brian's ex-wife Camilla Henderson."

"Someone murdered Brian's ex?" Danielle gasped.

Walt, who had placed Bella on the floor, sat on the sofa next to Danielle, while Chris took a seat on one chair across from them and told them what he knew about Heather's arrest.

"That explains some of the confused messages Hunny and Bella keep sending me," Walt said after the telling. He glanced down at Bella, who sat on the floor between his feet and Danielle's, while Hunny curled up by Chris's chair.

"I haven't heard from Mel yet, but Adam said she's at the station now. This whole thing is crazy, and on top of everything, that SOB was itching to shoot Hunny." Chris then elaborated on what had happened regarding Bowman and Hunny in Heather's office, and how Joe had intervened.

"Wow. Good for Joe," Danielle said. "That guy is freaking nuts."

"I'll have a talk with Hunny," Walt said. "I'll explain if she sees the man who took Heather again, to stay away from him. No barking, no acting aggressive. She needs to understand he carries a gun, and he has no problem using it at the slightest provocation."

Danielle glanced at the time and looked back at Chris. "We're going to have to leave soon to pick up the chief."

"What is he going to say about all this?" Chris asked.

"I don't even want to tell him," Danielle said. "I feel bad enough telling him about what happened at the station between me and Bowman. And we didn't say anything about what happened with you and Heather at the pharmacy and back at her house. But this. Crap. The guy just had major surgery."

"We can't keep it from him," Walt said. "All he has to do is read tomorrow's newspaper."

"You guys need to tell him. I agree, it sucks. The poor guy needs to focus on his recovery, but if you don't tell him, someone will. And if he thinks we're keeping things from him, that will make it worse."

Danielle was about to agree when snowflakes fell from the ceiling. They looked up briefly. "Hello, Eva," Danielle greeted.

"I'm here too," Marie announced. The next moment, the spirits of Marie Nichols and Eva Thorndike appeared in the middle of the parlor just as all the snowflakes vanished.

"We wanted to check on Edward," Marie explained. "When are you picking him up?"

"Heather was arrested," Chris blurted. Both spirits looked at him. Chris repeated all that he had told Walt and Danielle minutes earlier.

"Do they know when Camilla was murdered?" Marie asked.

"I didn't learn much from Bowman or Joe when they arrested Heather, other than she was being arrested for Camilla's murder. But after they left, I did some calling around and found out the last time they saw her was at Pier Café yesterday morning," Chris began. "According to Carla, Heather stopped in to use the bathroom during her morning jog, and she ran into Camilla. Carla didn't know what was said, but Bowman acted like the two had some sort of altercation in the bathroom. Camilla was having breakfast with her brother and sister. When they were done, Camilla left the restaurant and planned to walk home. Heather had already left by that time. Carla assumed, to continue her run. That was the last time Camilla was seen alive. They found her the next morning in the public restroom south of the pier. Someone stabbed her in the back."

"So, the time of death?" Danielle asked.

"Since Bowman believes Heather is the killer, I have to assume after Camilla left the restaurant and before eleven a.m., because Heather arrived at work at eleven," Chris said.

"Then Heather is innocent," Marie announced.

"We already know that," Chris snapped.

"I just mean I can prove it." Marie smiled at Chris. "Because I was with her yesterday morning. When she ran into Camilla in the bathroom at Pier Café, I was there. I stayed with her all morning, joining her on her run, and even drove along to work with her. I am her alibi."

"Yes, dear, but alibis from us don't count," Eva gently reminded her.

"Oh… that's right," Marie grumbled.

"But we will tell the chief what you said," Danielle promised.

"What can we do to help poor Heather?" Marie asked.

Chris looked at Marie. "I suggest you go to the station and keep her company. Mel told me Heather might have to spend the night in a cell. If that's the case, I'm sure she would appreciate your company."

"And considering what a jerk Chief Bowman is, it would be nice if someone like Marie was there to keep an eye on Heather," Danielle said. "Just don't do anything that she can be blamed for."

HEATHER SAT ALONE on the narrow bed in one cell in lockup, her feet up on a mattress, and her hands folded in her lap, as she leaned against a wall. The last time she had been in lockup, she had stood on the other side of the bars while convincing an inmate she was a witch. Heather smiled at the memory.

"I wish Marie were here with me now, like she was then," Heather said aloud. The next moment, snowflakes fell from the ceiling. She abruptly sat up, her feet now on the floor. "Eva?"

"We're here to keep you company!" Marie called out. The spirits of Eva and Marie appeared in her cell as all evidence of snowflakes vanished.

"I was just wishing you were here! And Eva's here too!"

"We couldn't leave you all alone while you deal with this," Marie said.

Eva and Marie joined Heather on the bed, with Eva sitting on Heather's right, and Marie on Heather's left.

"Chris told us what happened," Eva said.

"And we want to help," Marie added.

"I saw Camilla this morning. She was standing in front of my house. I spoke to her."

"It was her ghost," Marie said.

"Yep." Heather nodded. "I really need to figure out how to tell dead people from living people."

"We preferred to be called ghosts," Eva said.

"Unless you're Walt. Then you want to be called a spirit," Marie smirked.

They all laughed.

When the laughing stopped, Marie said, "I'm glad to see you still have your sense of humor. And I know this is going to work out. I understand my new granddaughter is on the case. And she's a brilliant attorney."

"Mel is terrific. She told me she's doing this pro bono. I can't believe how generous she is."

Eva tilted her head ever so slightly and said, "The Universe sees this as coming full circle. It's when you release blessings into the universe, sowing the field for future blessings."

Heather frowned at Eva. "What do you mean?"

"Yes, Eva, what do you mean? I'm not sure what blessing there is with poor Heather locked up in a cell and being accused of murder."

Eva chuckled. "I was talking about the gift of Melony's expertise she's passing on to Heather. Once it was Heather returning my emerald to its rightful owner. Danielle shared the emerald with the museum. And then Danielle happened across the Winterborne engagement ring, which ended up with Melony. And now Melony is helping Heather."

"Sort of like paying it forward," Heather said.

"Interesting perspective," Marie muttered.

"Do you know where Bella is?" Heather asked.

"Walt asked Bella where she wanted to stay until you got home. The choices were your house, Marlow House, or Chris's. Bella wanted to go home. She said she wanted to be there when you returned," Marie explained. "Chris said he will go over and feed her, clean her litter box, and make sure she has water."

Heather giggled.

"What's so funny?" Eva asked.

"There is just something funny about Chris Glandon cleaning my litter box."

Marie chuckled and then said, "Okay, let's get serious. What do you want us to do?"

"I'd like to talk to Camilla. Ask her who murdered her."

"You want us to find her?" Marie said.

Heather nodded. "Her ghost might be at the funeral home or her uncle's house. Or maybe she's hanging around Brian. It seems like she had some sort of obsession with him before someone murdered her."

"I can go look for her, and Marie can stay here with you, keep you company," Eva suggested.

ACROSS TOWN, Walt and Danielle Marlow sat with Chief MacDonald in his living room. The boys hadn't come home from school yet, and the chief sat in his recliner, with his feet elevated, a post-op knee brace secured in place, and his walker within arm's reach. They had updated the chief on all that had happened involving Heather, including what had gone down before the murder allegation.

The chief's cellphone buzzed. He picked it up off the side table next to his chair and looked at it. After reading the text message, he said, "That's the pharmacy. My meds are ready."

"I'll go get them," Walt offered.

After Walt left to get the chief's pain medication, Danielle stayed to keep the chief company.

"I really want to thank you and Walt for helping me today."

"Hey, that's what friends are for."

"But I'm regretting having this surgery. I wish I would have post-poned it."

Danielle let out a sigh. "No one saw this coming."

"I need to go down to the station tomorrow."

Danielle shook her head. "You need your rest. You just had major surgery."

"But an innocent woman is in lockup, charged with murder."

"Melony's on it. And Eva and Marie are keeping Heather company."

"Well, I'm going to tell Walt that if he wants to dump hot coffee in Bowman's lap again, he has my approval."

TWENTY-FIVE

F riday evening, Eva left Marie to stay with Heather while she took off in search of Camilla's spirit. Heather managed to get a decent night's rest, knowing Marie looked over her. The next morning, instead of being served breakfast in her jail cell, Brian greeted Heather with the news she could go home.

"Why?" Heather asked.

"I suspect Mel got to the DA," Brian suggested. "From what I understand, the DA didn't feel there was enough evidence to take this to trial."

Standing at the now open jail cell, Heather said, "One thing I thought was weird, I was never questioned. No one asked me where I was when Camilla was killed. No one asked me if I knew Camilla or what our relationship was. Nothing."

"What about when you were in the interrogation room with Bowman?" Brian asked.

"He didn't really ask me questions. I thought it was because Mel wasn't there yet. He just kept trying to talk me into confessing, telling me how much better off I would be to save money on bail and legal fees."

"How about after Mel arrived?" Brian asked.

Heather shook her head. "No. He didn't ask me anything. Not really. As far as he knew, I might have an airtight alibi during the time of death. He didn't know if I had a jogging partner who was with me that morning or if I was alone the entire time."

"You had one. Me," Marie chimed in.

Heather smiled at Marie. "True. And Marie, thanks again for staying with me last night. It really made it much easier."

"I'll walk you out before I go find Eva. I doubt she's found Camilla, since she hasn't been back, but perhaps she has a lead," Marie said.

THIRTY MINUTES EARLIER, across town in the Lyonses' garage apartment, the Bowman twins sat on the unmade sofa bed in the living room, still wearing their pajamas while each ate a bowl of cereal and watched cartoons.

In the kitchen area, a colorful vinyl tablecloth covered the small table, where Clay sat drinking his coffee and staring at the cellphone in his hand.

"Do you want eggs or cereal?" Debbie asked her husband for the second time. When he still didn't answer, she snapped, "Clay!"

Clay frowned up at his wife, who stood over him, her hands on her hips. "What?"

"I asked you, what do you want for breakfast?"

"I've got to go into the station."

Debbie frowned. "But it's Saturday. I thought we could do something together today, as a family."

Clay picked up his mug, finished the last of his coffee, and stood up. "I need to go down there. That call I just got. I have to release our prisoner."

"But she murdered someone. Right?"

"Apparently, her attorney convinced the DA that we don't have enough to hold her on."

"Can he do that? Just let a murderer go?"

WHEN CLAY PULLED into the police department parking lot on Saturday morning, he saw they had already released Heather. She walked with Brian, heading towards his car. Bowman pulled up beside the couple, rolled down his window, and stopped his vehicle.

"What did I tell you, Henderson?" Bowman barked.

Placing his right hand protectively on the middle of Heather's back, Brian turned to the police car. "What are you talking about?"

"You're to stay away from Donovan. She is a suspect in the murder of your ex-wife, and if you're trying to compromise our case, perhaps I need to charge you as an accomplice."

"And I imagine they'll drop those charges as fast as the ones against Heather," Brian snapped back.

"I know she killed your ex-wife." Clay turned his attention to Heather, who stood silently by Brian's side. "You're not to leave Frederickport, Miss Donovan. You're still a prime suspect in this case, and trust me, I'll be bringing you in again, this time with enough evidence to convince the DA to pursue this case."

Heather glared at Clay. "If you have anything to say to me, you can talk to my attorney."

Brian gave Heather's back a gentle nudge, and the two continued to his car.

MARIE RESISTED the temptation to give Clay Bowman a good kick in the backside. She had already gotten Heather into enough trouble by smacking Camilla at the funeral. Had she not done that, she doubted the story of the animosity between Heather and Camilla would have spread, thus saving Heather from being a suspect in Camilla's murder.

She watched as Clay drove away after harassing Heather and Brian. He parked in Chief MacDonald's space on the other side of the parking lot. Marie turned her attention back to Heather, who was now getting into Brian's car.

167

"You go home, get a good rest," Marie told Heather. "I'll go find Eva. Hopefully, she has a lead on our newest spirit."

Five minutes later, Marie stood in the parking lot and watched as Brian and Heather drove away. She looked back at the police station just as Bowman entered the building. Marie contemplated following Bowman instead of looking for Eva.

AFTER CLAY ENTERED THE BUILDING, he went straight to lockup, hoping no one had been arrested last night. He didn't want an audience when retrieving the voice-activated cassette recorder he had hidden in the cell. Ten minutes later, Clay entered his office and locked the door behind him. He walked to the desk and sat down, placing the recorder before him. He wanted to see if Henderson had ignored his orders and visited Heather last night. If he had, Clay wanted to know what they had talked about.

He hit the rewind button and discovered the recorder had captured something last night. He wondered whose voices would be on the tape. After the recorder finished rewinding, he hit play and listened.

"I wish Marie were here with me now, like she was then. Eva? I was just wishing you were here! And Eva's here too! I saw Camilla this morning. She was standing in front of my house. I spoke to her. Yep. I really need to figure out how to tell dead people from living people." *Laughter.*

Clay stopped the tape, rewound it, and then listened to it again. *Who is she talking to?*

"Mel is terrific. She told me she's doing this pro bono. I can't believe how generous she is. What do you mean? Sort of like paying it forward. Do you know where Bella is?" *Giggling.* "There is just something funny about Chris Glandon cleaning my litter box."

Once again, Clay stopped the tape. *Did she say Chris Glandon was cleaning her litter box? Is she talking to herself?* He hit play again.

"I'd like to talk to Camilla. Ask her who murdered her. Her ghost might be at the funeral home or her uncle's house. Or maybe she's hanging around Brian. It seems like she had some sort of obsession with him before someone murdered her."

MARIE HAD ENTERED Bowman's office not long after Clay pushed play on the recorder. It took Marie a minute to figure out what she was listening to. Bowman had obviously hidden a voice-activated recorder in Heather's jail cell last night. Since it was a voice-activated recorder, it had only recorded when Heather spoke or made some noise, and it stopped when Eva or Marie spoke. Because of this, it sounded as if Heather had been rambling incoherently when alone in her cell last night.

Furious at the invasion of Heather's privacy and rights, Marie focused her energy on the tape recorder. Just as the recording said, "It seems like she had some sort of obsession with him before someone murdered her..." the tape player's speed increased at such a rate the voice coming out of the machine sounded like an angry chipmunk.

Frowning, Clay looked down at the recorder and pressed pause. The compartment holding the tape flew open, spitting the cassette from the machine and, in doing so, sent narrow tape unraveling outside of the cassette. The cassette landed on the desk, a pile of tape spilling from its core.

"What the hell?" Clay muttered as he picked up the cassette. Gingerly touching the loose magnetic tape with his fingertips, he looked as if he was contemplating how to roll the tape back onto the cassette. The next moment his hands moved of their own volition, and his eyes widened as he stared down at his fingers as they pulled the rest of the magnetic tape from the cassette and then tore the tape into little bits, putting an end to any notion he might have had of rewinding the tape and listening to it again.

After his hands finished decimating the cassette, they dropped the tape onto the desktop. Clay sat paralyzed, staring down at the broken cassette and pile of tangled and torn magnetic tape. He raised his hands to his face and stared at them as if looking at the appendages for the first time. He took a deep breath, lowered his hands to the desk, and closed his eyes.

"Serves you right," Marie snapped at Clay. "You won't be listening to that now." Had a medium been in the room with Clay, they would have witnessed Marie vanish the next moment.

———

HIS HEART RACED; its wild beating filled his head. Clay told himself to calm down, and he took another deep breath. He remembered the coffee incident in Pier Café. The mug hadn't simply slipped from his hand. He remembered the distinct sensation of pressure against his hand as if someone took hold of his wrist and twisted it, making the mug turn upside down.

He searched his brain for an answer and remembered a problem he'd experienced several years earlier with his legs, where they twitched uncontrollably. The doctor had said it was muscle spasms, and had explained dehydration, too much coffee, not getting enough sleep, stress, or anxiety could cause the spasms. Clay had to admit, he had been experiencing both stress and anxiety, and he didn't get enough sleep, and he probably drank too much coffee.

After convincing himself he had diagnosed his problem—ignoring the fact spasms would not make his hands behave as they had—Clay picked up the ruined cassette, along with the recorder, and threw them all in the nearby trash can. He leaned back in the office chair, closed his eyes, and tried to recall what he had heard when playing the recording.

At first, it sounded as if Heather was talking to herself, a jumble of nonsense. He wished he could listen to the tape again. Was she simply crazy? Did she imagine someone was in the cell with her? Was that whom she was talking to, an imaginary friend? Then it came to him. She must have been talking on the phone. Perhaps her words weren't an incoherent jumble. Perhaps he only heard her side of the conversation, not the other person's. This meant someone at the police department had brought her a cellphone last night, against his orders.

It must have been a phone conversation; that would explain what he'd heard. The recorder only turned on when she spoke, and then turned off when she stopped talking and the person on the other end of the call spoke.

She mentioned someone named Eva. Was that whom she had talked to? *Who is Eva?*

TWENTY-SIX

W hile Clay sat down to listen to the tape in his office, before Marie helped him destroy it, Brian was driving Heather home. Brian had Saturday off, and Joe had worked a double shift, getting off work Saturday morning. Joe had been the one who got word charges against Heather had been dropped. He had first called Brian and didn't even consider calling Bowman to come in before someone checked Heather out. Bowman had Saturday off. Joe had left for home minutes before Bowman showed up at the police station on Saturday, avoiding any tantrum Bowman might have thrown regarding Heather's release.

Heather leaned back in the passenger seat in Brian's car, gazing out the side window. "I can't wait to shower."

"I can relate to that feeling."

Heather turned to Brian and smiled. "That's right, they arrested you for murder before I moved to town. She was one of your ex-lovers. Hmm... An ex-lover, now an ex-wife? Should I be afraid?"

Brian let out a snort. "You're a little flippant about all this."

Heather shrugged. "I'll blame Danielle's influence. She deflects to humor when crap like this happens."

"True. And for once Danielle doesn't seem to be in the center of the drama. Although now that I think about it, this is not your first time."

"Must be something in the water in Frederickport."

Brian let out a sigh. "While humor might be a way to deflect, the fact is, a woman has been murdered."

"A woman you spent over twenty-five years with." Heather's tone softened. She looked at Brian. "How are you doing? A woman you once loved has been murdered. Someone you spent a lot of years with. It's okay if you need to grieve."

Brian shrugged, his hands still firmly on the steering wheel. "I'm not sure how I feel."

"While murder is tragic and not funny, from my perspective, death is simply a door to the next leg of our journey."

"I doubt Camilla was ready to go through that door."

"Do you have any idea who might have killed her?" Heather asked.

Brian shook his head. "They always teach us to look at the people closest to the victim. While I haven't been close to Camilla for years, I was married to her. But I didn't do it, and you didn't."

"How can you be so sure about that?"

Brian glanced briefly at Heather and then looked back down the road. He smiled. "For one thing, I doubt you want my ex-wife to come back and haunt you."

Heather grinned. "True."

"While I don't want to consider we might have a psycho out there stabbing random women on the beach, I'd like you to promise not to go jogging unless Marie is with you."

"Yeah, Marie and I sorta talked about that last night. But let's assume it isn't some random killer. Could Camilla's brother or sister be involved? They're the only people in town who have a relationship with your ex."

"If you would have asked me that the other day, I would say no way."

Heather looked at Brian. "What do you say now?"

"I couldn't listen in when Bowman interrogated you. But I was

173

there when he interviewed Ted and Lucy. During Lucy's interview, she claimed you hit Camilla before she slapped you."

"I did no such thing!"

"I know that. I was there, remember?"

Heather frowned. "Why would she say that? Why would she tell such an ugly lie?"

Brian shook his head. "There is only one reason. She wants you arrested for her sister's murder."

"But she doesn't even know me!"

"True. But if she was responsible for Camilla's death and they arrested someone else for the murder, that's her get-out-of-jail-free card."

"That's horrible." Heather slumped back in the seat and looked down the road. "But what can you expect from a killer?"

"Actually, there is also another possibility."

Heather glanced at Brian. "What's that?"

"Maybe she sincerely believes you killed Camilla, and she wants to do all that she can to get you behind bars."

Heather rolled her eyes. "That's almost worse than framing someone else because you don't want to go to prison. What kind of person acts as judge and juror and gives false testimony? Dang, I wouldn't want to deal with that karma when it comes around to bite her."

Brian smiled and continued to steer his car down the road.

"If she lied because she's the killer, what's her motive?" Heather asked.

"The only motive I can come up with is money. Which is a motive for both her and Ted. Ted and Lucy wanted to sell Carter's house, but Camilla planned to move in. Carter's will wouldn't allow them to sell unless they all agree. So that is one motive. And if Camilla dies, it's entirely possible, as her closest relatives, they'll split her share of the estate, not to mention whatever she owns outside of what they inherit from Carter."

"Could they be in on it together?"

Brian shrugged. "It's hard for me to wrap my head around the possibility that either of them killed Camilla, much less the two plotting this together. And Ted didn't lie when Bowman interviewed him. At least, not about you hitting his sister. He said he thought you hit her, but he admitted he didn't see you do it."

"Someone killed your ex, and right now, her siblings look like the most likely suspects."

"We also need to remember, Camilla lived in Frederickport for a long time before she left," Brian reminded her. "I don't know if she stayed in contact with someone in town. Someone who had a grievance with her."

"Someone who wasn't happy that she came back?" Heather asked.

Brian nodded. "Exactly."

Heather cringed. "I have to admit, I hope it is someone who knew her, because I hate to think we have some crazy person going around stabbing strangers."

"You and me both."

"I wonder why Bowman was so determined to pin this on me."

"I've been thinking about that. You said he never properly interrogated you. That gave me an idea on why he might have been so intent on arresting you."

Heather looked at Brian. "And?"

"I think he was hot to solve this case. Not that he really cared about locking up Camilla's killer. But he wanted to look good in his new job. Think about it, he arrests someone within hours of a murder and gets her to confess. Wraps up the case. He probably figured he could get you to confess even if you were innocent."

Heather frowned at Brian. "Why would he think that?"

"I imagine he did a basic but quick background check on you. You don't have family. But you own a home and don't have a mortgage. He probably figured you bought your house with the money you inherited. You're a single woman working for a nonprofit. Joe says he doesn't know Chris is Chris Glandon, nor is he that familiar with the Glandon Foundation. Since nonprofits typically like to portray a flawless reputation, enabling them to bring in future donations, he figured they would likely let you go after your arrest. Then, with you facing legal fees and trying to get bail, you might be convinced to cut your losses, agree to a couple of years instead of burning up the equity in your home to pay for your legal fees."

"That rat," Heather grumbled. "But what surprises me is that he doesn't know more about the Glandon Foundation."

Brian shrugged. "One thing I remember about Bowman from when I worked with him back then, he wasn't a good listener. So even if Lyons told him about the Glandon Foundation moving here, or what it is, it's very possible it went in one ear and out the other."

WHEN BRIAN PULLED into Heather's driveway, they found Walt and Danielle standing by her back gate. Had they arrived moments earlier, they would have seen Walt and Danielle coming through the gate from Heather's yard.

"A welcoming committee?" Heather asked as she stepped out of Brian's car.

Danielle laughed. "Actually, we just came over so Walt could talk to Bella. Brian called us this morning, letting us know they had dropped the charges. We weren't sure when you'd get home, so Walt wanted to come over and tell Bella. She's been worried about you."

Heather grinned. "And people say cats don't care about their owners."

Walt chuckled. "Trust me, Bella does not consider you her owner. You are her human."

Heather's grin widened. "I'll take that."

Walt and Danielle each gave Heather a welcome-home hug, with Danielle's being a side hug because of her advanced baby belly.

"I bet you can't wait to shower," Danielle said after the hug ended.

Heather wrinkled her nose. "Do I stink?"

Brian laughed. "I imagine Danielle said that because, like you and me, she has also been arrested for murder and knows what it feels like spending time in that particular jail cell."

"Gosh, do we need to start a club?" Heather teased.

"Not sure about a club, but this evening, you and Brian need to come over for dinner. It's actually a welcome-home party for you," Danielle explained.

———

FLORA REMEMBERED the old manual typewriter she had seen in Homer Carter's attic. She waited for Ted and Lucy to leave. They told her they were going out to lunch, which meant she had time to do what she needed to do. As soon as they drove away in the rental car, Flora headed to the attic with the typing paper she found collecting dust in Homer's desk. Once in the attic, she pulled the typewriter from its shelf. Instead of bringing the typewriter down-stairs, she set it on a card table and inserted a piece of paper. She held her breath and prayed there was enough ink on the old type-writer's ribbon to create the necessary document. But if it had dried up, she would need to come up with a different plan. To her delight, she discovered there was enough life in the old typewriter ribbon to do what she needed to do.

When Flora finished with the typewriter, she returned it to its shelf in the attic and headed back downstairs. Her next stop was the church.

After arriving at the church, she found Pastor Chad there with some other parishioners, preparing for Sunday's Easter service. She made an excuse about needing to use the church library. They didn't pay her much attention and continued with what they were doing.

Once in the library, she began looking through some of the church records—the records open to the parishioners. They locked some up in cabinets, but she didn't need those. After taking a record book to a table, she started looking through the pages and pages of signatures—signatures of people who attended the church. After flipping through the pages for a few minutes, a name popped out at her.

Flora left the book opened to the desired page and walked to the library door and peeked outside. By the voices drifting in, she felt confident Pastor Chad and the others were still busy. Flora hurried back to the table, pulled out the paper she had typed on Homer's typewriter, and unfolded it. Looking back to the book, she studied the signature she had selected, before copying it onto the document, meticulously forging the signature.

TWENTY-SEVEN

When Clay pulled up into the driveway in front of the garage apartment, his brother-in-law greeted him. Fred walked up to the driver's side of the police car as Clay got out of the vehicle.

"I was hoping we could talk," Fred greeted.

"Sure. What about?" Clay slammed the car door shut.

Fred glanced up to the garage apartment and then back to Clay. "Robyn's up with Debbie and the boys, telling them about the Easter egg hunt."

"What Easter egg hunt?" Clay asked.

"Robyn read about it in the newspaper this morning. She wanted to ask Debbie if you all wanted to go tomorrow morning before we come back here for Easter dinner. From what the article said, there'll be a lot of activities, along with an Easter egg hunt. It would be a way for the boys to meet some kids."

"I imagine the boys would like to find some friends here. But I'm not sure what they'll think of an Easter egg hunt."

"Well, we can let the girls talk to them about it. I was hoping you and I could speak privately. We can go back to my house. I don't want to discuss this around them."

A few minutes later Clay sat at the breakfast bar in the Lyonses' kitchen as Fred poured them each a cup of coffee.

"I wanted to talk about this murder." Fred set a mug of coffee in front of Clay and then sat down next to him with a cup of coffee for himself.

"Certainly. What do you want to ask me?" Clay took a sip of his coffee.

"When I heard you had already arrested someone for the murder, I told myself I had made the right decision bringing you here. But then I found out they had dropped the charges."

"Do you regret hiring me?"

Fred shook his head. "No. No. Not at all. But I am concerned. If the person you arrested isn't the killer, does this mean we have a serial killer out there, and they're just getting started? I need to find out what steps you plan to take to find whoever murdered Camilla Henderson before someone else is killed."

"I'm confident I arrested our killer." Clay set his coffee mug on the breakfast bar. "Unfortunately, the DA isn't convinced we have enough evidence to indict, so it's my job to gather more evidence. Which I intend to do."

"You're convinced Heather Donovan is guilty?" Fred asked. "I'll confess, I'm having a hard time seeing her as a cold-blooded killer."

Clay frowned. "Do you know her?"

"Somewhat. I've met her several times. She's a little odd, I'll grant you that. But I never considered her dangerous. Why do you think she's the one who murdered Camilla Henderson?"

"To begin with, Camilla is the ex-wife of Brian Henderson, who is Donovan's boyfriend."

"I can't even imagine how Henderson is dealing with all this. His ex getting murdered and his girlfriend getting arrested. I don't envy you having to deal with all this since he's one of your officers. But to be honest, I never understood what someone like Henderson saw in a woman like that. I just figured he was going through some mid-life crisis."

"One way I've handled it, I've made it clear to Henderson he is to stay away from this case. If I could, I would keep him away from Donovan, but I don't seem to be able to do that at this point."

"So why are you convinced she's the killer?"

"She was not happy when she learned Brian's ex returned to town. She probably felt threatened, so much so that she attacked Camilla at Homer Carter's funeral."

Fred set his mug on the breakfast bar. "Robyn and I went to the funeral, and someone told us about the two having an issue. We didn't see anything. From what I was told, Camilla accused Heather of hitting her, but no one saw it."

"That's not true. Camilla's sister saw it. And then Donovan lied about it. I did a little digging. Camilla and Brian were married for twenty-five years. I suspect he never got over her leaving him, considering some of the women he got involved with after the divorce. I found out he hooked up with a married woman, who ended up being a murderer. In fact, he even got arrested for her murder."

"Yes. Darlene Gusarov."

"And then he got involved with a widow who killed her husband."

"Beverly Klein." Fred shook his head at the memory.

"And now Donovan. It's like Brian's a magnet for women with homicidal tendencies."

"Perhaps that describes Brian, but I am not sure why that proves Heather murdered Camilla."

"A couple of days before the murder, Camilla stopped in the station and talked to Brian. Brian told me about it when I interviewed him after we found her body. He said she wanted to extend an olive branch. She wanted to be friends. In my opinion, he saw that as a chance to get her back. It's entirely possible he never got over her. After all, he never remarried. Plus, Camilla's sister said Camilla still had feelings for Brian."

"Really?"

Clay nodded. "From what I've learned about Donovan, she's volatile. I suspect Brian might have mentioned something to Donovan about talking with Camilla at the station. Perhaps he even admitted having feelings for his ex. Donovan felt threatened. And then she ran into Camilla the next day, twice. The first time was at Pier Café, and according to what Camilla told her brother and sister after the encounter, Donovan was hostile. And then the second time was a little later that morning, down on the beach. I doubt Donovan expected to see her again during her jog, but when she saw her coming out of the bathroom, I suspect something in her just snapped. Or perhaps they had words. Camilla turned away, and Donovan attacked her."

Fred let out a heavy sigh. "I can see why you suspect her."

"Plus, she lied about seeing Camilla. She told Brian that Camilla had stopped by her house on Friday morning."

"That's the same day you found the body."

Clay nodded. "Exactly. The coroner says Camilla had been murdered hours before we found the body. Hours before Donovan claimed to see her on Beach Drive."

"Why would she say that if she killed Camilla and knew she was already dead?" Fred asked.

"There's few people on the beach right now. Donovan knows that, because according to Morelli, Donovan jogs along the beach every morning. I suspect she just wanted to confuse the autopsy results after the body was found. If you can't accurately determine the time of death, she probably figured it would be harder to convict her."

"Hmm… Interesting. Did you find the murder weapon yet?" Fred picked up his mug and took another sip of coffee.

"No. I suspect she threw it in the ocean. The victim's phone was also missing. But it seems nothing was taken from her wallet. Her credit cards were still there, along with a couple of hundred in cash, which tells me this was personal."

Fred looked at Clay. "From what I understand, the coroner believes she was killed with a knife. Your theory seems to be Heather came across her a second time during her run and snapped. If true, where did she get a knife?"

Clay shrugged. "I assume she carried some sort of switchblade with her, for protection. She routinely runs alone on the beach.

It's not uncommon for a woman to carry some type of protection."

"I wonder what the Glandon Foundation thinks about all this. Even with the charges dropped, that doesn't mean she's innocent." Fred set his mug back on the breakfast bar.

"What do you know about the Glandon Foundation?"

"They moved their headquarters here about five years ago, after buying Stoddard Gusarov's mansion. Eventually, they moved their corporate offices here, but I understand many of their employees work remotely and live all over the globe. They donate a lot locally. You can Google them."

"I did. From what I read, the owner of the company, Chris Glandon, travels all over the world. But according to Donovan's attorney, Chris Glandon was willing to pay Donovan's bail—no matter the cost. I found that odd."

Fred chuckled. "I imagine that was Chris Johnson's doing."

"What do you mean?"

"Chris Johnson runs the show over there. There are some rumors around town that Chris Glandon and Chris Johnson are the same, but I don't believe that. From what I've read about Glandon, he has a lot of issues. He was adopted at an older age. Went from poverty to Richie Rich. After his parents died in a boating accident, his uncles tried to steal his inheritance. In fact, he came to Frederickport one Christmas, stayed at Marlow House, and his uncles tried to kill him."

"Wow."

"I've never met him. But because of everything he's been through, he likes his privacy and is comfortable with Chris Johnson running things here."

"How did Donovan land a job with them? From what I've dug up on her, she doesn't have prior work experience or the education to explain how she got the job as assistant to Chris Johnson."

Fred laughed. "The story someone told me, she ran into Chris Johnson's new car. Not sure if she didn't have the money to pay her insurance's deductible, or if she didn't have adequate insurance, all I know is she needed money to pay for the repairs on Johnson's car and her own. He ended up hiring her, supposedly to help her pay for the repairs. But apparently, she did a fair job, so he kept her on."

"I wonder what Glandon would think if he knew what Heather Donovan is really like," Clay asked.

Fred shrugged. "While Glandon's come to town a few times over the years, I've never met him, but I assume he's met Heather. So what now?"

"I have to find enough evidence to convince the DA to pursue charges against Heather Donovan."

"In the meantime, we have a killer on the loose, which does not make me comfortable."

"Even if the DA hadn't dropped the charges, Donovan would probably be out on bail anyway," Clay reminded him. "Fortunately, I don't think she is a major risk to the community right now."

"I'm assuming you've already checked with the houses along the beach. It's possible a security camera caught something," Fred suggested.

"I'm on it. I have a question for you."

"What's that?"

"Do you know of anyone named Eva who lives in Frederickport?" Clay asked.

Fred frowned. "No. Why?"

Clay shrugged. "Just a lead I'm following up on."

"No. The only Eva I know around here is Eva Thorndike." Fred grinned.

"Who?"

"You don't remember Eva Thorndike? She was that silent screen star whose parents had a vacation home here. Her portrait's at the museum. Certainly, you've seen it. Of course, the museum wasn't open when you used to live here."

Clay shrugged. "I may have heard the name."

"Which reminds me, one of Heather's grandfathers—or great-grandfathers—helped steal the jewels out of the original Missing Thorndike. Surely, you remember the Missing Thorndike?"

Clay shrugged again. "Yeah, I remember now. I also remember

reading how they found it a few years back behind some wall paneling or floorboard at Marlow House."

"Apparently, this ancestor of Heather's was in cahoots with Eva's ex-husband and helped steal the diamonds and emeralds from the necklace. Heather found one of the stolen emeralds in her grandfather's things and gave it back to its rightful owner." Fred paused a moment and then added, "Which could say something about her character."

"It might prove Donovan isn't a thief, but it doesn't prove she's not a murderer."

"Back to this Eva you're looking for regarding this case. How does she fit in?"

"I don't want to say where I heard it, but I was told someone brought Donovan a phone to her cell last night, and she called someone named Eva. I'd like to find out why."

"Have you asked Heather?"

Clay smiled. "I don't want her to know what I know. With me stepping into this position, I must tread carefully. Many, such as Joe Morelli, have loyalty to Brian and might not be candid when it comes to Donovan."

"My experience with Joe, he is straight by the book. And he doesn't let personal feelings interfere with the job."

"Maybe that's true. But someone slipped a cellphone to Donovan, yet according to the logs, no one visited her, which tells me one of the people who was on shift last night intentionally defied my orders. I can't ask her about the phone."

"Because it will expose your inside source?" Fred asked.

Clay nodded. "Exactly. I used to have a lot of respect for MacDonald. But he seems to have changed since losing his wife. I don't believe he's paying attention to what's going on in his department. I hate to say that, but it's the truth."

TWENTY-EIGHT

On Saturday evening, Heather stood in Marlow House's living room, a glass of wine in her hand, as she gazed out the front window, reflecting on how her life had changed since moving to Frederickport a little over four years ago. Yesterday afternoon, after being led out of her office in handcuffs, she'd felt overwhelmed and terrified. But then her friends had come to her rescue, reminding her she was not alone. They believed in her innocence, even before Marie had offered her an alibi.

She and Brian had arrived at Marlow House before the other guests. Walt stood at the bar with Brian, talking. Danielle had left the room a few minutes earlier—Heather assumed to use the bathroom. Danielle seemed to do that a lot these days.

When Chris's car pulled up to the front of the house a moment later, Heather turned from the window, set her glass of wine on the table, and rushed out of the room. Just as Chris opened the front door, Heather threw herself into his arms.

"Whoa!" Chris laughed, accepting Heather's hug. "I'm glad to see you, too." He stood in the still open doorway. Danielle stepped out of the downstairs powder room just as Heather released her hold on Chris.

With tear-filled eyes, Heather looked into Chris's face. "I want to thank you."

Chris frowned. "What did I do?"

Curious, Danielle walked to the pair instead of returning to the living room.

"Mel told that Bowman jerk you were covering my bail. No matter the cost."

Chris grinned. "Hey, I would not let them lock you up until your trial. I felt sorry for those poor inmates who might be locked up with you. Don't they have enough problems? It would be inhumane for them. Torture."

"Oh, you brat!" Heather laughed and gave Chris a playful swat.

Chris wrapped his arm around Heather, pulling her close before kissing the top of her head. "Thankfully, it didn't go as far as bail."

When Chris entered the living room a few minutes later, he had Heather on his right and Danielle on his left, with an arm draped around the shoulder of each woman. Walt and Brian looked up when they saw the three enter the room.

Walt arched his brow and lifted his glass of brandy as if preparing to toast, and Brian asked, "Do you think we need to be jealous?"

Walt shrugged. "Well, he is pretty cute. Can you blame them?"

THE REST of the guests started showing up five minutes later. Lily and Ian arrived with Connor, followed by Olivia, who lived in the house between Marlow House and Heather's. Joe and Kelly showed up next, and to Heather's pleasant surprise, both showed Heather tremendous support, with Kelly making disparaging comments about Clay Bowman. The last to arrive were Mel and Adam.

"How is Eddy doing?" Melony asked Danielle as she and Adam stood at the bar while Walt made them each a cocktail. Melony was the only one in their group to call the chief Eddy, as she had been the best friend of his late wife and had known him before he had moved to Frederickport to take the job as police chief.

"He's doing okay, considering the stress this is putting on him," Danielle said. "He wanted to come tonight, but there was no way. He needs his rest. Last night, he slept in his recliner. He said that's the only way he can get comfortable. I imagine he's going to be sleeping there tonight."

"That poor guy." Melony accepted the cocktail Walt had just handed her.

"Tomorrow, Walt and I are taking Evan to the Easter egg hunt at the beach park. Eddy Junior didn't want to go, said he would rather stay home and take care of his dad."

They talked about MacDonald a few more minutes, but the conversation shifted when Adam said, "Guess who came into my office right before closing yesterday."

"Who?" Danielle asked.

"Camilla's brother, Ted. He wanted to talk to me about listing his uncle's house."

"I understood they weren't selling the house," Danielle said.

"That's only because Camilla wanted to move in. But now, with her gone, they're selling," Adam explained.

Joe, who had just stepped up to the group, overheard the conversation and said, "That's quick. He just found out his sister was killed."

Adam shrugged. "I know they always wanted to sell the house. I ran into Camilla the other day at Lucy's Diner and met her brother. He was trying to convince her to sell the house then. He was insistent on listing it, but she wasn't having it. Apparently, he's now the trustee on the estate, with Camilla gone."

While Joe and Adam discussed the recent change involving Homer Carter's estate, Heather sat on the sofa with Brian, while Chris and Olivia sat on the chairs across from them, chatting. Lily and Ian stood by the window, talking to Kelly while Connor played on the floor nearby.

MINUTES AFTER CAMILLA walked through Heather's door, a voice demanded to know why she was there. Yet it wasn't exactly a voice. Adding to Camilla's confusion, the voice, not-quite-a-voice, seemed to come from a perturbed calico cat sitting on the living room sofa's right arm.

"I have something to tell Heather Donovan." Camilla wasn't sure if she thought the words or said them, but the next thing she heard was something about Heather being at Marlow House.

Camilla turned from the cat and walked back through Heather's door. A few minutes later, she stood in front of Marlow House's living room window. She looked inside and saw a group of people, including her ex-husband and Heather Donovan. Without thought, she stepped inside the house.

Pockets of conversations drifted to Camilla from various parts of the room. Three adults next to her continued talking and ignored her, but a young child playing with toy trucks on the floor nearby looked up at her. Across the room on the sofa sat Brian and Heather, engaged in a discussion with the people sitting across from them. And next to what looked like a makeshift bar stood another group, also talking, their incoherent words drifting her way.

Camilla focused her attention on Heather and shouted, "Heather Donovan!"

Faces turned in Camilla's direction. Brian obviously hadn't heard her, but Heather and the man sitting across from her looked her way, as did several people at the bar, while others kept talking as if she weren't there.

"Heather Donovan," Camilla repeated. "I'm dead. And I know you can see me! I also know you killed me!"

HUNNY AND SADIE had been curled up by the fireplace when Camilla entered through the front wall of Marlow House's living room. But it wasn't until she yelled at Heather that the dogs started barking. They immediately quieted when Walt silently gave them

189

the command to stop. While no longer making noise, the two dogs sat down and stared at Camilla.

The non-mediums in the room looked at the dogs. "What was that all about?" Joe asked.

Kelly, Lily, and Ian, who stood next to Camilla, looked to Hunny and Sadie. "Why are they staring at us like that?" Kelly asked, not knowing the dogs were looking at the nearby ghost.

Ian glanced down at his son playing on the floor. The boy, like the dogs, stared curiously at the space next to them. Unsettled by the behavior of the dogs and his son, Ian promptly walked to the boy and swooped him up in his arms and, in doing so, stepped through Camilla.

"I can't believe you just did that!" Camilla shouted at Ian. While Ian failed to react to her words, Connor peeked over his father's shoulder at the ranting spirit. About to say more, Camilla suddenly froze when two women walked through the same wall she had moved through minutes earlier.

"Marie Nichols?" Camilla gasped.

"Hello, Camilla," Marie greeted. "We stopped by Heather's, and Bella told us you stopped by."

The non-mediums in the room started talking again, some returning to their prior conversations, while others speculated on the dogs' odd behavior. The mediums attempted to behave normally while paying attention to what the spirits were saying.

Marie motioned for Camilla to follow her. "Come, we can talk in the parlor." Marie led Camilla and Eva out of the living room.

TWENTY-NINE

After entering the parlor, Camilla looked at Marie and blurted, "You're dead."

"What do you think you are?" Marie asked.

"Dead, obviously. This is a little overwhelming. I never imagined I'd run into someone I knew who had also died." Camilla turned from Marie to Eva, who had been standing quietly in the background. She studied the spirit for a moment before blurting, "You're Eva Thorndike! Are you Eva Thorndike?"

Eva smiled at Camilla. "Yes, I am."

"I don't believe it!" She looked back to Marie and asked, "Is this what happens when we die? We become invisible and stick around? Except, not invisible to everyone. Heather Donovan can see me. She talked to me after she killed me."

"Heather did not kill you." Marie pointed to the nearby sofa. "Sit down."

"She most certainly did!" Camilla insisted.

"Please sit down," Eva asked.

Reluctantly, Camilla took a seat on the sofa, while Marie sat next to her, and Eva sat across from them on a chair.

"I was with Heather the day you were killed," Marie said. "I was in the women's bathroom at Pier Café when you ran into Heather. For the next few hours, until she went to work, I stayed with Heather. She never saw you again after she left Pier Café."

Camilla stubbornly shook her head. "No. You have to be wrong."

"Why are you so insistent Heather killed you?" Eva asked.

Camilla looked to Eva. "You really are Eva Thorndike, aren't you?"

"Yes, I am."

"I understand your portrait is at the museum. But I haven't been to the museum yet. I read some online articles about you and your portrait," Camilla explained.

"Why don't you answer Eva's question?" Marie asked.

Camilla looked at Marie and frowned. "I remember you were always bossy. I heard someone murdered you. Smothered with a pillow, right?"

"Yes, and they arrested my killer. We'd like to see yours arrested as well. But you are making it difficult by not answering Eva's question."

"I already told you who killed me. And I also want my killer arrested. Actually, she already was, but they let her go. I want her arrested again, and this time sent to prison."

"If that happens, the wrong person would be punished for your murder. Please answer Eva's question. Why do you insist Heather killed you? I understand someone stabbed you in the back. Tell us what you saw."

"You mean when I was murdered?"

Marie nodded.

Camilla shrugged. "Nothing. I stopped to use the public restroom along the beach. After I came back outside, I felt a horrible pain in my back and folded over and fell to the ground. I assumed I'd passed out, and when I woke up, I was outside and no longer hurt. I walked back into the bathroom to look in the mirror to straighten my hair. But when I stepped inside, there was a woman on the floor, blood covering her back."

"It was you," Marie said.

192

Camilla nodded. "I didn't realize that then. I was confused and tried to get help, but everyone ignored me. At least, I assumed they were ignoring me. I didn't realize they couldn't see or hear me. It got dark. Then the sun came up. I ended up in front of Heather Donovan's house. I spoke to her, and unlike the others, she answered me. It felt all wrong. I ran off and eventually ended up back on the beach. And then I ran into Joe Morelli and Clay Bowman walking along the ocean. I tried asking them for help. But like the others, they ignored me. And we ended up back in the public restroom. I followed Clay into the bathroom, and she was still there. But then, I realized who it really was. I had been murdered."

"You still haven't explained why you insist it was Heather," Marie said.

Camilla looked to Marie. "I eventually returned to Uncle Homer's house. My sister and brother were there talking. Ted said Heather had followed me after I left the restaurant and stabbed me after I walked out of the bathroom. My sister didn't understand why they let her go after arresting her."

———

HEATHER WHISPERED to Brian why the dogs had been barking. She excused herself, stood up, and headed for the doorway leading to the entry hall.

Moments later, Heather walked into the parlor and shut the door behind her. She found Camilla and Marie sitting on the sofa with Eva sitting across from her. The three spirits looked up at Heather when she walked into the room.

Camilla stood and pointed to Heather. "You! You killed me!"

"Sit down, Camilla," Marie ordered. "Heather did not kill you. I told you I was with her when someone killed you."

"And why would I kill you?" Heather asked. "So your annoying spirit can barge into my house whenever it wants, and there's nothing I can do about it?"

"You hit me at my uncle's funeral."

"She didn't hit you. I did," Marie confessed.

Camilla looked down at Marie but said nothing. Instead, she marched over to Heather and slapped her across the face. Fortunately for Heather, Camilla's hand moved effortlessly through Heather's face without inflicting pain.

"What was that for?" Heather asked.

"To prove a point." Camilla turned to Marie. "I may be new at this, but I know once you become a… what are we… a ghost?"

Marie shrugged. "A good enough name."

"When we become a ghost, it's impossible to hit someone. I certainly know that, considering the frustration I've experienced since this woman took my life." Camilla flashed Heather a glare. "People not listening to me, and at the time I did not know why. I confess, I started throwing hands, but it never seemed to matter. Nothing. That's why I know you couldn't have hit me. Because, like me, you're a ghost."

Marie let out a sigh. "You have a lot to learn, dear." The sofa Marie sat on rose into the air. Camilla's eyes widened at the sight. The next moment, the sofa lowered back to its original spot on the floor.

"What just happened?" Camilla demanded.

"Some of us spirits—or, as you called us, ghosts—can harness energy. Just as I lifted the sofa, I can move energy so it feels like a slap. I shouldn't have done it. I realize that now. Because Heather did not deserve to be slapped at your uncle's funeral. I know you would not have struck her had I not hit you. For that I apologize."

AFTER HEATHER LEFT the living room, Danielle walked over to the sofa and sat down next to Brian. Brian leaned over to Danielle and whispered, "Camilla was just here?"

Danielle nodded. "So were Eva and Marie. They headed to the parlor. I assume that's where Heather is."

"Did Camilla say who killed her?" Brian asked.

Danielle cringed. "Sort of."

"What did she say?"

"She claimed Heather killed her."

Brian turned toward Danielle. "What?"

With a smile, Danielle reached out and touched Brian's wrist. "It doesn't mean Heather killed her. Remember, someone stabbed Camilla in the back, and it's possible she didn't see who did it."

"But why would she claim Heather killed her?" Brian asked.

Danielle shrugged. "Probably for the same reason Stoddard insisted I murdered him when I didn't. And like I had an alibi back then, so does Heather. Marie was with her during the time Camilla was killed."

"I wasn't suggesting Heather killed Camilla. Never thought that for a moment. I just wondered why Camilla would say something like that. While my ex-wife and I had our differences, the woman I knew when we were married would never falsely accuse someone of murder."

"She would if she sincerely believed Heather had murdered her," Danielle reminded him.

———

CURIOUS TO FIND out what was going on, Brian excused himself and left the living room. When he stepped into the parlor a few minutes later, he found Heather standing by the small desk.

He shut the door behind him and asked, "Are you alone?"

Heather shook her head. "No. Marie and Eva are here with Camilla."

"Where?"

Heather pointed to a spot several feet away. "Camilla's standing right there. Marie's on the sofa, and Eva's on one chair across from the sofa."

"Does Camilla still think you killed her?" Brian asked.

Heather smiled. "Who told you?"

"Danielle. Does Camilla still believe you murdered her?"

Heather looked at Camilla. "Do you, Camilla? Has Marie convinced you, or do you still think I killed you?"

Brian waited for the answer. After a moment, Heather looked at

195

Brian and cringed. "Apparently, she does. Claims no one else would want her dead."

"Tell her—" Brian began, only to be interrupted by Heather, who said, "She just left."

"Oh dear, there is someone else who wanted her dead," Marie said.

Heather looked at Marie. "Who?"

"Her brother." Marie then told Heather what she had overheard the brother say on the phone at Lucy's Diner.

THIRTY

Across town, silence filled what had once been Homer Carter's living room. Ted sat on the worn recliner, a glass of brandy in his right hand. He stared blankly across the room, lost in thought. Lucy lounged on the nearby sofa, her stockinged feet propped on a throw pillow with her shoes abandoned under the sofa. Before sitting down, Ted had poured her a glass of chardonnay.

Lucy cupped her glass between her hands and stared down into what remained of the wine. "I wish I were on that flight."

Ted looked up at his sister. They had planned to fly back this evening so they could be home for Easter. But after their sister's murder, they had cancelled their flights. "The police didn't say we needed to stick around, so I don't know why we can't get out of here as soon as we have the house listed. I need to talk to the attorney on Monday and find out what we need to do, if we need to do anything, now that Cam's dead."

"Do you think he'll know if she has a will?" Lucy asked.

"I have no idea. But I doubt she does. Back when Uncle Homer set up the trust, I said something to Cam about how I was glad he'd created a trust, and that I intended to do the same for my family.

She said she didn't want to spend money making a will, since she didn't have kids."

"Uncle Homer didn't have kids," Lucy reminded him.

"Cam once said the only reason Homer set up the revokable trust was to make sure someone took care of him when he got too old to take care of himself." Ted took a sip of his brandy.

Lucy absently ran a fingertip along the edge of the wineglass and looked up at her brother. "Who did Cam think would take care of her when she got old?"

"It doesn't really matter now, does it?"

"If she doesn't have a will, then who inherits her estate?"

"Us." Ted lifted his glass in mock salute and took another sip of brandy.

"Are you sure?" Lucy asked.

"In the state of Oregon, when you die without a will, your estate goes to your next of kin. You and I are her next of kin."

"When settling her estate, does it go by Oregon law, where she died, or where she lived?"

"From Cam's perspective, she had moved back to Oregon," Ted reminded her.

"But is she legally considered a resident of Oregon? There is no way she got an Oregon driver's license already. I don't know when she would have done it."

"I doubt it matters. I'm pretty sure the state she lived in has similar inheritance laws to Oregon, but I'll ask Homer's attorney when we see him next week."

Lucy glanced toward Flora's bedroom. The caretaker had been in her room for most of the evening. "What are we going to do about her?"

"I told her she could stay until the house sells, providing she cooperates with the Realtor and keeps the place neat."

"What did she say?" Lucy asked.

"She didn't really say anything. But I'm going to talk to the lawyer about that too. We need to make sure there's not a problem getting her out before the house closes escrow. And we don't need her sabotaging the sale."

Lucy let out a deep sigh, finished the last of her wine, and set the glass on the nearby coffee table. She looked at her brother. "Are we doing the right thing by not having a funeral?"

"What's the point? Who would go? She hadn't lived here for ten years. Seems a needless waste of money."

Lucy leaned back on the sofa, stretched out her legs, and crossed her ankles. "I imagine Cam would agree with you. About the money thing, at least."

"Excuse me." Flora's voice intruded on the conversation. Both Ted and Lucy looked at Flora. They hadn't heard her enter the room.

"Did you need something?" Ted asked.

"Umm… we need to talk. I have been putting this off," Flora explained.

Lucy sat up on the sofa, putting her feet on the floor. "What about?"

Flora walked over to the empty rocking chair and sat down. It was then Ted and Lucy noticed the folded sheets of paper in Flora's hand. "We've already discussed the promises Camilla made when she hired me to care for your uncle."

"Yes. And Cam said it was a misunderstanding, and you admitted she put nothing in writing," Ted reminded her.

Flora smiled at Ted. "That's true. Sort of."

"Sort of?" Lucy frowned.

"I made an appointment with an attorney for next week. Camilla had given me something. You might consider it collateral on her promise. I didn't remind Camilla of this because I wasn't sure it would help me."

"What did she give you?" Lucy asked.

Flora stood up. "I made two copies. One for each of you. I have the original someplace safe. I'll be taking that to the attorney next week." Flora walked to Lucy, handed her a copy of the document, and then walked over to Ted and handed him the same.

Picking up his reading glasses from the end table, Ted slipped on his glasses when Lucy, who stared at the paper Flora had handed her, blurted, "Is this a will?"

Flora sat back down on the rocking chair. "Yes."

Ted looked at the document Flora had handed him. "*I, Camilla Henderson, leave my share of Homer Carter's estate to Flora Bennett.*"

Both Ted and Lucy looked at Flora. "Camilla wouldn't do this," Lucy said.

"Your sister didn't plan on dying," Flora said. "When she asked me to trust her to do the right thing when your uncle died, because she said she couldn't write a contract giving away part of his estate until after he was gone, I told her while I might trust her, I didn't know either of you. And if something was to happen to her, like dying in a car accident, then I'd be screwed. So she wrote that up and said if something happened to her, this would protect me. It even has a witness signature."

Ted read the name of the witness out loud, "*Agatha Pine.*" He frowned at Flora. "Was this a friend of my sister's?"

Flora shook her head. "No. She was just someone from your uncle's church. Agatha wasn't a friend of mine, nor of your sister's. Since your sister didn't want to take the time to notarize the document, I wanted to have an impartial witness sign it."

"And Agatha will verify this?" Ted asked.

"I'm sure she would if she were still alive. Unfortunately, Agatha died about four years ago. But you can verify the signature."

THE SUN HAD SET hours earlier. Camilla sat in a cherry tree across the street from Marlow House. She hadn't climbed a tree since she was twelve. Nor had she climbed one tonight. She had basically floated up onto the tree's branch, an interesting trick that she wasn't sure how she had accomplished. From this location, she could see into Marlow House's living room window. Lights were on inside.

She found the guest list interesting. Never would she have imagined Brian running in the same social circles as Adam Nichols. Of course, she couldn't imagine Brian—*her Brian*—dating someone who not only looked young enough to be his daughter, but looked like someone he would be more likely to arrest as opposed to date.

Camilla wondered if Eva and Marie were still inside Marlow House. She thought about what Marie had said, about being with Heather until she went to work at eleven. If true, Heather could not be her killer. If not Heather, then who?

People in Marlow House's living room started moving around. Camilla considered going closer to see what was going on, but she didn't want to be seen. Marie and Eva had told her something interesting that evening before Heather barged into the parlor. Apparently, several mediums lived on Beach Drive. Heather, it seemed, was a medium, which was why she could see Camilla the morning after her murder. But Heather was not the only one. Marie told her Walt and Danielle Marlow, along with Chris Johnson, who worked with Heather, were also mediums.

The front door to Marlow House opened, and Camilla watched as the people began to leave. Apparently, the party was over. The party, in Camilla's opinion, was in poor taste. Marie had called it a celebration of Heather's release from jail. Even if Heather hadn't been responsible for her death, having any sort of celebration because of something that only happened because of her murder didn't seem right.

The last couple to leave the party were Brian and Heather. She watched as Brian draped an arm around Heather's shoulders as the two walked down the street toward Heather's house. Camilla frowned at the sight. None of it made sense. What did her Brian see in that woman?

ACROSS TOWN, over at Uncle Homer's house, after Flora had dropped her bombshell, she returned to her bedroom and shut her door. Ted and Lucy decided to go somewhere and talk. They each changed their clothes and, less than an hour later, sat in a quiet booth in the bar section of Pearl Cove.

"I can't believe Camilla left that woman her portion of Uncle Homer's estate," Lucy said before tasting her wine.

"I can. And remember what Flora said, Cam didn't expect to die," Ted reminded her.

About to take another sip of her drink, Lucy paused and looked across the table to Ted. "What does that have to do with anything?"

"I can see Cam giving her something like that to convince Flora she'd take care of her after Uncle Homer died, while knowing full well all she had to do was write a new will. And one thing about Flora's will, there is nothing in the document suggesting the will is a show of good faith should Cam die before Homer. Nothing. I doubt Flora could use that as evidence to prove Cam made a verbal promise. All Cam had to say was that she wasn't sure whom she wanted to leave her share of Uncle Homer's estate to, so she left it to Flora and then changed her mind. People change their minds about wills all the time. Nothing wrong with that."

Lucy sat in the booth, her hands on the tabletop, wrapped around her beverage glass. "Do you think Cam made a new will? I sure hope so. When I heard Uncle Homer had died, I assumed his estate would be so easy to settle, and now this. I can't afford to contest Flora's will, and I could really use half of Cam's share. And I don't want to share it with someone we don't even know."

Ted reached across the table and patted Lucy's hands. "Don't worry, little sister. Flora won't be getting any of Uncle Homer's estate."

Lucy frowned. "Why? Do you think Cam wrote another will?"

Ted shrugged. "Even if she did, that doesn't mean she left her estate to us. Actually, it might be better if Flora's will is the only one out there. Remember, when you murder someone, you can't benefit from their death."

"What are you suggesting?"

"I need to think about this. Tomorrow is Easter. But on Monday, it might be a good idea to take this little document to the police. We could be handing them a much better motive for murder than what Heather Donovan had for killing our sister. And we both know Donovan never touched Cam."

THIRTY-ONE

P astor Chad's church sponsored the Easter egg hunt at the beach park, beginning with a sunrise service. Not everyone who attended the Easter egg hunt came early to listen to Pastor Chad. Some attended Easter services at their own church, or others, like Walt and Danielle, slept in that morning. Before going to the park, Walt and Danielle drove over to Chief MacDonald's house to pick up Evan.

Evan sat in the back seat of the car while Walt drove them from Evan's house to the park. On the way there, Evan said, "Dad was talking to Aunt Sissy about Heather being arrested."

Danielle glanced to the back seat and Evan, and asked, "Does your dad know you overheard?"

Evan shook his head. "No. I was hiding behind the sofa."

Walt chuckled while Danielle asked, "Evan, do you think it's nice to eavesdrop on your father?"

"It's the only way I learn stuff. Aunt Sissy thinks Heather killed the lady, but Dad told her she didn't and they let her go. But I don't think Aunt Sissy likes Heather."

Walt glanced briefly at the rearview mirror. "Your dad's right.

Heather's innocent. Marie was with her all morning when the murder happened. Plus, I can't imagine Heather killing anyone."

"No way. The person would just come back as a ghost and haunt her!" Evan said.

LILY AND IAN arrived at the park before Walt and Danielle. They brought Connor, along with Ian's sister, Kelly, as Kelly's husband, Joe, had to work. The sunrise service had long since ended, and people gathered around picnic tables covered with brightly colored Easter-themed vinyl tablecloths. Arranged neatly on the tables were stacks of napkins, cups, paper plates, trays of donuts and pastries, along with coffee, tea, and single-serve cartons of milk and juice.

Lily took a carton of milk and a donut to share with Connor, while Ian and Kelly each poured themselves a cup of coffee. They stood about ten feet from the tables, so as not to block the area from other people wanting access to the food and beverages. Lily had shoved the unopened carton of milk in the purse hanging from her shoulder and was about to tear the donut in half when a voice said, "Ian Bartley, I'd like to introduce you and your wife to my sister-in-law and her husband."

Lily looked up to see Fred Lyons now shaking hands with Ian. While she hadn't met him yet, Lily recognized the stocky man standing next to Fred as the infamous Clay Bowman. She flashed Fred a smile, tore the donut in half, and handed one piece to her son.

She listened as introductions continued. Fred's small group included his wife, Robyn, whom Lily had met before, along with Clay and his wife, whom she hadn't. Fred motioned toward the table of food, saying something about his nephews. Lily glanced at the tables and spied the two boys she had seen at Beach Taco. They didn't seem to behave much better than they had at the restaurant. The twins indiscriminately handled the donuts, making her grateful she had snagged one before their germy little hands had gotten to them.

"Ian is the one I told you about. He writes under the pen name Jon Altar," Fred explained.

"Jon Altar?" Bowman sounded impressed. He enthusiastically shook Ian's hand. "I'm a fan."

With sticky donut frosting covering her fingers, and fussing with Connor, Lily was spared shaking hands, but gave a smile and nod when they introduced her to the new police chief and his wife.

"This is my sister, Kelly," Ian introduced.

"Oh, yes." Fred turned to Clay and said, "Her husband is one of your men."

"One of his men?" Lily snickered before licking off the frosting from her fingers. Both Fred and Clay looked at Lily. By their expressions, they didn't understand her comment.

Lily removed the carton of milk from her purse, opened it, handed it to Connor, and then noticed the two men still staring at her, as if waiting for an explanation. Unfazed, she looked at them and smiled. "It just struck me as funny. *His men*. Sounds so… possessive. Like he owns Joe or something." Lily's gaze met Clay's. He didn't look amused.

"I just meant, Joe's a police officer, and now that Clay is the police chief…" Fred muttered awkwardly.

"Joe? Would that be Joe Morelli?" Clay asked. His tone was as unfriendly as his expression.

"He's the only Joe in the department," Lily answered. "But I guess you're still getting to know everyone." Lily smiled sweetly. "Oh, I heard the chief is doing great, by the way. Surgery went well; he's already up and around. He's probably going to be back to work before you know it."

"I had knee replacement surgery two years ago." Fred gave one of his knees a pat. "It can take from six months to a year for a full recovery. Chief MacDonald has weeks of physical therapy ahead of him."

Lily looked at Clay and asked, "Any new leads on the murderer we have on the loose?"

"They arrested the killer, but the DA released her!" Debbie blurted.

As Clay hushed his wife, Lily looked at Debbie and shook her head. "No, they released Heather Donovan, who isn't the killer. Heather is the last person to kill anyone."

"Do you know her?" Debbie asked.

"Yes. She's a good friend and a neighbor. She watches our son all the time," Lily said.

Clay looked at Lily. "You might reconsider allowing that woman to watch your child. We're gathering evidence now. She's still the prime suspect."

"If that's true, then you're wasting your time, which doesn't make me feel very good, since that means you aren't looking for the actual killer." Lily's voice grew louder.

Ian draped an arm around his wife's shoulder and looked at Clay and said, "I have to agree with my wife."

"It's probably best we not discuss an open case," Fred blurted.

After Fred and his companions walked away a few moments later, Ian turned to his wife and said under his breath, only loud enough for Kelly to hear, "You were such a bitch."

"Yeah, I was." Lily grinned.

Ian laughed and hugged his wife.

"I kinda loved that," Kelly confessed after Ian released Lily from the hug. "That jerk has been making Joe's life miserable since he got here."

Lily looked at her sister-in-law and smiled. "Yes, I know. Family and friends need to stick together." Lily linked an arm with Kelly's, and Ian picked up Connor.

"There's Dani!" With one arm still linked with Kelly's, Lily pointed toward the parking lot, where the Ford Flex had just pulled in.

WHILE WALT and Danielle chatted with Lily, Ian, and Kelly, Evan ran off to snag himself a donut. When he got to the tables, he saw two boys, obviously twins, each eating a donut while poking the other donuts on the tray and then laughing when sprinkles fell off.

Evan frowned at the boys. "Hey, don't touch them all. That's gross."

The boys turned to Evan. While a year younger than Evan, they looked closer to his age because of their size.

"You can't tell us what to do," one boy said.

"Yeah. Our dad is the police chief. We can get you arrested for bothering us!" the other boy said.

"Your dad is not Police Chief MacDonald," Evan said.

Both boys laughed. The boy who had bragged about his father being chief said, "No, you're stupid. That was the old police chief. Our dad is the new one."

"Chief MacDonald is still the police chief," Evan argued. "He's just not working right now because he had an operation on his leg."

"No," the braggart argued. "He's not coming back. Our dad is the new chief, and if you don't leave us alone, we're going to get you in trouble! Just see if we don't." The boy shoved Evan, making him fall to the ground. The twins ran off laughing.

While no living adult noticed the encounter, Marie, who had just arrived, witnessed the exchange.

"Who were those little hooligans?" Marie asked as Evan got to his feet and dusted off his pants.

"The guy who's replacing Dad, I guess those are his kids," Evan grumbled.

Marie looked over to the nearby playground equipment where the two boys had run off to. Evan, who now held a chocolate donut, stood by Marie's side as they watched the twins push other children from the playground equipment so they could climb up the hanging bars.

A few moments later, the twins held onto the overhead bars. They dangled from the equipment, their shoes not touching the ground as they kicked their feet to keep the other kids away. Those who had been pushed aside glared at the two boys.

"Watch this," Marie told Evan, who silently ate his donut.

The next moment, the twins' pants unbuttoned, unzipped, and slid down to their ankles, exposing their not-so-white tighty-whities. Horrified at hanging in their underwear, the twins let go of the overhead bars, fell to the sand, and quickly hiked up their pants as they got to their feet. They scrambled off, still zipping up their pants, while the children around them laughed and pointed in their direction.

Marie watched as the twins ran toward their parents. By the parents' expressions, Marie guessed they had witnessed what had just happened on the climbing bars. Curious to hear what the parents might say, Marie told Evan she would be right back.

THE MOMENT the twins reached their parents, their mother grabbed them each by a wrist and began dragging them toward the restrooms.

"Mom!" they both cried, each digging their shoes into the ground to slow her down.

Furious, Debbie twirled around and faced her sons, still clutching their wrists. "You do not know how angry I am at you two!"

Confused, Zack asked, "Why are you mad at us? What did we do?"

"Dropping your pants like that, for everyone to see! What were you thinking? You weren't thinking! Your father has an important job in this town, and your actions reflect on him!"

"But Mom, it wasn't our fault!" Eric insisted.

"It wasn't your fault? Are you saying your pants just happened to fall down? At the same time?"

Both boys nodded.

MARIE RETURNED TO EVAN, who now stood with Walt, Danielle, and Ian. Lily and Kelly had taken Connor to see the Easter Bunny, who was actually Pastor Chad's nephew dressed up in a bunny costume. While Connor was off meeting the Easter Bunny,

Evan was telling Walt, Danielle, and Ian about his encounter with the Bowman twins and what Marie had done.

"Picking on little boys," Danielle playfully chided Marie when she appeared.

"I admit, I feel a little guilty. Their mother saw what happened on the climbing bars, and she thought they did it on purpose, and now they have to sit on a bench for twenty minutes before they can get up. But I suppose it's karma for pushing Evan down."

EVAN LEFT to go to the restroom. When he stepped out of the bathroom ten minutes later, he glanced toward the twins' mother. She kept looking over to see if her boys remained sitting on the bench, but the others in her small group didn't seem to be paying attention and chatted amongst themselves.

Evan walked over to the bench, stopping about six feet from it, and stared at the twins.

Zack glared at Evan. "What are you looking at?"

"You have to sit there for twenty minutes," Evan said.

"How do you know that?" Eric asked.

Evan shrugged. "I just do."

"He doesn't know nothing," Zack snapped.

"It's karma," Evan said.

"What's karma?" Zack asked.

"If you hadn't pushed me, your pants wouldn't have fallen down. And if your pants wouldn't have fallen down, you wouldn't have to sit here. That's karma." Evan smiled and walked away.

THIRTY-TWO

Camilla had been wandering up and down the beaches of Frederickport since leaving Marlow House, seeking answers regarding her premature demise. She considered what Marie had said regarding Heather's innocence. While Camilla hadn't known Marie well when they had both been alive, she didn't imagine Marie was the type who would lie for a killer.

But if Heather wasn't the killer, there was only one other possibility. Frederickport had a cold-blooded murderer on the loose—someone who targeted women alone on the beach. That had to be the answer, because Camilla couldn't imagine anyone she knew personally would actually want her dead. If not Heather, then it had to be a total stranger. It was one reason she moved up and down the beach. Perhaps her killer was still out there, preparing to attack another innocent victim.

When Camilla reached the beach park, there was a crowd gathered. They hadn't been there the last time she had passed by. Moving closer, she spied the giant Easter Bunny, or more accurately, someone dressed up in an Easter Bunny costume.

Moving closer, Camilla noticed everyone seemed to be smiling—talking—having a good time. *The world moves on without me,* Camilla thought. It was then she recognized a familiar face—Debbie Bowman. She had only met Debbie a few times back when she was still married to Brian.

The first time she had met Debbie, she wondered how a virile man like Clay Bowman had ever married such a timid and plain woman. Camilla stood along the breakers and watched as the woman standing with Debbie grabbed her wrist and pulled her away from their group, as if she had a secret to share. Curious, Camilla moved closer. While it did not thrill her to find herself dead, Camilla found some aspects of being a ghost interesting, such as the ability to eavesdrop on conversations. She intended to eavesdrop on Debbie, but then she changed her mind when someone else showed up by Debbie's side—Marie Nichols.

"HOW ARE YOU HOLDING UP?" Robyn asked her sister. The two women stood together out of earshot of their husbands—but not from Marie's ghost.

"I just wish the DA hadn't released that Heather person. Clay was convinced she'd plead guilty for a lighter sentence. Even if her attorney got her off, she'd end up losing her home to pay for legal fees, not to mention bail. Clay said she might only get a couple of years if she confessed, because it obviously wasn't premeditated."

"It's a shame Camilla came back," Robyn said. "She should have had the decency to stay away."

Debbie shrugged. "I can understand her coming back for her uncle's funeral. But for her to move back at the same time we do. No. That wasn't going to happen."

"When I heard she was dead, I thought that would take care of things," Robyn said.

"While I'm glad she's dead, I regret..." Debbie looked out to the ocean and didn't finish the sentence.

Robyn placed a hand on her sister's shoulder. "I understand. A car accident would have been better. Anything but an obvious murder."

"People might ask too many questions. I don't need that humiliation. My boys don't deserve that."

———

WHILE MARIE LISTENED in to Debbie and Robyn's conversation, Camilla drifted to Clay and Fred, who chatted with two other men. Just as Camilla reached them, the two men they had been talking with moved on, leaving Clay alone with his brother-in-law.

After the men's departure, Clay noticed Lily Bartley standing some distance away with a small group of people, including Danielle Marlow.

"I see Ian Bartley's wife is also chummy with the Marlow woman." Clay gave a nod toward Lily and Danielle.

Fred glanced toward the two women and then looked back at Clay. "I thought I told you they're best friends. They live across the street from each other. Danielle and Lily were friends before they moved to Oregon."

"I knew they lived across the street from each other, but I didn't realize they were close friends. Hell, I lived for four years at our last place, and I never met our neighbors," Clay said with a snort.

"Are you really that convinced Heather killed Camilla Henderson? She has a lot of friends in this town."

Clay turned to Fred. "I wouldn't be doing my job if I walked away from a suspect because that person is popular. A good, innocent woman was murdered. I will not allow the killer to go free. Camilla deserves someone to stand up for her. To make her killer accountable. It won't bring her back, but it is the very least I can do. And I believe Heather Donovan killed Camilla during a fit of jealousy."

"Did she really have a reason to be jealous?"

"Let's be honest, if you were Brian Henderson, who would you rather be with, someone who looked like Camilla Henderson or a skanky version of Elvira? From what her brother and sister said, it seems Camilla wanted to get back with Brian, and even Brian admitted Camilla came to the station to see him. He described it as extending an olive branch. But I think it was more. And I think he mentioned it to Donovan. And when she ran into Camilla not just once, but twice the next day, I think Donovan snapped."

Camilla, who had been listening to Clay, reached out her hand to touch him, but it moved through his arm, with him never noticing her presence. She quickly pulled back her hand and let out a sigh.

"Thank you for saying that. It means a lot to me," Camilla said to deaf ears. "While you're wrong about Heather's guilt, as I was, a part of me appreciates all that you just said. Thank you for that, Clay."

"WHAT ARE YOU DOING HERE?" Marie asked Camilla when she suddenly appeared by her side. Startled, Camilla turned from Fred and Clay to Marie. "Eavesdropping?"

"I saw you eavesdropping too," Camilla said.

Fred, who noticed someone else he wanted to introduce Clay to, pulled his brother-in-law away, leaving Marie and Camilla standing alone.

"It is one perk of being a ghost. I'm curious, how long do you plan to stick around?" Marie asked.

"Why? Obviously, there's no rush; you're still here. Not to mention Eva. She died, what, like, a hundred years ago or something?"

"So you do plan to stick around? Do a little haunting?" Marie asked.

Camilla shrugged. "No. But I can't go just yet."

"You want to find out who killed you?"

Camilla nodded. "Yes."

Marie pointed toward Robyn and Debbie, who now walked toward their husbands. "What's the deal between you and Debbie Bowman?"

"Me and Debbie Bowman? I barely know the woman. Sure, I

obviously met her back when I was married to Brian. I knew who she was. But we weren't friends."

"She seems to have strong feelings about you."

Camilla frowned and looked to Debbie, who now stood some distance away, by Clay's side. "Why? Did she say something?"

"She didn't seem the least upset about your passing. In fact, her exact words, *I'm glad she's dead.*"

Camilla looked from Debbie to Marie. Silently she stared at Marie for a moment, who looked as if she expected an explanation for what she had overheard Debbie say. Instead of giving an explanation, Camilla vanished.

WITH A COLORFUL, small bucket in hand, Evan helped Connor hunt for Easter eggs while Walt and Danielle sat with Connor's parents at a nearby picnic table. Kelly was off taking photographs of the event to use on her blog.

As the four adults chatted while keeping an eye on the two boys, Marie appeared at the table and shared with Walt and Danielle what she had overheard Debbie and Robyn discuss regarding the murder, along with Camilla's reaction.

After repeating Marie's words to Ian and Lily, Danielle said, "When my time comes, it would really make me feel bad if I overheard someone say they were glad I was dead. That sucks. I wonder why Debbie disliked Camilla so much."

"According to Camilla, she and Debbie barely knew each other," Marie said.

After Danielle repeated Marie's words, Lily said, "Who knows what happened back then when Camilla was married to Brian? Camilla and Debbie were both married to cops at the same station. They obviously had some interaction. It might not have been a big deal to Camilla; she might have even forgotten about it. But it's something that really bothered Debbie, so much so that she's glad the woman is dead."

Danielle turned to Marie. "Didn't you say Camilla was a flirt?"

214

"Yes. She was quite a flirt back then." Marie nodded.

"Are you suggesting Camilla used to flirt with Clay when she was married to Brian?" Lily asked Danielle, hearing only her comments on flirting, not Marie's response.

Danielle shrugged. "Marie said she was a big flirt. Some women really don't appreciate another woman giving their husband that type of attention. And if it was something Camilla did with other men, she probably doesn't remember flirting with Clay, or thinking it was a big deal. And like I said, some women get pissed when another woman flirts with their man."

"Yeah, but enough to want them dead?" Lily asked. "I remember Heather was a little flirty with Ian when she first moved here."

"She had a crush on him," Walt reminded her.

"But I never wanted her dead," Lily said.

"You knew she wasn't a threat," Ian reminded her.

"I didn't want Danielle's cousin Cheryl dead either, and she more than flirted," Lily remembered.

Ian reached over and patted his wife's hand. "Again, still not a threat."

Lily shook her head. "Still, even if a woman came on to you— one that I considered to be a threat—I wouldn't want her dead. That's kind of a me problem. If our relationship can't survive another woman coming on to you, is there a relationship?"

THIRTY-THREE

On Monday morning, Ted took his copy of the will Flora had given him to the Frederickport Police Station. Initially, he intended to give it to Chief Bowman, as he was the one who had interviewed him after discovering Camilla's body. According to Bowman, he would personally handle his sister's case. But when he arrived at the station, Colleen told him they did not expect Bowman in for another hour.

"By any chance is Brian Henderson here?" Ted asked.

"Yes. Would you like to see him?" Colleen asked.

Ten minutes later, Ted sat with his ex-brother-in-law in the interrogation room, looking over the will.

"If there was ever a motive for murder, there you have it," Ted said as he sat across the table from Brian, who read over the document.

Brian looked up to Ted. "You no longer think Heather killed Camilla?"

Ted shifted in his chair. "She's your girlfriend. Drove Cam crazy when she saw who you were dating. After my sister's murder, I couldn't imagine who would want Cam dead. Chief Bowman was convinced Heather Donovan killed her. And as far as motives, she

216

was the only one who had one aside from now." Ted pointed to the document in Brian's hand.

Brian tossed the will on the table and folded his hands atop it. "That's not true. You and Lucy had just as much of a motive as Flora. Until Flora gave you this, I'm assuming you figured you would inherit her estate."

"I wouldn't kill Cam for money. You know me better than that."

"Someone overheard you talking on the phone. You said, and I quote, '*I could kill my sister.*'"

Ted stared at Brian. "Who told you that?"

"I can't say. But you were at Lucy's Diner, having lunch with your sisters. Adam Nichols had joined you. After they all left, you got a phone call, and you reportedly said that to whomever you were talking to." Brian couldn't say who told him because the information came from Marie.

Ted closed his eyes and took a deep breath. He opened his eyes. "Yeah. I remember that now. I said that. But I didn't mean it. I was talking to my wife. Pissed that Cam refused to sell the house. But I didn't mean it. Anyway. Lucy and I were together after Cam left us at Pier Café that morning. We even stopped at the store; people saw us there. We have an alibi."

"Did you ever tell that to Bowman?" Brian asked. "Where you were when Camilla was killed?"

Ted shrugged. "No. He never asked us for an alibi. I assume because he figured Donovan was the killer."

Brian pointed to the will. "Can I make a copy of that?"

Ted nodded. "Sure."

Brian took out his cellphone and took a picture of the will. After taking the photo, he shoved the document toward Ted. "Why would Lucy lie about Heather slapping Cam at the funeral?"

Ted stared at Brian, reluctant to answer the question.

"Bowman asked you about it. Lucy claimed to have seen Heather hit Camilla. I was right there when Camilla slapped Heather. Heather never touched Camilla. It didn't happen. Lucy lied. Why?"

Ted moved uneasily in the chair. "You should ask Lucy. I just came in here to give you that. It's a motive for murder. You should be happy; it helps your girlfriend."

The door to the interrogation room opened, and Chief Bowman walked in. "What is going on in here?"

When Brian tried to explain why he was talking to Ted, Bowman interrupted by saying, "I told you to stay out of this case. You're too close to both the victim and the prime suspect. I want you to leave now, and if you interfere with this case again, you will be suspended indefinitely. Do you understand?"

After Brian left the room, Ted immediately apologized for getting Brian in trouble, insisting it was his fault. He then handed the will to Bowman while giving him a quick rundown on how it came about.

Still standing and holding the document in one hand, Bowman glanced over the will, gave a shrug, and then tossed the document back to Ted. "I'm not sure what you want me to do with that. If you want to contest the will, talk to an attorney."

"No… that's not what this is about. This is a motive for murder. Flora may have murdered my sister."

Bowman gave a snort. "If this is a motive for murder, then I should be arresting you and your sister, because as far as I know, you assumed you and your sister inherited her estate. Go home. Let the police do our jobs. Stop trying to play detective."

After Ted left the station, Bowman tracked down Brian and handed him a large box of files he had been going through to familiarize himself with the cases over the last five years.

"I need you to file these," Bowman told him.

Confused, Brian looked down at the box now in his hands. "You want me to file?"

"I figure it will keep you busy and out of trouble. You obviously have too much time on your hands."

DANIELLE, with Marie's help, made several batches of chocolate chip cookies on Monday morning. Instead of freezing all the cookies, Danielle decided to take a plate over to Heather's and check on her. Chris had encouraged Heather to take a few days off, considering recent events. Marie insisted she accompany Danielle to Heather's, knowing a killer was on the loose.

"Marie must really like you," Heather said as she sat in her living room, munching on a cookie. Danielle and Marie sat across from her on the sofa.

"Of course I like Danielle," Marie scoffed.

Danielle laughed. "You mean because she helped me bake cookies?"

Heather nodded. "She always told me she didn't like to bake."

Marie shrugged. "It wasn't so bad."

"You're all here," a voice blurted from the entry. The three looked toward the front door and saw Camilla standing just inside the doorway. They all understood she had walked through the door.

"What are you doing here?" Heather asked. "Why haven't you moved on by now?"

Camilla stepped into the room. "I can't move on until I find out who killed me."

"It wasn't me," Heather said.

Camilla nodded. "Yes. I realize that now."

"So why are you here?" Heather asked. "I certainly can't help you find your killer. I wish I could. It would solve some of my problems."

"I'm here because I'm curious. I need to understand the thing between you and Brian. You aren't his type."

Their conversation stopped the next moment when Brian came walking into the room from the kitchen. He had obviously parked in the back and entered through the kitchen door.

After entering the living room, Brian looked at the sofa and paused. "Oh, Danielle's here."

"Hey, Brian," Danielle greeted.

"Are you playing hooky?" Heather asked.

Brian's gaze shifted from Danielle to the plate of cookies on the coffee table.

"Whose cookies?" Brian asked.

"Danielle brought them. I guess they're mine now." Heather grinned.

Brian walked straight to the coffee table and grabbed a cookie from the plate. "Can I have one?" Brian took a bite of the cookie before waiting for an answer and then said, "I need to vent."

"You left work to vent? This must be serious," Heather said. "But I need to warn you, Marie's here, and she's with someone."

Brian glanced around the room. "Eva?"

Heather shook her head. "Camilla."

Brian looked around the room again. "Where?"

Heather pointed to where Camilla stood.

"I can't comprehend how he accepts all this," Camilla muttered, still staring at Brian.

Brian looked toward the front door. "Camilla, I'm sorry you were killed. Really. I want to help find your killer. But tell me, why in the world would you leave your share of Carter's estate to Flora? You only met the woman once in your life."

"What are you talking about?" Camilla said.

"She doesn't know what you're talking about," Heather told Brian.

"Flora gave Ted and Lucy a will she says you wrote. Leaves your share of Carter's estate to her," Brian explained.

"It's obviously a forgery. I never wrote a will leaving anything to Flora!"

Heather repeated Camilla's words for Brian.

"Really?" Brian popped the last of the cookie in his mouth and started to sit on the sofa when Danielle stopped him, telling him to sit on the other side, because Marie sat there. Without missing a beat, Brian moved to the other end of the sofa and said while sitting down, "I found the witness an interesting choice. Agatha Pine."

"Agatha Pine? She's dead," Danielle said.

"Yes. But she was alive when the will was supposedly written," Brian said.

"As I said, I never wrote a will leaving anything to Flora. If I had written a will, I can't imagine a scenario where I'd ask Agatha Pine to witness a document for me." Camilla shook her head at the thought.

"Did you know Agatha?" Danielle asked.

Camilla looked at Danielle. "Yes. I used to attend Christmas service with Uncle Homer. Agatha went to his church, and he introduced us. I only remember her because it always fascinated me how her daughter and grandchildren treated her with such reverence."

Brian, who hadn't heard Camilla's views on Agatha Pine, said, "If it's a forgery, that puts a new spin on this, especially since Bowman doesn't seem to think the will is a motive for murder." He then went on to tell them Bowman's reaction to finding Brian talking to Ted about the case.

"He didn't think it was a motive?" Heather asked.

Brian shook his head. "Ted called me after he left the station. He said Bowman didn't seem to think it was a motive, and he didn't even make a copy of the will."

"But if it's fake, then it sure seems like a motive to me," Heather said.

"But how do we prove it's fake? Only two people signed that document, and they're both dead," Brian said.

"I'd like to see the document," Danielle said.

"Me too," Camilla added.

"I can show you." Brian took out his phone and opened his photos app. He got up from the chair, walked to Danielle, and handed her his phone. Holding Brian's cellphone in her hand, Danielle studied the photograph while Camilla peeked over her shoulder. Using two fingers, Danielle touched the phone's screen and enlarged the photograph. She continued to study it while everyone silently watched.

"I bet this was typed on a typewriter. Not printed from a computer," Danielle said.

"Which wouldn't surprise me, because I know Flora doesn't know how to use a computer. She uses a smartphone, but I know she's basically computer illiterate." Camilla grew silent a moment, considering what she had just said while Heather served as a ghost translator. After Heather finished repeating her words, Camilla blurted, "Oh my god, Flora murdered me!"

Danielle turned to Camilla. "Why would Flora think she can pass off an un-notarized will? Even if Bowman doesn't think the will is a motive for murder, certainly your brother and sister would contest the will. Who's going to believe you left your share of your uncle's estate to her? The will isn't even notarized, and the two people who signed it are dead. How hard would it be to forge two signatures? Unless she could show there was a reason to leave that money to her and not family, I don't understand how she thought she would get away with it."

"Well... I might know why," Camilla said with a sigh. Everyone but Brian looked her way. "I suppose, now that I'm... dead... well, according to what Marie and Eva told me, it's better to be as forthright as possible before moving on. Something about penance and judgment on the other side."

Marie looked at Camilla. "What did you do?"

"Yeah, judgment for what?" Heather asked. Brian, who now realized Camilla must be talking, sat patiently and waited for someone to fill him in.

"I suppose when I hired Flora, I may have suggested there would be a pension of sorts after my uncle passed if she kept taking care of him until then."

"And you didn't give her one?" Heather asked. Camilla shrugged in reply.

"Were your brother and sister aware of this?" Danielle asked.

Camilla nodded. Heather quickly recounted Camilla's words for Brian.

"Even if the will is forged, it doesn't mean Flora killed Camilla," Danielle said. They all turned to Danielle.

"Why do you say that?" Camilla asked.

"It's possible that after you were killed, Flora saw an opportunity to compensate for the money she felt you owed her by forging a will. Since your brother and sister had been told about your promises to Flora, they might assume the will was legitimate."

"But it isn't legitimate," Camilla insisted.

THIRTY-FOUR

C amilla paced Heather's living room. "I don't want my killer to inherit any of my estate!"

"I'm not convinced Flora is your killer," Danielle said. "I bet Flora forged the will after Camilla's murder, to get something she felt entitled to. It sort of reminds me of crab tamales."

Camilla stopped pacing and stared at Danielle. "Crab tamales?"

Heather chuckled. "Yeah, one of Brian's old girlfriends offed her cheating husband with crab tamales. He was allergic."

"She was not my girlfriend," Brian grumbled.

Heather shrugged, and Danielle continued with her explanation. "At first, the wife wasn't blamed for his death. Everyone thought the person who initially gave her husband the tamales was the killer because he had a motive to kill him. But I always thought crab tamales were an unreliable murder weapon. After all, it wasn't the crab that killed him, it was falling into the ocean after he ate them. No one could predict he would fall into the ocean."

Camilla stared dumbly at Danielle. Finally, she said, "I have absolutely no idea what you're talking about."

"Maybe it's just me, but I'm not sure what Steve Klein's case has to do with Camilla's," Brian muttered under his breath.

Heather chuckled. "Actually, I sorta understand what she's saying."

"Even if Flora didn't murder me, I don't want her to inherit one cent of my money!"

"One way to prove the will is a fraud. Find the typewriter she wrote it on, and then link it to her," Danielle suggested. "I bet she made the will after Mr. Carter died. The typewriter has to be around somewhere."

"That won't help," Brian said.

They all looked at Brian. "Why?" Heather asked.

"Because I have a good idea which typewriter she used. Homer had a manual typewriter, and it's probably still at the house. So if Danielle's right, and that document was typed as opposed to printed off from a computer, then I imagine the typewriter was the one already in the house."

"Then find it and see if her fingerprints are on it," Heather suggested.

"Even if Flora's are the only fingerprints on the typewriter, that proves nothing," Brian said. "Remember, that will was supposedly written when Flora first came to work for Carter. So it wouldn't be suspicious if Flora's were the only fingerprints on the typewriter now."

Heather slumped down in the chair. "Oh. You're right."

Heather's cellphone rang. She sat up, grabbed the phone from the side table, looked at it, and said, "It's Chris."

While Heather talked to Chris on the phone, Brian and Danielle agreed they needed to discuss the matter with Chief MacDonald. When Heather got off the phone, she said, "I'm babysitting Hunny tonight."

"Why?" Danielle asked.

"Chris has to go to Portland. Something came up. So he's going to drop her off in about fifteen minutes. I kind of like having Hunny here. Because if Flora didn't kill Camilla, then we have a psycho killer on the loose."

"If Flora killed me, she's a psycho," Camilla snapped.

Heather looked at Camilla. "We can argue that anyone who kills a person, not out of self-defense, is a psycho. But if she is the killer, it's because she had a motive. The type of psycho killer I'm talking about is someone who likes to kill random strangers. Until they catch the killer, I won't be jogging on the beach alone or leaving my doors unlocked. And if Bowman keeps obsessing over me instead of looking for the person who killed you, I don't see that happening anytime soon."

Brian stood. "I need to get back to the station before Bowman realizes I'm missing. I'm supposed to be filing."

Heather frowned. "Filing?"

Brian shrugged. "It's my punishment for talking to Ted."

Danielle stood. "I'm going to see if Walt will go to the chief's house with me. We need to let him know what's going on."

"I'd go with you, but I need to stay here and wait for Chris to drop off Hunny," Heather said.

"I think I'll tag along with Walt and Danielle. I'd like to see how the chief is doing," Marie said.

Everyone left Heather except for Camilla. Heather looked at the ghost of her boyfriend's ex-wife, who now sat on the sofa Danielle and Marie had been occupying minutes earlier.

"Did you want to talk about something?" Heather asked.

"I'm just trying to understand you and Brian."

"Has anyone told you how we got together?" Heather asked.

Camilla shrugged. "Marie said you and Brian shared a harrowing experience and got together after that. But she didn't really go into it."

Heather stood up, grabbed two cookies off the plate from the coffee table, and sat back down in her chair. She looked at Camilla, took a bite of a cookie, and said, "Let me tell you a story."

CLAY BOWMAN HAD LEFT the police station after talking to Camilla's brother, Ted, that morning. When he returned, he noticed both Joe's and Brian's cars in the parking lot. Instead of going right to his office after entering the building, he headed for the break room to grab a cup of coffee. But just as he reached the open door, he heard Joe's and Brian's voices coming from inside the room. Curious to learn what the two were up to, he remained in the hallway yet stepped out of sight, listening.

"I don't know where Bowman took off to," Joe said.

"If we're lucky, he won't come back." Both men laughed.

"Where have you been?" Joe asked.

"I stopped by Heather's."

"At her work?"

"No. At her house. Chris told her to take a few days off. He had to go to Portland, so he's not even in the office."

"How is Heather doing?"

"How would you feel if someone arrested you for murder? Not terrific. But Danielle was over there trying to cheer her up with her chocolate chip cookies."

"Danielle's chocolate chip cookies could cheer me up." Joe laughed. "So, is she staying with Heather?"

"No. Danielle left the same time I did. She and Walt are going over to check on the chief. She's probably going to take him some cookies, too."

"You want to grab some lunch a little later?" Joe asked.

"No, I can't. Bowman gave me a ton of filing I have to do before I leave work today. It's going to take me a couple of hours, at least."

"Filing? Why?"

Brian then told Joe about his morning encounter with Ted and Bowman.

Trying not to make a sound, Bowman backed away from the open doorway to the break room, careful not to let Joe or Brian know he had been listening. He hurried down the hallway. But just as he was about to open his office door, an idea came to him.

DANIELLE, Walt, and Marie sat with Chief MacDonald in his living room, with the chief in his recliner and his legs elevated. Minutes earlier, Eddy and Evan had said their hellos, with Evan giving a silent nod to Marie before going to their rooms to play video games.

After the boys left the living room, Danielle recounted what had occurred at the police station between Brian, Bowman, and Camilla's brother.

The chief shook his head in disbelief. "That sounds like the Bowman I remember. I could kick myself for not telling Lyons I didn't want to work with his brother-in-law. But to be honest, I never imagined Bowman would actually be able to accept the job. I figured he'd need to give two weeks' notice, at least. I know he left fairly quickly the first time he worked for us, but he didn't have a supervisory position like he had at his last job."

"What do you mean the Bowman you remember?" Danielle asked.

"Just that when he got something in his head, he was like a freaking bulldog. Wouldn't let it go or step back to see if he was wrong. He's obviously fixated on Heather being guilty. Not a good trait for someone in his position."

"I just remembered something we should tell Edward," Marie said. "Danielle, tell him about the conversation I overheard at the Easter egg hunt, between Clay's wife and her sister." Danielle did her best to repeat what Marie had told her at the Easter egg hunt.

"That's interesting," the chief muttered when Danielle finished the retelling.

"Can you think of any reason Clay's wife would have such strong feelings about Camilla?" Danielle asked. "Marie said Camilla was a flirt, and we wondered if Camilla had flirted with Clay, and it made Debbie mad. Or maybe you remember something that happened between the two women."

Edward leaned back in his chair and considered the question for a moment. "I don't remember anything happening between Debbie and Camilla back then. In fact, I don't recall any specific interaction between the two over the years. Nothing stands out. Although, now that I think about it, I remember something Cindy once told me."

"Your wife knew both of them?" Danielle said.

Edward nodded. "Yes. This was before Cindy got sick. She was just getting ready to have Evan when Clay quit and announced he'd found another job. Around that same period, Brian and Camilla split up, and she moved from town. And, of course, Brian was a mess. He never saw it coming."

"Wasn't it, like, six months after their twenty-fifth anniversary?" Danielle asked.

"Yes. I think Cindy was about three months pregnant when we attended their anniversary party."

"What was it that Cindy told you?" Danielle asked.

"There was an event at the library. I can't remember what it was for, but Cindy attended. So did Camilla. They were serving champagne, and of course, Cindy didn't have any because she was well into her pregnancy with Evan. Cindy said Camilla was drinking more than her share of the champagne."

"Camilla was tipsy?" Danielle asked.

Edward nodded. "Yes. Clay was there in an official capacity, and his wife didn't attend. Cindy said she was going to the restroom and accidentally walked into one of the meeting rooms. And there was Clay and Camilla."

"There how?" Marie asked.

Danielle repeated Marie's question for the chief.

"Cindy opened the door to the meeting room, and she walked in on Clay and Camilla embracing. Clay immediately saw Cindy, pushed Camilla away, and said something about Camilla having too much to drink."

"Are you saying Camilla and Clay were having an affair?" Danielle asked.

Edward shrugged. "Cindy and I talked about it that night, and she thought it was entirely possible Camilla had instigated what happened in the meeting room. Apparently, Camilla was already tipsy when Clay arrived at the library. From the moment he got there, Camilla started flirting, and Cindy thought he looked uncomfortable with her attention even before Cindy walked into the meeting room and caught them."

"Do you think Debbie knew about what happened in the library?" Danielle asked.

"It's likely someone else who was there told Debbie how Camilla was coming onto her husband," the chief said.

"Camilla was always a flirt," Marie said. Danielle repeated Marie's words for the chief.

"She never flirted with me," the chief said. "But after that incident at the library, I noticed how Camilla would watch Clay when she'd come to the station to see Brian. At the time, I wondered if she was worried he might say something to Brian about what she had done at the library. I don't know."

"Camilla left Brian not long after that," Danielle reminded him.

"True. In fact, Cindy had heard through the wife grapevine that Camilla was leaving town with another man. After hearing she left Brian, that wouldn't have surprised me."

THIRTY-FIVE

Clay sat in his police car in front of the station. Before proceeding, he wanted to make sure his wife hadn't changed her plans. He picked up his phone and called Debbie.

She answered her cellphone. "Hi, Clay, is anything wrong?"

"No, just calling to see if you wanted to meet me for lunch."

"I'd love to. But did you forget? My sister and I are at the museum with the boys. Remember, they're sponsoring art projects for the kids all week long because of spring break."

"Oh, I forgot. That's today?"

"Yes. In fact, we're here now, and I really need to go."

"How long are you going to be there?" Clay asked.

"It's around three hours, according to the brochure. And we got here about five minutes ago."

"You guys have fun."

"Thanks, Clay. We will."

Tossing his cellphone on the passenger seat, Clay inserted his key in the ignition and started his car. Ten minutes later, he pulled up in front of the garage apartment. He knew Fred was at work, and his wife was with Debbie. So no one was at the main house or at the garage apartment.

After getting out of the vehicle, Clay sprinted up the stairs and into the garage apartment, slamming the door behind him. The first thing needed was tools necessary to pick a lock. It couldn't look like a break-in. He found what he needed and headed to the bedroom. In the bedroom, he took his knapsack out of the closet and filled it with a change of clothes, knit hat, and leather gloves. Atop of those, he placed the tools to pick a lock.

Moving from the living room to the kitchen, he spied a felt-tip pen sitting on the kitchen table. He picked it up and removed its cap before testing the pen on a paper napkin someone had left on the kitchen table. He wanted to make sure the pen hadn't dried out. Satisfied that it would serve his purpose, he dropped the pen in the knapsack after replacing its cap.

He remembered seeing a rope in the utility closet when they had first moved in and hoped Debbie or the boys hadn't moved it. After opening the door to the utility closet, Clay smiled when he saw the rope still rolled neatly in the corner. He leaned into the closet and picked up the rope. Before adding it to the knapsack, he checked to see if it was long enough to do the job.

Clay started for the front door with the knapsack when he started worrying that Heather Donovan might not have any writing paper, and he didn't want to waste time looking for some. After dropping the knapsack to the floor, he walked to the small file cabinet in the living room where Debbie stored her homeschool supplies.

After rummaging through a drawer, he found a package of small notebooks still in their cellophane. He removed one notebook and tossed it with the other items he had collected. Satisfied he had everything he needed, Clay picked up the knapsack and headed outside to his car.

Fifteen minutes later, Clay pulled up to the public restrooms north of the pier. Fortunately, no one seemed to be around. He took the knapsack and went into the bathroom and changed out of his uniform and dressed in the clothes he'd brought from home. He decided if someone saw him and later asked why he had changed his clothes at the restrooms, he would claim he wanted to go undercover to find leads on the killer. Because if the killer was someone not known by Camilla Henderson, the only real clue they had was the fact the killer targeted people coming out of restrooms along the beach.

After shoving his gun under his belt, he slipped on his jacket. Clay wiped off any fingerprints from the felt-tip pen and slipped it into an outer jacket pocket with the tools he needed to pick the lock. He slipped the small notebook into one of the wider jacket pockets, not overly concerned about leaving fingerprints. He intended to tear the paper from the notebook after he had gloves on and not leave the notebook behind.

In the largest inner pocket of the jacket, he shoved the rolled-up piece of rope. It barely fit, with half of the rope protruding above the pocket. Yet with the jacket closed, it concealed the rope.

Before stepping outside the restroom, he looked out to see if he was still alone. Confident he was, Clay walked to the police car, opened the back hatch, shoved the knapsack now holding his uniform into the trunk of the police vehicle, slammed the hatch closed, and set out on foot to Heather Donovan's house.

Clay had initially considered changing his clothes at the garage apartment and leaving the police car there rather than at a public restroom. Yet he worried the boys might act up at the library, forcing their mother to bring them home early. He didn't need Debbie and his sister-in-law wondering why the police car was at the garage apartment without him. Nor did he want either of them asking questions when he returned home on foot.

He pulled on his knit cap, buttoned up his jacket, dug his hands deep into his pockets, and continued down the road, while keeping his head down as much as possible. It didn't take him long to reach the alley behind Heather's house. When walking past Marlow's house, he peeked in the garage window and only saw the Packard. The other car was gone. He assumed they were still at MacDonald's house.

There was no car in the driveway behind the house between Marlow House and Donovan's. Clay knew that neighbor worked at the library, and he assumed she was at work.

When he reached Donovan's house, hers was the only car in the driveway. Unbuttoning his jacket, he started up the back walk to her rear kitchen door.

CAMILLA WAS STILL at Heather's house when Chris had showed up with Hunny an hour earlier. Seeing Chris had made Camilla wonder if she should stick around instead of moving on after finding her killer. She wouldn't mind haunting someone who looked like Chris Glandon.

Eva and Marie had already told her all about Chris Glandon, aka Chris Johnson. The fact he was also a medium made him even more intriguing. She also found it interesting how spirits could communicate with dogs and cats.

When alive, she had never considered herself a dog or cat person. She'd had no desire to own a pet. Like children, animals were something that required a commitment and cost money. However, after Chris had dropped off Hunny, she found herself in a fascinating conversation—if you could call it a conversation—with the pit bull and then with Heather's cat, Bella. While Camilla had never been cruel toward animals, she had never been particularly interested in having one—until now. Of course, now was too late. It was too late for everything now.

Chris had already left for Portland, and Hunny napped behind the sofa, out of sight of Heather's small calico, who had wandered into the kitchen to get something to eat.

"I'm wondering if I would still be alive if I had given Flora what she asked for," Camilla asked.

"You can't do anything about it now. Do you really think Flora killed you?"

"I don't know who else it could be. No one wanted me dead."

"If you're determined to find your killer before you move on, maybe you should start haunting everyone you know in Frederick-port. It's one way to find your killer. The killer might say or do something that only you'll see or overhear, and then you can pass that information on to the mediums. You should try it. Now. Like right now. Go." Heather smiled.

"Do you want me to leave?" Camilla asked.

Heather let out a sigh. "It's just a little strange, having my boyfriend's ex-wife sitting in my living room."

"You mean your boyfriend's dead ex-wife?" Camilla snarked.

Heather chuckled. "Yeah, that too."

Camilla settled back on the sofa. "Before I leave… I just want to say I appreciate you telling me how you and Brian got together. I would've loved watching Brian handle all that—Walt talking to a cougar and flying rattlesnakes."

Heather smiled. "He took it all in stride. But I think over the last five years, since Danielle moved to town, Brian saw a lot of things that didn't fit what many consider normal."

Camilla nodded. "You know, after Uncle Homer died and I moved back to town, I hoped to get back with Brian."

"After ten years?"

Camilla shrugged. "I knew I had broken his heart back then. He never remarried. I figured he never got over me."

"Why did you want him back now? You could have come back any time during the last ten years. I understand you didn't remarry, either."

Camilla smiled sadly. "I suppose I was on a search for greener grass."

"Greener grass? Are you talking about the grass is always greener on the other side?"

Camilla nodded. "I think I was just restless. Bored. I was at a point in life when many women my age were watching their kids leave home. I never had children to leave home."

"Did you regret not having children?"

Camilla shook her head. "No, it wasn't that I regretted not having children, it was that it didn't live up to my expectations."

Heather frowned. "I don't understand?"

"I suppose I thought not having children would mean I'd lead a more exciting life. I wanted something more."

"That's why you left Brian?"

Camilla let out a long sigh. "I'll just say it—I left Brian because I fell madly in love with someone else. And he and I were going to run off together and live an exciting life. The life I imagined when I decided motherhood was not for me."

"You left Brian for another man?"

"Yes. Brian suspected there was another man, but those suspicions were never confirmed. I know there was some gossip around town—in some circles. Even my brother and sister assumed I had left Brian for another man. It surprised my sister, Lucy, when she visited me not long after my divorce and discovered I was living alone and there wasn't any sign that I had a man in my life."

"What happened?" Heather asked.

"Let's just say his marriage wasn't as easy to end as mine."

Heather arched her brows. "Ohh…"

Camilla shrugged. "But the fact is, it was lust—not love. It took me a while to realize that fact. And after a series of failed relationships after him, I came to understand the grass had never been greener on the other side. I eventually regretted divorcing Brian… throwing everything away."

"I imagine it was quite a shock to find Brian with someone… like me."

Camilla smiled and then chuckled. "Yes. That might be an understatement. You were a surprise." Camilla grew serious and then said, "Eva and Marie speak highly of you. I remember Marie Nichols when I was married to Brian, and she was not someone who gave her loyalty lightly. She's quite fond of you."

Heather smiled. "I'm quite fond of her, too. And Eva."

"I'm not sure I'll ever completely understand you and Brian. But I regret hurting him…"

Before Camilla finished her sentence, a crashing sound came from the kitchen. Camilla stopped talking, and both women turned to face the doorway leading to the kitchen. Heather's first thought was that Bella had pushed something off the counter, which was why she hadn't jumped up from her chair. But then a man burst into the room. He held a gun in his right hand, now pointed at Heather's head.

THIRTY-SIX

C amilla recognized him first. "Clay? What are you doing with that gun?"

Heather's eyes widened. She remained seated in her chair, unable to move. Finally, she asked, "What are you doing here? Are you here to arrest me again?"

Clay moved closer to Heather and pulled something from his coat pocket. He tossed it toward her. She looked dumbly at a small pad of paper and pen Clay had just dropped on her lap, and then she glanced up to him, the gun now pointed at her face.

"Listen carefully. I want you to write: *Brian, I love you. I'm sorry.* And then sign it *Heather*," Clay ordered.

HUNNY, who had been napping behind the sofa, woke up when a crashing sound startled her. She assumed Bella was up to some mischievous prank, so she decided not to investigate. The sleepy canine found it cozy behind Heather's sofa, and she wanted to nap.

But then a familiar voice caught her attention. If she was not mistaken, that voice belonged to the man Walt had instructed her to avoid. She crawled to one end of the sofa, peeked out into the living room, and saw a man who resembled the one Walt had warned her about. Hunny moved back behind the sofa, out of sight, trying her best to obey Walt. He had sternly conveyed to Hunny that if she ever encountered the man again, she must do whatever necessary to stay out of his sight and, no matter what he did, not to engage because the man would hurt Hunny.

"YOU WANT me to write a love letter to Brian?" Heather frowned.

Camilla, no longer on the sofa, stood next to Heather, watching Clay. "What are you doing, Clay? Put that gun away!"

"Do as I say!" Clay pointed the gun briefly at the pad of paper and pen on Heather's lap and then pointed it back to her head, unaware of Camilla's ghostly presence.

"Clay, she didn't kill me!" Camilla shouted. "I know you're angry because they let her go. But please don't do this. She's innocent."

Both terrified and curious, Heather glanced from Clay to Camilla and back to Clay. Heather hadn't immediately recognized Clay when he had burst into the room moments earlier. But when Camilla said his name and Heather realized who it was, she thought he had come to arrest her again. Perhaps he'd found additional evidence that he believed supported a case against her. Yet in the next breath, she wondered why he wasn't wearing his uniform. But when he asked her to write a note, her already pounding heart dropped.

A meow broke Heather's concentration and caught Clay's attention. He looked down at the calico cat now weaving in and out between his feet.

"Bella, go," Heather blurted.

Clay gripped the gun aimed at Heather and then quickly glanced at the feline at his feet. Without hesitation, his free hand reached down and grabbed the cat by the scruff of her neck. Bella let out a hiss in protest and tried attacking the gloved hand yet could not reach her captor's skin.

"Let her go!" Heather cried out. "You're hurting her!"

"Clay, let the cat go. You shouldn't hold her like that. She's not a kitten!" Camilla begged.

"You don't want me to hurt the cat, then write the note. When you do, I'll let her go. And if I have to let this damn cat go before you write the note, I'll kill it first."

Fearing for Bella's life, Heather reluctantly picked up the pen and pad of paper. She opened the pad of paper to the first page, set it on the end table, and wrote out the words Clay had given her. After she finished, she looked at Clay. "Let her go now."

"First, let me see the note," he ordered.

Heather held up the note for him to read.

Clay nodded. "Okay, set the notebook on the table next to you and stand up. Once you do, I'll drop the cat."

Heather quickly complied, and the moment she stood up, he dropped the cat. Once Bella's paws hit the floor, she flew across the room and under the sofa.

HUNNY REMAINED hidden behind the sofa, listening to the jumble of human words she couldn't understand. When she had heard Bella's hissing, she didn't think too much about it because Bella loved to hiss at her. And then she wondered if Walt had warned Bella about the man. Or perhaps the man only had an issue with dogs, not cats.

As Hunny speculated on what might be going on in the living room, a bundle of hissing fur rocketed under the sofa straight in her direction. To Hunny's surprise, Bella's hissing stopped, and instead of initiating a game of torment the pitty, Bella snuggled up next to Hunny's side. Curious about what was going on in the living room, Hunny nudged Bella with her nose before crawling to the edge of the sofa. She peeked out and focused on Camilla, attempting to get her attention.

IT WASN'T until Clay released Bella and the cat flew under the sofa did Heather remember that not only was Hunny at her house—she slept behind the sofa. For a moment Heather had been relieved when Clay released Bella, but now she was terrified that sweet little Hunny might come poking her head out from behind the sofa and get herself shot.

Heather didn't have long to worry about Hunny or Bella, because the next moment Clay ordered her to go upstairs with him.

"Why do you want her to go upstairs?" Camilla asked.

Heather might have voiced the same question as Camilla, but did what Clay asked, considering the gun pointed at her. Plus, she didn't want to create a ruckus that might tempt Hunny out from behind the sofa. Heather knew Clay would shoot the dog if given the opportunity.

Heart racing, her right hand clutching the rail, Heather walked up the stairs with Clay right behind her. She wished Marie would show up and then remembered Camilla. Perhaps Camilla didn't have Marie's powers, but she had the power to get Marie.

"Camilla, please get Marie, now! Quick!" Heather called out.

"Acting crazy won't help you." Clay laughed, nudging Heather along with the barrel's end of his gun.

"If he could just hear me," Camilla cried. "He's doing this for me."

"I don't care why he's doing this; go get Marie!" Heather snapped. "She's at Chief MacDonald's house. You know where that is?" Clay laughed at Heather's ramblings.

They had already reached the top of the stairs and had only walked a few steps down the hallway when Clay pushed Heather onto the floor. Heather rolled onto her back and looked up at Clay, who had just tucked his gun into his belt. She tried getting up, but he pushed her down with one booted foot.

"What are you doing?" Heather screamed.

Clay smiled and then pulled a rope from an inside pocket of his jacket. "Haven't you figured it out? You wrote your suicide note. They'll find it when they find you hanging from the top of your staircase." He held the rope with both hands and began fashioning a noose.

"Why would I kill myself?" Heather asked as she tried scooting away, only to be held in place by his foot.

"Because you loved Brian so much and were so jealous of his beautiful ex-wife that you couldn't help yourself. It would have been easier had you simply confessed. You would have saved not just your home, but your life."

"But she didn't kill me. Don't do this, Clay!" Camilla pleaded to deaf ears.

"I didn't kill Camilla. I didn't! Damn it, Camilla, go get Marie!"

Clay laughed. "I know you didn't kill her, you stupid woman. Because I killed her." He knelt down, holding Heather in place, using his body's weight while trying to loop the noose around her head.

Heather refused to die, as Walt had died during his first lifetime. She let out an unholy scream from the depths of her soul while flailing her limbs and body in all directions. Camilla's screams along with her own filled Heather's head as she fought with her attacker.

Heather glimpsed her savior from the corner of her eye as the pit bull, who had just raced up the staircase, jumped onto Clay's back and dug her teeth into his right shoulder.

Clay let out a scream that rivaled the one Heather had made moments earlier. With Clay now on the floor with the pit bull still in attack mode, Heather stumbled to her feet and looked down at the man now fighting for his life.

To Heather's horror, Clay grabbed his gun from beneath his belt, and while still on his back while sprawled on the floor, he aimed his gun not at Heather, but at the dog, who viciously and relentlessly attacked his leg.

Without hesitation, Heather grabbed her bronze statue of Artemis from the hall table, intending to stop Clay from shooting

Hunny by hitting him over the head. Heather brought the statue down on Clay's head at the same time he pulled the trigger. Both man and dog went limp simultaneously.

Heather stood over the man and dog, unable to move, the hallway eerily quiet until a timid meow broke the silence. Heather looked toward the stairs and saw Bella's head peeking up from the top step.

Heather dropped to her knees by Hunny and cried, believing Clay had shot a fatal bullet. But the moment she pressed her face against Hunny's fur, she felt a heartbeat.

"She's alive," Heather sobbed.

"So is he," Camilla, who knelt by Clay, warned.

Heather jumped up and grabbed Clay's gun, gingerly holding it with two fingers before setting it on the table that had moments earlier held the bronze statue. She picked up the rope Clay had brought and began securing the unconscious man's hands behind his back. While securing his hands, she looked at Camilla and snapped, "Now please get Marie!"

"I would have, but I don't know where Chief MacDonald lives!"

Heather quickly rattled off the location of Chief MacDonald's house. The next moment, Camilla disappeared. Heather now stood alone in her hallway. She looked down to Hunny and saw a concerned Bella circling Hunny, gently butting her head against the pit bull's fur, trying to wake her. She also saw the dog's blood, yet not the wound.

Uncomfortable with Clay's proximity to the injured animal, knowing he could regain consciousness at any moment and finish Hunny with several quick kicks from his heavy boots, she had to move one of them, and she couldn't wait for Marie.

Heather understood it was too risky to move Hunny. She pushed Clay's body onto one end of the hall runner and rolled him up in the long, narrow carpet like a burrito. She had secured his arms behind his back, but she also wanted to immobilize his legs. When she reached the end of the runner, Clay moaned as he slowly regained consciousness.

Heather left Clay at the far end of the hallway, stood up, and raced toward the staircase and Hunny. When she reached the dog's side, Bella looked up at her and cried pitifully.

Heather dropped to Hunny's side and located the gunshot wound. She pulled off her blouse and pressed the fabric against the wound to stop the blood while she prayed for Marie to arrive.

The next minute, Heather's prayers were answered.

THIRTY-SEVEN

The apparitions of Marie and Camilla appeared in the middle of Heather's upstairs hallway. They found Heather wearing a black bra and stretch pants, kneeling by Hunny's side, pressing her wadded-up blouse into Hunny's wound to stop the bleeding. Heather looked up to the two spirits in relief and then noticed motion behind them.

Clay had figured out that if he moved his body in one direction, he could unroll himself from the confining carpet runner. As he unrolled himself, getting closer to Heather and the spirits, Heather called out, "Turn around! He's getting away!"

Marie turned toward Clay and promptly used her energy to send him rolling away from them back into the carpet. Clay let out a scream. Without missing a beat, Marie's energy lifted the heavy trunk Heather kept at the end of the hallway. The trunk moved several feet from the wall. The rolled-up carpet holding Clay lifted into the air and moved toward the back wall, dropping behind the trunk. Marie's energy pushed the trunk back toward the wall, securing Clay between the trunk and the wall.

Marie turned back to Heather. "That should keep him for now."

She rushed to Hunny. Kneeling by the dog's side, Marie stared at her. "Hunny's not answering me."

"Her heart's still beating. I need to call the vet. And Brian." Heather glanced down the hall at the man trapped behind the trunk. "But my cellphone is downstairs."

Marie pointed to the wadded-up blouse. "Go. I'll hold that for you. And I'll keep an eye on him." Marie glanced briefly at Clay and back to Hunny. "Get your phone." Marie kept the now blood-soaked blouse in place while Heather ran down the stairs. She hadn't noticed Bella when she had first arrived, but now she spied the cat curled up next to Hunny's side. Marie smiled at Bella's apparent concern.

By the time Heather made it back upstairs, she had already called Brian, unlocked the front door, and was currently on the phone with the vet, begging him to make a house call. The vet agreed, not because he knew Chris Johnson was good for what might be a high medical bill considering the injury, but because of the money Chris and Heather had helped raise for the humane society through the Glandon Foundation.

When Heather got off the phone after calling the vet, Marie told her she should probably go put on a blouse before everyone started showing up. Heather, who had forgotten her partial state of undress, dashed to her bedroom and grabbed the T-shirt she had worn to sleep in the previous night.

Five minutes later, Heather knelt by Hunny, Marie and Bella by her side. "I should have gone to work today. Then this probably wouldn't have happened."

"Before you tell me what happened, who's wrapped up in the hall carpet?" Marie asked. "All I know, Camilla showed up at Edwards and told me I needed to get to your house because you were in danger."

TEN MINUTES EARLIER, Brian had been filing papers at the police station when his cellphone rang.

As soon as he answered the call, he heard Danielle's voice. "Camilla's spirit just showed up at the chief's house and told Marie she needed to go to Heather's because she's in danger. Marie is probably already there, but you need to check on Heather."

Abandoning the files, Brian left the police station and headed for Beach Drive. He was almost there when Heather called. Brian was just pulling up to the front of her house when she finished explaining what had happened. As soon as they ended their call, he called Joe for backup.

Brian was getting out of his car when Walt pulled up in the Ford Flex. He was alone. Unbeknownst to Brian, Walt had left Danielle at the chief's house. Together, Walt and Brian rushed up the front walk toward Heather's front door.

"We're up here!" Heather called out as soon as she heard the front door open.

Walt and Brian raced up the stairs yet stopped abruptly when they saw the unconscious pit bull sprawled near the top step of the second-floor landing. Heather, once again holding the wadded-up blouse to Hunny's wound, looked up to Walt and Brian. "She's been shot."

"Who in the hell shot her?" Walt demanded.

"Clay Bowman," Brian answered for Heather. During their phone call minutes earlier, Heather had already told him the abbreviated version of Bowman's break-in.

Camilla, who had remained silent since bringing Marie to Heather's, stood off to the side and watched.

"Henderson? Brian Henderson, is that you?" Clay shouted from the other end of the hall.

While Walt knelt beside Hunny with Heather, Brian walked toward Clay. "Yes, it's me, Bowman."

"It's Chief Bowman!" Clay shouted. "And get me out of here! Your crazy girlfriend has done it now! I'm locking her up once and for all!"

Hands on hips, Brian stood over Bowman and looked down. "You shot Hunny."

"Damn right I shot that animal! It attacked me. I'm suing Johnson, and who knows, the Glandon Foundation might come to his rescue too and pay for the settlement he's going to be owing me. Now get me out of here! Now!" Bowman shouted. Once again, fighting against his restraints, Clay pushed the trunk out from the wall a few inches.

"We'll get you out of there in a minute," Brian said before turning away from Bowman and walking back toward Heather and the others.

Furious, Clay screamed, "Don't walk away, Henderson! You heard me! Get me out of here now, or I'll make sure you never work in law enforcement again!"

Joe and the veterinarian showed up at the same time. While the vet went upstairs to look at Hunny, Walt and Marie monitored Bowman, and Heather and Brian headed downstairs to explain to Joe what had happened.

"I don't understand. Why would he do this?" Joe asked after Heather finished her telling.

As Heather explained, Bowman continued to shout out that someone needed to untie him.

"He confessed to killing Camilla," Heather said. "I think initially he wanted me to believe I was going to be convicted of the murder, so he tried convincing me I'd be better off taking a plea deal, spending a couple of years in prison, and saving my home. That way, with someone serving time in prison for the murder, he'd be in the clear. When that would not work, he decided I'd commit suicide because I felt so guilty that I killed Brian's ex. You'll find the suicide note he made me write downstairs in the living room."

"Did he say why he killed Camilla?" Joe asked.

Heather glanced up the stairs and saw Camilla standing on the top step, watching the commotion. Heather looked back at Brian. "Maybe you guys should bring him downstairs, and I'll tell you what I know. I imagine the vet is getting a little uneasy up there with some guy shouting to be untied."

"I should call for more backup," Joe said.

JOE AND BRIAN walked to the end of the hall. Bowman was now on his back, his head sticking out from one end of the rolled-up carpet. "Morelli, good, you're here. Get me out of this thing."

"Let us move this trunk first," Joe said.

Bowman smiled and seemed to relax, believing Joe, unlike Henderson, knew how to follow orders.

"How did Heather get him behind here?" Joe asked as he and Brian slowly pushed the trunk to one side, freeing Clay so that he was no longer pressed between the trunk and the wall.

"She must have used her weight to slide it over," Brian said, knowing full well Marie had moved the trunk. Once Clay was no longer trapped behind the trunk, Joe and Brian picked him up, set him on his feet, and unwound him from the runner. Once free, Clay demanded they remove the rope from his wrists.

Joe moved behind Clay and untied the rope holding his wrists together. Meanwhile, Clay glared into Brian's eyes, a smug smile on his face. But the smirk vanished when Joe slapped on handcuffs just as the rope came off.

"Hey! What are you doing?" Clay jerked around to Joe.

"We need to go downstairs and get some answers," Joe told Clay.

"Have you forgotten who I am?" Clay demanded.

FURIOUS TO BE LED down the hallway in handcuffs by two of his officers, Clay's angry gaze fixed on the dog staining the wood floor with its blood. The animal had ruined his plans. Everything had gone brilliantly until the dog appeared out of nowhere. It should be dead—it looked dead—but the man identified as a veterinarian worked to save its miserable life.

There was no way Clay would allow the dog's life to be saved. One good kick could deliver a final blow. Morelli and Henderson had to walk him around the dog to get to the staircase. He would make it happen so fast, there would be nothing they could do. What was the punishment for kicking an already dying dog? He didn't care at this point.

But what Clay hadn't counted on were the observant eyes of Marie and Walt. Clay's brain told his foot when to kick the dog, but instead of it kicking outward, Clay cried out in pain and stumbled. It felt as if someone had grabbed hold of his ankle just as it moved to kick the dog and then mercilessly twisted the ankle. Joe and Brian kept Clay from falling and walked him down the stairs.

Once they reached the first-floor landing, Brian's cellphone rang. He looked at it. It was the chief.

"Joe, I need to take this. It's the chief."

Joe walked Clay over to a chair and told him to sit down. Reluctantly, Clay sat, yet he found it impossible to get comfortable with his hands behind his back.

Brian moved out of earshot of Joe and Clay, yet kept a close eye on the two, just in case Clay tried something.

"What's going on over there?" MacDonald asked.

Brian quickly updated Chief MacDonald on what had occurred.

"Is Hunny going to be okay?"

"I don't know. The vet is working on her, and I didn't want to bother him with questions. Heather and Walt are talking with him, and I assume know more. I have no idea if Hunny needs surgery, or if she'll be staying here with Heather. I don't know when Chris is expected back, and he doesn't know what happened to Hunny. Joe and I were just getting ready to question Clay. We brought him downstairs. He's sitting in a chair with Joe watching him now."

"I don't want you to question Clay at Heather's house. Bring him to the station. Danielle's going to use my car and bring me down there now. Put him in the interrogation room. I want to talk to him."

"But, Chief, are you up to it?"

"I'll be there. And tell Heather I want her to come down to the station so I can talk to her. Danielle can drop me off and then head over to Heather's house to help with Hunny."

When Brian got off the phone, he walked over to Joe and told him what the chief had said just as two more officers entered

Heather's house. Seeing the new arrivals, Clay reminded everyone that he was the police chief, not MacDonald. Yet his rants went ignored as Joe and the two officers took Clay out to the squad car while Brian sprinted upstairs to tell Heather what was going on.

Heather was already standing on the top of the step when Brian reached her.

"How's Hunny?" Brian asked.

"She needs surgery. The vet's on his phone right now, setting up things with his office. Walt will help get her downstairs."

"I need you to come down to the station as soon as you can," Brian said. "The chief wants to talk to you. Danielle's dropping him off at the station and then coming here to help with Hunny."

Heather nodded and then glanced over to Hunny with concern.

"And I need to gather some evidence before I go," Brian said. "Like the note he had you write."

Heather looked back at Brian. "You might want to take his gun, too."

THIRTY-EIGHT

Heather stood on the sidewalk in front of her house, Bella in her arms, Camilla by her side, as they watched Walt and Danielle drive off, following the van carrying Hunny to the veterinarian's office for surgery.

Bella let out a pitiful meow.

"She's worried about her friend," Camilla told Heather.

Heather glanced down at Bella. "Friend? Did she tell you that?"

"In her own way. I'm trying to get used to how they send me their thoughts. But yes, Bella loves Hunny."

Heather smiled down at Bella. "Sometimes it takes almost losing someone to realize what they mean to us. We can't lose Hunny." Heather gave Bella a gentle squeeze, kissed the top of her furry head, and turned toward her house.

Camilla looked at Heather. "I'm sorry about the dog."

Now walking toward her house, still holding Bella, Heather glanced back at Camilla. "I have to go to the police station. But before I do, I need you to do something for me."

"What?"

Heather stopped at her front door and faced Camilla. "I need

250

you to tell me everything you didn't tell us about Clay. You know why he killed you, don't you?"

WHEN HEATHER ARRIVED at the police station, an anxious and excited Colleen greeted her. "It's crazy down here. Chief MacDonald showed up about fifteen minutes ago. He's using a walker. They arrested Chief Bowman, but I assume you already know that because Brian said they arrested him at your house. Fred Lyons showed up a few minutes ago, and he's super mad. He's in the chief's office with him—although I'm not sure who's the chief and whose office it is."

"Why is Fred Lyons here?" Heather asked.

"When they brought Chief Bowman in, Chief MacDonald wasn't here yet. Chief Bowman insisted on his phone call. So they let him, and apparently he called Mr. Lyons."

"Where is Bowman now?"

"He hates when anyone calls him Bowman," Colleen whispered. "He doesn't even like Mr. Bowman. Only Chief Bowman."

Heather let out a snort. "Not sure how that's going to play behind bars."

"Do you think he could really go to jail? What did he do?"

"Why don't you call the chief, tell him I'm here," Heather said.

"YOU SHOULDN'T EVEN BE HERE," Fred told MacDonald, who sat in the chair behind the desk, his walker by his side. "You're supposed to be out on medical leave. I think Clay is right. We have a serious problem in Frederickport. The number of capital crimes has spiked in the last five years. And while we have another killer on the loose, our police officers are arresting their own chief! What is going on?"

"I hope to find out," MacDonald said.

The phone rang on the chief's desk. MacDonald answered it,

251

spoke quietly a few moments to whomever was on the other side, and hung up. He looked up at Fred. "Heather Donovan's here. I need to speak to her."

"Are you putting her under arrest?" Fred asked.

MacDonald frowned. "Why would I put her under arrest?"

"When Clay called me, asking to contact an attorney for him, he explained he had been investigating Camilla Henderson's murder. He went undercover because he'd lost all confidence in your officers. In fact, he was beginning to believe Brian was someway involved, especially considering how he attempted to sabotage Clay at every turn."

"Sabotage?"

Fred nodded. "Clay decided to talk to Donovan again. She let him into her house and seemed quite willing to talk to him. He asked her a few questions, and she told him there was something she needed to show him that Brian had left at the house. He walked upstairs with her, and before he realized what was happening, she set a pit bull on him. The dog would have probably killed him if he hadn't shot it. Unfortunately, after he shot the dog, Donovan hit Clay over the head with something. Knocked him out."

MacDonald arched his brows. "Really?"

"When he came to, he was being arrested. Clay suspects the only reason she called the police is because he shot the dog. Clay figures Donovan planned to get rid of his body later. But with the dog shot—a dog that belongs to her boss—she had to come up with a story explaining the injured animal."

"Exactly why did Heather want Clay dead?" MacDonald asked.

"Because she understood Clay would not let her get away with murder."

"Well, that's quite a fascinating story. Clay has already told us he will not be talking to anyone until he speaks to his attorney. But I'm going to let you and Clay stay in the office next to the interrogation room while I question Heather. Of course, Joe and Brian will need to be in there too."

HEATHER SAT in the interrogation room, waiting for the chief to arrive. She kept looking at the clock, wondering how Hunny's surgery was going. Her cellphone buzzed, showing an incoming message. Assuming it was Walt or Danielle giving her a Hunny update, she checked her phone. The text was from Brian.

"FYI. Joe and I are in the next office, with Fred Lyons and Clay. Watching."

Heather set her phone on the table and glanced over to the one-way mirror. The next minute, the chief shuffled into the room with his walker.

"Ahh, Chief, how is your leg?" Heather asked.

"I'm okay." MacDonald shuffled to the table, pulled out a chair, and sat down, awkwardly keeping his right leg straight. "I need you to tell me everything that happened today."

"I was alone at home. Well, except for Hunny and Bella. Bella was in the kitchen, and Hunny was behind the sofa, sleeping. I heard a crash in the kitchen. I thought Bella knocked something over. The next minute Clay Bowman barges into my living room, demanding I write a note to Brian, telling him I love him and that I'm sorry."

"Why would he want you to write a note to Brian?"

"I didn't think too much about why he wanted the note; I kept looking at that gun pointed at me. Bella came into the living room, and Clay grabbed her, threatened to kill her if I didn't write the note. So I wrote it. At that point, it didn't dawn on me; I was writing my suicide note. I found out a few minutes later he intended to kill me."

"Why would he want to kill you?"

"Because he killed Camilla. He wanted to frame me for the murder."

"He told you that?"

"He said something about how I'd just written my suicide note —because I was remorseful for killing my boyfriend's ex. I told him I hadn't killed Camilla. He laughed and admitted he killed her. And then, he just started talking, like he wanted to tell someone, and I guess he figured I'd be dead in a few minutes after he dragged me upstairs and hung me from the banister, so I'd be the perfect one to tell. You see, he and Camilla used to be lovers."

IN THE NEXT ROOM, Clay bolted up from the chair he had been sitting on, while shouting, "I never told her that!" Joe hushed Clay and pushed him back down on the chair.

The men continued to watch Heather, who sat primly in the chair facing MacDonald, her hands folded neatly on the table.

"I don't think Clay expected to run into Camilla when he moved back to Frederickport. But then Camilla's uncle died, and she came back to town and decided to stay. Clay told me Camilla barged into his office one day and told him she didn't want him in Frederickport. That she'd left town once because of him, screwed up her life, and she was coming back and wanted to get back with Brian. She couldn't do it with him here. She told him to find an excuse to leave town, or she would tell Debbie everything. That's why he killed her." Heather folded her arms over her chest and leaned back in the chair and smiled.

"SHE'S LYING! I never said any of that!" Clay shouted.

Fred told Clay to calm down because he had an idea. He picked up his cellphone and called the chief. The men in the room with Fred watched as the chief answered his phone and then listened as Fred said, "Clay insists she's lying. He's willing to take a lie detector test. Is Donovan willing?"

The chief looked from his phone to the one-way mirror and then back to Heather. Reluctantly, he repeated Fred's demand to Heather.

Heather considered for a moment and then smiled. She looked in the mirror. "I'll take a lie detector test under one condition. Bowman takes it first—yet instead of asking him if he told me those things, ask him if he did those things. If he agrees to that, then okay."

In the other room, Clay stared dumbly at the window, looking into the interrogation room. Finally, he said, "I can't do anything until I speak to my attorney."

THEY TOOK Clay back to a cell, and to Fred's chagrin, they brought Debbie into the station to be questioned. Fred asked to watch from the office next to the interrogation room, as he had with Heather.

"WHAT'S GOING ON? Is my husband okay?" Debbie asked when she was brought into the interrogation room and found Chief MacDonald sitting at the table with a walker by his side.

"We have arrested your husband for the murder of Camilla Henderson," he explained.

Debbie let out a gasp and then sat down without being told. She closed her eyes for a few moments and took a deep breath before exhaling. She looked at the chief.

"Were you aware of your husband's affair with Camilla Henderson?"

Debbie closed her eyes again and took another deep breath.

"Debbie? Did you know?" the chief asked.

Debbie opened her eyes and nodded. "Yes. I did. But it wasn't really Clay's fault. We had been trying to get pregnant forever. And when I couldn't get pregnant, I started keeping track of my cycles, taking my temperature. Sex for me became about making a baby, and unless it was the exact time in my cycle, I didn't want us to. I think that's when the cheating started."

"So you knew about Camilla?"

"Yes. But it wasn't serious, him and Camilla. She was older than him. It's not like he was going to leave me for her, because she couldn't have kids. It wasn't just her age, but someone once told me she'd had a hysterectomy. Clay always wanted kids."

"Did Clay know you knew about Camilla?"

Debbie shook her head. "No. I don't think he had any idea that I even suspected his affair. But after I found out I was pregnant, he started talking about how we should leave Frederickport. He said he wanted to get a better job now that we were starting a family. But I understood why he really wanted to move. He wanted to get away from Camilla, make a clean break. I didn't really want to go, move so far away from my sister, but I realized it was probably the best thing for our marriage."

"How did you feel when you saw Camilla had moved back to town?"

"I didn't like it. Because she was still single, looked great, and I worried Clay might cheat again. The fact she couldn't have kids, Clay would probably see as a plus now. The twins are a handful. Not that he doesn't love them, but having a woman like Camilla in such close proximity, who can't get pregnant, well, that's simply too convenient. After all, Clay is just a man. But I didn't kill her. Honest. And I don't believe Clay would kill her either."

THIRTY-NINE

With pillows propped behind her back and head, Danielle leaned against the headboard in the downstairs bedroom. Next to her on the mattress sprawled Hunny, who had been dozing off and on for the last hour, her head resting on Danielle's right thigh. Max curled up on the end of the bed, napping.

Absently stroking the pit bull's head, Danielle watched Hunny's steady breathing. Occasionally, the dog would open her eyes and look at Danielle, as if wanting to be reassured Danielle was still in the bed with her. Once she saw Danielle, Hunny would close her eyes again.

"You sailed through that surgery like the brave pup you are," Danielle whispered to the sleeping dog, her hand still stroking Hunny's neck. "You're lucky you don't have to wear one of those horrid cones. Walt's little talk seemed to have worked better than a cone."

With a deep sigh, Danielle stopped stroking the dog, yet left her hand resting on Hunny's neck. She closed her eyes, and like the dog and cat sharing the bed with her, she fell asleep.

WALT, who had been sitting in the living room, trying to read a book—something he couldn't seem to do with his mind on the dog in the next room—glanced up to the front window when a flash of color caught his attention. He immediately recognized it as Chris hurrying up to the front door from the street, where he had parked his car.

Tossing the book on the end table, Walt stood and walked to the doorway leading to the entry hall. He had just taken a few steps into the entry when Chris came barreling through the front doorway.

"Where's Hunny?" Chris shouted.

Walt motioned for Chris to lower his voice and whispered, "Not so loud. She's sleeping, and you don't want to wake her. She needs her rest."

"Where is she?" Chris asked in a quieter voice.

Walt motioned for Chris to follow him. When they reached the closed door of the downstairs bedroom, Walt briefly pressed his right index finger against his own lips before gently opening the door.

Standing at the open doorway, both men looked into the dimly lit bedroom, the blinds closed and the overhead light off. Danielle lay sleeping on the bed, the state of her pregnancy obvious. Hunny, her body bandaged, slept next to her. The pit bull rested her sleeping head on one of Danielle's legs, while Max continued to nap at the foot of the bed.

The men watched the three for several minutes before Walt gently closed the door, leaving it open a few inches so Max could get out if he woke up, and motioned for Chris to follow him to the kitchen.

"I couldn't believe Heather's phone call," Chris said once they walked into the kitchen. "I was going to stay overnight, but I came right home."

"The good news, Hunny came through surgery like a champ. Fortunately, the bullet did minimal damage. The vet said we could bring her home, providing we keep a close eye on her for the next twelve hours." Walt walked to the refrigerator and grabbed two beers. He handed one to Chris, who absently accepted it. The two men sat down at the kitchen table.

"You'll help me get her home?" Chris opened his can of beer.

"Of course. But leave her where she is. There's no reason to move her. She can just sleep in the downstairs bedroom while she recovers. It'll be easier for everyone. If she has any sort of pain, she can tell me. And when she needs to go out, I can move her outside —without straining my back or yours."

"Walt, would you mind if I stayed here? I'll sleep in the room with Hunny."

Walt chuckled. "Danielle and I already talked about that. We assumed you'd want to. No problem."

"So what happened, anyway? Much of what Heather told me made little sense."

Walt told Chris about the day's events, beginning with Clay breaking into Heather's house, up to his arrest. He then told about Hunny's time at the vet. "When we first brought Hunny home, she was out of it. Ian came down to the vet hospital to help me load Hunny into the car. Or should I say give the appearance of helping me? When we moved Hunny from Heather's house, it would have been easier had everyone stayed out of my way, but obviously, that wasn't going to happen."

Chris gave a snort and took a sip of his beer.

"Once we got Hunny settled in the downstairs bedroom, she started coming out of her fog. I explained to her what had happened and told her if she left her bandage alone, she wouldn't have to wear an uncomfortable cone on her head."

Chris chuckled at both the absurdity and convenience of Walt's special gift.

"After I explained to her what had happened, the first thing she wanted to know, was Heather all right. Then she apologized for not obeying my orders to stay away from the man—but she said she had to help Heather. You have a brave little girl there. She knew the risk of helping Heather. But she didn't care."

Tears filled Chris's eyes. He set his beer on the table and looked at Walt. "She apologized?"

Walt nodded. "Hunny just wants love. She wants to please us. And she's fiercely protective of those she loves."

"It's funny, I initially got Hunny after that fiasco with the hijacking because I decided to get a guard dog instead of hiring a security detail. People always say pit bulls are ferocious." Chris absently stared at his hand holding the beer can.

Walt chuckled. "When you brought her home, I told myself, this puppy will never be guard-dog material. She had so many fears. She still does."

"Hunny rose to the occasion." Chris looked up at Walt. "I didn't even ask, what kind of damage did she do to Clay?"

Walt shrugged. "Nothing that warranted stitches. Fortunately for Clay, he was wearing a heavy jacket and denims. While I imagine the bites didn't feel good, Hunny didn't break any flesh. She didn't have enough time to do real damage aside from some shredded clothes."

"Any news on what's going to happen to Bowman?" Chris asked.

Walt shrugged. "No. Heather's still down at the police station. She's been there all afternoon. She hasn't called."

DANIELLE WAS STILL SLEEPING in the room with Hunny when Brian and Heather arrived. They entered through the kitchen door, with Heather carrying Bella.

"How is she?" Heather asked the moment she entered the house.

"She's doing good," Walt said. "She's sleeping with Danielle and Max in the downstairs bedroom."

Heather looked at Chris. "How are you? I'm sorry about everything."

Chris's weary eyes looked up at Heather. "It's not your fault. I'm just glad you're both okay."

Walt silently motioned to Brian, asking him if he wanted a beer, to which Brian nodded. Just as Walt handed Brian the beer, Bella meowed pitifully. Walt looked at the cat, and the two stared at each other for a few moments until Bella leapt from Heather's arms and raced out of the kitchen.

"Bella!" Heather called out before going after her. She followed the calico to the downstairs bedroom. By the time she got there, Bella was already up on the bed, nuzzling the top of the now awake pit bull's head before grooming the dog's face.

Heather paused in the doorway and watched. A moment later, Chris, Walt, and Brian joined her, standing by her side. In the bed, a sleepy Danielle opened her eyes and looked surprised to find an audience watching them. She rubbed her eyes and then looked down at Hunny now being attentively groomed by Bella.

"Is Hunny okay with Bella up there?" Brian asked, knowing the cat's history of tormenting the dog.

Walt chuckled. "Don't worry, Hunny doesn't mind, and Bella is extremely grateful Hunny saved her human."

ON MONDAY EVENING, Chris ordered Chinese food for dinner, but instead of picking it up, he had them deliver it to Marlow House; he didn't want to leave Hunny. Chris ordered enough food to feed half the people on Beach Drive.

Ian, Lily, Connor, and Sadie arrived before the food. An hour earlier, Danielle had woken up and had gone upstairs to shower and change her clothes, and she was still upstairs. Chris had been sitting by Hunny's side when the Bartleys arrived.

After Walt greeted the Bartleys at the front door, he explained to Sadie what had happened to Hunny. Without waiting for Walt's permission, the golden retriever raced from the entry to the downstairs bedroom. By the time Walt and the others arrived at the open doorway to the bedroom, they found the golden retriever standing by the bed, licking Hunny's ear.

Chris, who sat on the bedside next to the patient, glanced over at Walt and the others as they stood by the open doorway. "By the way Hunny started wagging her tail when Sadie showed up; I think she's happy to see her."

"She is," Walt confirmed.

"WHAT'S GOING to happen to Bowman now?" Lily asked as they all sat around the living room, each holding a plate of food on their laps.

"He has a lawyer, and I imagine he'll be getting out on bail," Brian said.

"Bail? They're going to let him out on bail? He killed Camilla, and he tried to kill Heather," Lily said.

Brian shrugged. "I'm sorry to say it's Clay's word against Heather's. He's sticking to the story he gave his brother-in-law."

"Is he even going to make bail if they set it?" Ian asked.

"I have a feeling Lyons will post bail. He seems to buy Clay's story," Brian said.

"Didn't Debbie admit Clay had an affair with Camilla?" Danielle asked.

Brian nodded. "Yes, but Lyons doesn't believe that's motive for murder. He's convinced Clay knew Debbie found out about the affair, so there is no motive to kill Camilla."

"But didn't Debbie say Clay didn't know she knew?" Danielle asked.

"Yes. But later she walked that back a bit, saying she initially didn't think Clay knew she found out, but after thinking about it, and things that happened over the years, she thinks he probably knew she'd found out. And because of that, he didn't have a motive to kill an ex-lover to keep her quiet."

"I'm just trying to figure out what all this means for me if he gets off," Heather grumbled.

"Or Hunny," Chris said. "I don't want them to come after Hunny for attacking him. If that happens, Hunny goes in hiding."

The conversation moved to Chief MacDonald and the fact he had to return to the station so soon after his surgery. "How did the chief get home?" Danielle asked.

"Joe said he'd take him home when he was ready. But when we

left, the chief was still arguing with Lyons, who felt they needed to suspend Bowman with pay."

"With pay?" Lily squeaked. "Is he serious?"

"Lyons obviously thinks his brother-in-law is innocent," Ian said.

"Which means he actually thinks I'm capable of trying to murder a cop with a loaded pit bull and then dispose of the body." Heather scoffed. "And how was I going to do that alone? Drag him into my bathtub and chop him up?"

Lily looked to Heather. "Then the Glandon Foundation could host a charity barbecue and pull a *Fried Green Tomatoes*?"

"Oh, good idea." Heather grinned.

"That's disgusting," Chris grumbled. "Seriously, disgusting."

"Not to change the disgusting subject, but what happened to Camilla?" Danielle asked.

"She came to the station with me," Heather said. "And after she listened to what Bowman had to say to Lyons, his side of what happened, she decided it was time to move on."

"She never knew Bowman killed her?" Lily asked.

Heather shook her head. "No. She thought he was going after me so hard because he believed I was the killer. And because of that, she got this fanciful notion that he harbored love for her all these years but denied it because of his children."

"Some love," Lily snarked.

"From what Camilla told me," Heather continued, "when Camilla asked Brian for a divorce, she thought Clay was going to ask Debbie for a divorce, and then the two of them could ride off into the sunset together. But I guess Clay just upped and moved, without telling her, and then she heard his wife was pregnant. She figured that's why Clay stayed with his wife."

"Things make a lot more sense now," Brian said with a shrug.

"I guess I was right about Flora," Danielle said.

Lily looked at Danielle. "What do you mean?"

"Carter's caregiver," Brian explained. "She claims to have a will that Camilla wrote, leaving Camilla's share of Carter's estate to her. Camilla claims it's fake, and the witness to the will was Agatha Pine."

"Agatha Pine?" Lily cringed.

Brian continued, "Camilla and her brother thought Flora's fake will was a motive for murder, but Danielle wasn't convinced."

Heather turned to Brian. "With all the commotion, I forgot to tell you something Camilla told me before she left. Her family doesn't have to worry about proving the will's a forgery. Apparently, Camilla actually had a will—one that was notarized and updated last year, which would supersede Flora's, even if Flora's wasn't fake. She left everything to her brother and sister. A copy of the will is in a box of her personal papers that are with the rest of her things waiting to be shipped here."

"Why didn't she mention that when we were trying to figure out how to prove Flora's will was fake?" Brian asked.

Heather shrugged. "It wouldn't have really proved Flora's will was fake, just that it was no longer valid. Although Camilla kept telling me how she didn't want Flora to inherit her money. Not sure how it slipped her mind until later that she had a will that would have prevented Flora from inheriting."

"A spirit rarely thinks clearly so soon after death, especially after such a dramatic death," Danielle reminded her.

FORTY

"You and your friends certainly have had an eventful week," a loving voice told Danielle.

Danielle opened her eyes and found herself sitting on the rocking chair in the nursery. Her mother sat nearby, on the toy box positioned between the rocking chair and crib.

"Mom?" Danielle jumped up from her chair and gave her mother a hug. Her mother, still sitting on the toy box, laughed happily and embraced Danielle. When the hug ended, Danielle sat back down on the rocking chair.

Danielle grinned. "This is a dream hop, isn't it?"

Her mother reached over and patted Danielle's right hand, which rested on the arm of the rocking chair. "You know the answer to that."

"I'm so glad to see you. Is there any special reason for your visit?"

"I know you've been worried about labor. The first time can be frightening, especially in your situation, with twins. But I want to assure you, everything is going to be fine. And don't worry, you won't need a C-section. These babies are going to come quickly. You won't be in labor long."

Danielle smiled. "Really?"

"Oh yes. Those two are quite eager to begin their new adventure with you and their father."

"You've met them?"

Danielle's mother laughed. "Of course I have. And I will warn you, they are going to be a handful."

"So that's why you're here, to tell me not to worry?"

"That, and to suggest you might want to finish getting this room ready. You're going to need it sooner than you think."

Danielle opened her eyes, sat up in bed, looked around, and saw that she was alone in the bedroom. Even Max, whom she normally found sleeping on the foot of the mattress each morning, was not there. She looked at the clock on the nightstand. It was a few minutes past nine a.m. She had slept in. Then she remembered Hunny, who had been shot the previous day and slept downstairs. Danielle threw back the covers and climbed out of bed.

WHEN DANIELLE MADE it downstairs fifteen minutes later, dressed for the day in stretch pants and a long T-shirt, the door to the downstairs bedroom was open. She peeked inside and found Hunny on the center of the bed, with Sadie curled up on her right side, and Bella curled up on her left side, and Max at the foot of the bed. They all seemed to be sleeping.

Turning from the room, she walked to the kitchen, where she discovered a bustle of activity. Walt stood at the stove, cooking bacon; Chris poured batter into the waffle maker; Heather washed dishes while Ian dried; Connor sat in the highchair, eating loose Cheerios from the highchair tray; and Lily sat at the kitchen table, reading the newspaper.

Danielle walked all the way into the kitchen. "Good morning."

Walt looked at his wife. "Morning, sleepyhead." The others glanced at Danielle, each offering a greeting.

Danielle walked to the refrigerator, opened its door, and pulled out the pitcher of juice. She shut the refrigerator door and headed to the counter. But before she reached it, Ian snatched the pitcher from her hands, poured her a glass of juice in a glass he had just dried, and then handed the full glass to her as she said, "Thank you." She walked toward the table with the glass of juice and said, "I see they're having a slumber party in the downstairs bedroom."

Folding the newspaper, Lily looked over at Danielle. "When we got up this morning, there was a message from Marie on the board in Connor's room, letting us know Sadie was anxious to see Hunny this morning." Lily set the folded newspaper on the table.

Danielle sat down next to Lily and looked over at Chris. "How did she do last night?"

"Slept through the night. I think it was the pain meds. Walt came in and took her out about six."

"Sadie wasn't the only one eager to see Hunny," Heather said from the sink. "From the time she got up this morning, Bella started meowing and pawing at the kitchen door. She doesn't normally do that, so I figured it must be about Hunny."

"Any news about Bowman?" Danielle asked.

Heather shook her head. "No. I haven't talked to Brian this morning."

"Well, I got some news this morning." Danielle sipped her juice.

Heather glanced from the sink to Danielle. "Did you talk to the chief?"

"No. It wasn't about Bowman. It was about the twins. Mom claims they're coming early," Danielle announced. "Walt, she said we might want to finish the nursery."

Danielle's announcement incited a flurry of questions, with Lily wondering how early since Danielle's baby shower was on Saturday. After breakfast, Walt and Danielle went shopping to purchase what they needed to complete the nursery. They left their friends at Marlow House.

Lily had asked to hang out in Marlow House's living room with Connor, since the construction crew would arrive at her house within the hour. Ian headed back across the street, leaving Sadie with Hunny, while Chris used the parlor desk for his makeshift office so he could monitor Hunny, with Heather as his assistant.

AFTER WALT and Danielle finished their shopping, they stopped at Pier Café for lunch. When they stepped in the restaurant, it reminded them it was spring break, considering all the full tables. Not wanting to wait for a table, they turned around and were about to leave when someone called their names. Turning back around, Walt spied Joe and Kelly sitting in a booth by a window. Joe waved them over, asking them to join them.

"We just got here ourselves," Kelly explained when Walt and Danielle sat down. "We haven't even ordered yet." Kelly handed them each a menu.

"Thanks." Danielle flashed Kelly a smile. "I can't believe how busy it is."

"It is spring break." Kelly shrugged and opened her menu.

"How are you feeling?" Joe asked Danielle.

"Fat?" Danielle grinned.

Kelly rolled her eyes. "You are not fat. Yes, you're wearing what looks like a basketball in front, but the rest of you looks trim."

"Thanks." Danielle closed her menu and set it on the table.

"Any news on Bowman?" Walt asked Joe.

"Oh yes," Kelly said, looking over at Joe to explain.

Joe flashed a brief reprimanding glance to Kelly and then looked back at Walt. "Let's not mention this to Carla when she comes to take our order. But, considering what the chief confides to your wife, I don't think he'll mind if I tell you."

"What?" Danielle asked.

"That notebook Clay gave Heather to write her suicide letter on?" Kelly answered before Joe had a chance. "They're pretty sure it came from Clay's house."

"I thought I was supposed to tell this?" Joe asked.

Kelly shrugged. "Sorry."

"The chief got a search warrant last night for Lyons's guest house," Joe explained. "The notebook Heather said Bowman gave her to write the suicide note on. It apparently came from a package of notebooks found in a trunk where Debbie Bowman kept her homeschool supplies. Same brand, same covers. They don't sell them in Oregon. She brought them with her."

"Why would Clay use a notebook they could trace?" Danielle asked.

"I assume he intended to take the notebook, leave the paper. The paper looks like regular lined notebook paper. It's the cover that's unique. But Hunny stopped his plans."

"How is Hunny?" Kelly asked.

Danielle looked at Kelly. "She's doing good."

Kelly smiled. "Hunny saved Heather's life. That's amazing."

"So what does this mean now? Does the notebook prove Heather's version over Bowman's?" Walt asked.

"Considering the amount of glowing character references that have been flooding our email since late yesterday afternoon for Heather, compared to the not-so-flattering feedback the chief got from Bowman's last employer when he called them this morning, I'd say the notebook is the icing on his indictment," Joe said.

"Character references from who? And how did they know to send them?" Danielle asked.

Joe took a sip of his water before explaining, "Apparently, the people who work at the vet office where Hunny was taken are fans of the Glandon Foundation—Heather in particular—because of all she's done for animals in our community and beyond. They apparently got on the phone, started calling fellow animal lovers. And the fact Bowman shot Hunny really made those people angry. Many of them know Hunny. I guess she's become something of a mascot for the Glandon Foundation. Bowman's just lucky they were only asked to write emails. I imagine they might have been willing to take up pitchforks if asked." Joe chuckled.

FORTY-ONE

By Wednesday afternoon, Walt had put the finishing touches on the nursery, and Lily helped Danielle arrange the items she had purchased on Tuesday, which included diapers, wipes, receiving blankets, and other necessities. Hunny was ready to go home and no longer needed Walt's help to go outside to do her business.

On Thursday, they got word Clay Bowman was out on bail.

On Friday they got word Clay Bowman had disappeared—along with his brother-in-law's coin collection valued at over thirty thousand dollars. While Fred had kept the coin collection in a safe in his den, he had foolishly left the combination to the safe in his top desk drawer, in the same den.

Clay had left behind his wife and twins. By Saturday, Fred was willing to let Clay keep his coin collection if he would just pick up Debbie and his sons, especially after his wife informed him her sister would be staying in the garage apartment indefinitely, because she had nowhere else to go.

Also on Saturday was Danielle's baby shower, hosted at Adam and Melony's new house.

ADAM DIDN'T QUITE UNDERSTAND CO-ED baby showers. Initially he assumed the men would go out to a bar for cocktails and watch a game while the ladies ate finger sandwiches, cake, and gave the mother-to-be presents fancily wrapped in pink and blue pastel paper. Melony soon dispelled that idea and let him know he would help her with the shower.

He didn't put up too much of a fight when he learned she intended to have a full bar and knowing he wouldn't be the only guy at the shower. Plus, this would be the first time they would entertain in their new home.

Melony had Pearl Cove cater the event yet purchased the cake from Old Salts Bakery. She had also set up a card table near the sofa to hold the gifts. Before the guests arrived, she had covered the card table with a lace tablecloth that had belonged to Adam's grandmother Marie.

The guest list included primarily their close-knit friendship group, along with Ian's parents. Chris had asked to bring Hunny with him, as he didn't want to leave her alone. There was no way Adam would tell Chris no, and Melony welcomed Hunny, calling her a hero for saving Heather.

Chief MacDonald was the only one of their close friends not at the shower. He had originally planned to come. But he had been overdoing it the last few days, going into the office for a few hours each day since Bowman's arrest. Danielle had told him she wanted him to stay home and get some rest, so when Joe and Kelly showed up for the shower, they had the chief's gift for the twins with them.

WALT AND DANIELLE sat together on the sofa in Adam and Melony's new family room. The room, located at the back of the house, overlooked the ocean. It was the first time in weeks that Danielle had dressed up. She wore makeup and wove her hair into a fishtail braid instead of a ponytail. Instead of wearing stretch pants, she wore a floor-length maternity dress that she'd found online.

When Lily saw it, she told Danielle it reminded her of something a pregnant Jane Austin character might wear.

After the guests started arriving, Melony gave them a tour of her and Adam's new home. She placed their shower gifts on the card table, and Adam played bartender, not knowing his grandmother and Eva Thorndike sat nearby on imaginary chairs.

Everyone had finally arrived and settled down, each finding a place to sit. Melony hadn't planned shower games and intended for Danielle to open her gifts after lunch, during dessert. Before lunch, guests munched on appetizers and enjoyed beverages.

Marie sat next to Eva, watching Melony bring out more appetizers while the room buzzed with friendly conversation. Much to Marie's surprise, Eva bolted from her chair and went straight to Danielle.

"Excuse yourself to go to the bathroom. Now," Eva implored Danielle.

Confused, but not willing to argue with Eva, Danielle mumbled something to Walt and stood up, while the mediums wondered why Eva had demanded Danielle go to the bathroom.

Leaving the family room, Danielle walked down the long entry hall toward the guest bathroom located near the front door. When Danielle stepped into the bathroom a few minutes later, shutting the door behind her, she looked at Eva, who had followed her into the room.

"Why did you want me to come in here?"

Eva cringed. "You might want to sit on the toilet."

"I don't have to go to the bathroom."

The next moment, Danielle's eyes widened when she felt water on her legs. She looked down.

Eva shrugged. "I just thought it better if your water broke over the toilet instead of the floor. But at least it didn't break on Melony and Adam's new sofa."

Danielle pulled up her dress and looked down at the floor. "My water broke." She grabbed a towel from the nearby cabinet and awkwardly wiped up her legs and attempted to wipe up the floor.

"What's going on in here?" Marie asked when she appeared a moment later.

Eva looked at Marie. "Danielle's water broke."

"And you're letting her mop up the floor?" Marie scolded Eva as she snatched the towel from Danielle and finished wiping up the floor.

"I'm not very good with towels," Eva reminded her. "They just slip through my fingers."

Danielle looked down at Marie. "I need to go to the hospital."

"Dear, you will not make it to the hospital," Eva said.

"Of course she's going to make it to the hospital. Don't scare the girl." Marie tossed the now wet towel in the bathtub.

"No. They're impatient. They told me they're not waiting any longer," Eva said.

Danielle started to say something but instead bent over in pain and let out a cry.

"I'll get Walt," Eva said. "You might want to make her comfortable, Marie."

By the time Walt got to the bathroom, Danielle's underwear had been removed, and she sat on the floor, leaning against the wall with her knees apart. When Eva had come out to the living room and announced to Walt that Danielle was giving birth to the twins—*now* —Chris and Heather had also heard.

Heather knew of only one person in the room who had ever helped deliver a baby before. She stood and said, "I forgot something in the car. Brian, I need your help." She grabbed Brian's arm and jerked him toward the entry hall, which was also on the way to the guest bathroom.

While Heather dragged a confused Brian with her, Chris quietly left the living room and called 911, requesting an ambulance, while the non-medium shower guests remained clueless regarding the current bathroom drama. The hosts and most of the guests assumed the mother-to-be had simply gone to the bathroom—something that mothers-to-be were known to do frequently, and believed Walt had gone to check on her. They continued chatting and enjoying the appetizers and drinks.

Ten minutes later, they all heard sirens.

"That sounds close," Kelly said before the sirens stopped. Believing the sirens had gone to a neighbor's house, the conversations resumed.

"Where did the guests of honor run off to?" Adam finally asked fifteen minutes later. They had been so engrossed in a discussion of the Clay Bowman drama that Adam and the others hadn't noticed the missing parents-to-be hadn't yet returned.

The next moment, Heather walked out into the living room carrying something bundled in a towel and announced, "I'm afraid the baby shower is going to have to be cut short. I'd like to introduce Addison Marie Marlow. Her mama, along with her brother, is still being checked out by the paramedics. But don't come too close. She doesn't need your germs."

LILY AND IAN'S shower gift had been a rocking chair that matched the one Walt and Danielle had already purchased for the nursery. Lily felt that with two babies, Danielle needed two rockers, one for her and one for Walt.

Danielle sat in one rocking chair, nursing Addison, while Walt sat in the second rocking chair, holding his sleeping son.

"They are so beautiful," Walt said in awe.

"And impatient."

Walt smiled.

"According to Mel, Adam can't get over the fact I had the babies in their bathroom." Danielle chuckled.

"Neither can I."

"But you know what really surprises me?" Danielle asked.

"What?"

"I can't believe I wasn't embarrassed—mortified—that Brian helped deliver our babies. But at that moment, I was so afraid, despite Eva and you reassuring me it was going to be okay. Modesty just flew out the window."

"I have to admit, Brian was extremely professional, took over like he knew exactly what he needed to do."

"Lily and I were talking about how my labor was as easy as hers with Connor. And a lot quicker."

"Does that mean you might consider doing this again?" Walt teased.

Danielle looked up from her nursing baby to Walt. "You should probably ask me that in three years. Because, according to Mom, these two are going to be a handful."

They both laughed.

THE GHOST AND THE POLTERGEIST

RETURN TO MARLOW HOUSE
The Ghost and the Poltergeist
HAUNTING DANIELLE, BOOK 34

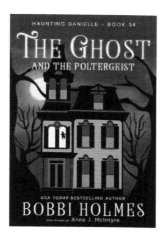

Living in a haunted house is nothing new to Danielle. In fact, she's rather fond of the ghosts who visit Marlow House.

But after she brings home the twins, unexplained paranormal activities in the nursery perplex not just her, but the ghosts who frequently visit Marlow House.

BOOKS BY ANNA J. MCINTYRE

COULSON FAMILY SAGA

COULSON'S WIFE

COULSON'S CRUCIBLE

COULSON'S LESSONS

COULSON'S SECRET

COULSON'S RECKONING

Now available in Audiobook Format

UNLOCKED HEARTS

SUNDERED HEARTS

AFTER SUNDOWN

WHILE SNOWBOUND

SUGAR RUSH

NON-FICTION BY
BOBBI ANN JOHNSON HOLMES

Havasu Palms, A Hostile Takeover
Where the Road Ends, Recipes & Remembrances
Motherhood, a book of poetry
The Story of the Christmas Village

Printed in Great Britain
by Amazon

31305942R00164